A former scriptwriter, foreign cor[...] reader and literary critic, Greg Flyr[...] public relations.

In his PR career, Greg has worked in Britain, the US, Asia and Australia. Greg travelled to Berlin and New York several times to research *The Berlin Cross*.

THE
BERLIN
CROSS

GREG FLYNN

BANTAM

SYDNEY AUCKLAND TORONTO NEW YORK LONDON

THE BERLIN CROSS
A BANTAM BOOK

First published in Australia and New Zealand in 2005
by Bantam

National Library of Australia
Cataloguing-in-Publication Entry

Flynn, Greg F.
The Berlin cross.

ISBN 1 86325 555 9.

1. Murder – Fiction. I. Title.

A823.4

Transworld Publishers,
a division of Random House Australia Pty Ltd
20 Alfred Street, Milsons Point, NSW 2061
http://www.randomhouse.com.au

Random House New Zealand Limited
18 Poland Road, Glenfield, Auckland

Transworld Publishers,
a division of The Random House Group Ltd
61–63 Uxbridge Road, Ealing, London W5 5SA

Random House Inc
1745 Broadway, New York, New York 10036

Typeset in Berling Roman, by Midland Typesetters Australia.
Printed and bound by Griffin Press, Netley, South Australia

10 9 8 7 6 5 4 3 2 1

To Wendy, Claire and Lucienne . . . with love

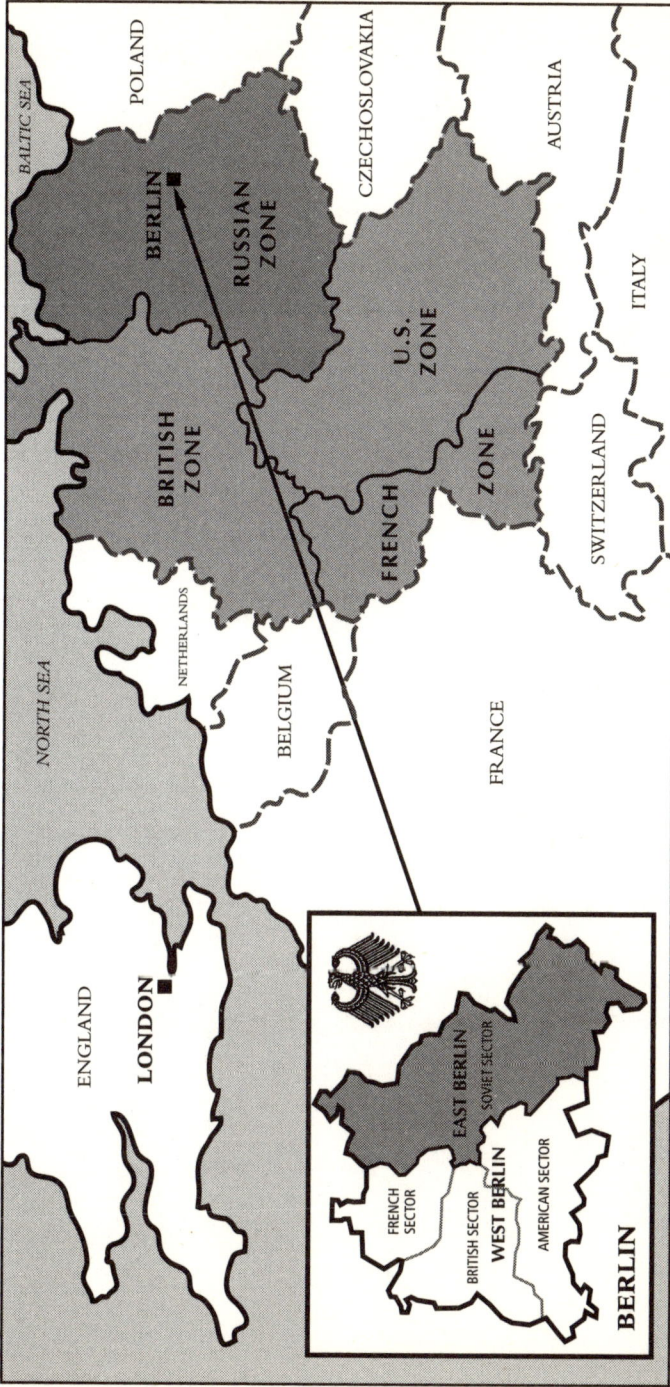

GERMANY 1948

BALTIC SEA

POLAND

CZECHOSLOVAKIA

AUSTRIA

BERLIN

RUSSIAN ZONE

U.S. ZONE

ITALY

BRITISH ZONE

FRENCH ZONE

SWITZERLAND

NORTH SEA

NETHERLANDS

BELGIUM

FRANCE

ENGLAND

LONDON

EAST BERLIN

SOVIET SECTOR

FRENCH SECTOR

BRITISH SECTOR

WEST BERLIN

AMERICAN SECTOR

BERLIN

AUTHOR'S NOTE

Although *The Berlin Cross* is fiction, some real people have been woven into the plot. I hope that they would have enjoyed being part of the action.

EINS

British Sector, Berlin, 26 May 1948

Beauchamp flipped over the dead man's silk tie. Hermès. Using a fountain pen cap, he eased back the shirt collar. Hannes Münch. The single shoe was Johnston & Murphy and the suit Kilgour French Stanbury. This wasn't a man who shopped at the stalls in Potsdamer Platz. Where could you find a tailor in Berlin these days who cared enough to line the crotch?

He stood up, thoughtful, slowly swinging the shoe backwards and forwards. A final benediction with a fashion crucible. The corpse looked undignified with one arm in his suit coat and his trousers around his knees. A pair of cotton boxer shorts was exposed. Munsingwear.

Beauchamp was tempted to pull the trousers back up. Instead he dropped the shoe into a glassine bag and handed it to Corporal White who scribbled a note on a cardboard tag and gently placed the bag on the bare, dusty floor next to a scattering of used condoms and a small pile of rusted rifle cartridges. The cartridges were Wehrmacht Karabiner 98K.

Beauchamp moved one of the condoms with the highly polished toe of his boot.

'It looks British,' said White, watching him.

'More in your area of expertise than mine, corporal. But we better have the lab make the identification. Bag the ones closest to the body.'

Using the spent rifle cartridges as makeshift tweezers, White started the distasteful process while Beauchamp went back to studying the body.

Rain drizzling through a 15-foot hole in the hotel roof had done a poor job of washing the victim. The once white cotton shirt with its cutaway collar was still stained with blood from a wound where, if the left ear was anything to go by, the right ear had stood out prominently from the head. One foot was bare, with several toes missing – the remaining toes were bruised. There was a blackened hole in the centre of the man's forehead.

After he had pincered the final condom into the bag White stood up. 'Single shot, close range and fatal,' he said, then paused. 'What do you think, captain?'

'I'd say he was murdered.'

Corporal White let out a sigh. As the months went by, the captain's jokes were becoming just a little predictable. 'If you say so, sir,' he muttered before pulling a heavy camera from a canvas bag. In a moment of barracks-room boredom the previous week, he'd drawn a Royal Military Police badge on the side of the bag using a red crayon. He admired his artwork as he absently screwed a fresh bulb into the camera's flash. The bulb popped and the room lit up to reveal a dark woollen blanket spread out in the corner, condoms scattered around it. There was a pale outline of a watch strap on the victim's tanned left wrist but the watch was nowhere to be seen.

As White snapped a close-up photograph of the wrist, Beauchamp looked up through the torn roof. A DC-3 hammered overhead on its descent into Gatow. Grey wings on a grey sky.

It's nearly summer, he thought, and since the bloody sun never seems to shine here, where did the victim get the tan? He took off his red cap, wiped his forearm across the flat, raindrop-flecked top and polished the badge with his elbow. The room suddenly brightened. My God, the sun's coming out, thought Beauchamp, this is a first. The body was now spot-lit in the centre of the room.

He peered around the shattered room and found a pile of dry rubble to sit on and then took a packet of Chesterfields from his pocket and lit up, studying the ciga-rette's branding as he did so. American. He wondered what type had burnt those scorch marks into the dead man's crotch. French, with first a hint of romance and then hali-tosis? Perhaps a sweet, smooth American cigarette had been used or, for the less discerning torturer, a dry British brand. Beauchamp had a theory that only the British would smoke their nation's cigarettes in a city where everything was for sale. Corporal White's first sweep of the room had identified that the freshest butts near the body were French, while those in the corner where the prostitute had laid out her blanket were British. There was no trace of fresh blood in the room. The victim had obviously been killed elsewhere and his body moved to this empty hotel. He had been dragged up the stairs and dumped in a room favoured by local tarts.

Robbery was unlikely, mused Beauchamp – no one in Berlin had the time or the patience to torture a victim for a wristwatch or the contents of a wallet. There'd been no attempt to disguise the identity of the victim. Some toes were missing but the fingertips were intact and currently being pressed onto an inkpad by an impassive Corporal White. The limbs still had some flexibility so the prostitute who'd found the body might have seen the killers.

Heavily built, the dead man clearly had not been a stranger to the delights of the dessert trolley. It would have taken two or more men to have hefted the body up the staircase and into the far corner of the room.

Standing up, Beauchamp brushed the seat of his trousers before going back to the body. He crouched down and did a final search.

'Only a Yank could afford those clothes,' White said, pulling a thread off the patch pocket of his own dowdy battle dress jacket.

Beauchamp didn't comment. While the dead man's clothes were extravagant and expensive, his dental work was almost certainly European. Smart suit, lousy teeth. French? Italian? German? He watched Corporal White circle the body, lining up each photographic shot with the care of a Cartier-Bresson. The popping of flashbulbs was the only sound in the room.

Beauchamp scratched his chin with his middle finger, a nervous gesture that had once, many years ago now, angered his nanny. Most ungentlemanly using that finger, she used to scold him. He stubbed out his half-smoked cigarette on a cement slab well clear of the body, pushed the stub back into the packet and went across to a small, frameless window. Shielding his eyes against the glare from the wet street, he could see across the Landwehr-kanal the saw-toothed wreckage of Potsdamer Platz. The Wertheim department store and Palasthotel had been flattened, but a green clock tower stood perkily in the centre, marking the corners of the British, American and Russian sectors.

He didn't wait for White who was packing up his gear. Down in the street, the mud, broken masonry, weeds and rain-slicked roadway were glistening in the sunlight.

It had been three years since the last Allied artillery round hit this neighbourhood and it was still a shambles. The exterior of the hotel was pockmarked from heavy-calibre gunfire. The hotel's name was gone, together with the east wing of the building. Along the street there were only three shops operating, the rest were shells. He could hear children playing somewhere out of sight.

Beauchamp opened his notebook and flicked dried blood off his fountain pen before writing himself a reminder: 'Plaster mould: tyre tracks.'

The prostitute who had found the body was leaning against a wall near where two Royal Military Police vehicles were parked. She was wearing a black woollen coat over a striped, belted dressing gown that almost reached the ground. The partially opened gown revealed hints of grey underwear. It had been quite a few months since Beauchamp had seen a woman's underwear, but he didn't find the sight particularly arousing. Her would-be client, a dishevelled Royal Scots Fusiliers sergeant, stood a few feet away, ignoring the woman and trying to make conversation with a young RMP lance corporal.

As Beauchamp approached, the sergeant and the woman looked at him with contempt. He was used to it. To the woman he was just another policeman cutting into her morning's work. To the off-duty sergeant, he was an umpire, an outsider, an intruder on the good times.

The lance corporal, his webbing and holster starkly white in the grey street, straightened up. He saluted Beauchamp and astonished him by pronouncing his name correctly: *Beech-um*. He was agreeably surprised if anyone in the army got his name right. On the day he had signed up, the recruiting sergeant reading Beauchamp's application form had mispronounced his name and then commented on Beauchamp having been to Magdalen College at Oxford. The sergeant pronounced it *Mag-da-lene*.

Beauchamp replied as politely as possible. 'Actually, my name's *Beech-um* and I went to *Maudlen*.'

The sergeant had put his pen down, pinched his

forelock between two fingers and asked, 'And how the fuck, milord, would you like me to pronounce *Oxford*?'

It was just one example of his countrymen's pre-occupation with class. Personally, Beauchamp didn't care about social rank. He was quite happy to be suspicious of most people regardless of their family connections or what school they'd been to. In the Royal Military Police, starting from a basis of mistrust when dealing with people saved a lot of disappointment later.

'The sergeant says he has to be back at the barracks by midday,' whispered the lance corporal.

Beauchamp snapped out of his reverie. 'If he hadn't been so keen on a quickie he could already be tucking into morning tea by now.'

Ignoring the sergeant he approached the woman who, as he neared, shifted her weight onto one foot and quietly broke wind.

'Could we have a word?' he asked, gesturing towards a doorway well clear of the lance corporal and the sergeant. Corporal White had said the woman spoke English. If so it had to be better than his German.

She didn't move.

He told her his name and rank and then added that he was with the Royal Military Police. She gave a slight shrug of her shoulders as if to say 'another policeman, another title'. Beauchamp decided on straightforward bribery and pulled out his cigarette packet, holding it towards her in the same way he would coax a Cocker Spaniel with food.

She stepped forward and withdrew a cigarette confidently. She could afford to. She weighed twice as much as he did.

Beauchamp retrieved his half-smoked stub, lit both cigarettes and waited a few seconds while she blew smoke at him.

'Is this your, ah, business address?' he asked, waving the smoke out of his face before gesturing towards the hotel.

'*Ja*. I would prefer the Fürstenhof but you bombed it.'

'Not personally.' He quickly changed the subject before she could sidetrack him into a discussion on the morality of carpet bombing. 'So, you found the body. Did you see anyone enter or leave the premises?'

'Premises?'

He had to stop sounding like an English copper. '*Hottel*,' he said, giving the word 'hotel' the German pronunciation.

'*Nein*. I have seen *nichts*. Just the body.'

'Very thoughtless for somebody to leave a dead man there and disrupt your work. Whoever left the body in the hotel must have known that it would eventually be found,' said Beauchamp, probing.

'A warning perhaps?' she suggested.

'To whom?'

She shrugged and blew more smoke at him. 'You are the policeman.'

The sergeant came over at a trot, appearing contrite. 'I have to return to barracks soon, sir.'

'You'll have the perfect excuse for why you were late.'

The sergeant looked anxious.

Beauchamp gave him a moment to regain his composure. 'Take me through what happened, but spare me any of the sex.'

'I met her two streets away,' said the sergeant. 'We agreed on a price and she suggested this hotel. I was in a hurry and she didn't want to do it in the open.'

'I like a woman with standards,' Beauchamp said.

'We went up the stairs and found the body,' continued the sergeant quickly, uncertain if the captain was teasing him. 'I told her to wait while I went for help.'

Beauchamp didn't bother pressing the sergeant as to why he hadn't turned to the Berlin police instead of the RMP. The local force was still being rebuilt. Understaffed and under pressure from four occupying powers, the *Schutzpolizei* could barely cope with traffic duties. Either way, Beauchamp knew the case would have come to him eventually. If a British serviceman found a corpse dumped in the British sector then it was definitely an issue for the RMP.

Corporal White emerged from the building carrying his crayon-etched bag and walkie-talkie. 'The morgue cart will be here in five minutes. I just need to make plaster casts of the tyre tracks.' Looking across at the prostitute and the sergeant, White added, 'Do you want to take these two to HQ?'

'No,' Beauchamp replied, 'we've got about as much as we can out of them – for now.'

The sergeant relaxed. The woman seemed puzzled and asked if she was free to leave.

It was Beauchamp's turn to shrug. 'What's the point of arresting you? You'd be back at your military relief work by midnight. Before you go, you might like to tell Corporal White your prices. He could do with a little relaxation. In the meantime he needs to do some plastering.'

ZWEI

New York, New York, 28 May 1948

Docker tried to stretch. The wardrobe was cramped and smelt of perfume, BO and naphthalene. This was no place for a claustrophobic moth let alone a grown man. He lifted the camera and rested it on his right thigh, then checked the luminous hands on his service-issue watch. It was 5.30 a.m. and he'd been in the wardrobe since just after 3. They were late. The bellhop had been wrong. Five bucks richer but nevertheless wrong.

He clenched and unclenched his fingers. He'd give the couple another hour. That was one more hour to consider how he'd been reduced to this: waiting around to listen to some philandering millionaire testing bedsprings with his secretary.

Suddenly he heard laughter, a key in the lock and the sound of the hotel door slamming. A giggle and a growl followed by the creak of a bed. The camera dug into his stomach and he wondered if he should loosen his gun in its holster, but he couldn't reach it. He shouldn't have bothered to bring it. Whatever the man in the hotel room had in his hand was unlikely to shoot back.

Soon there was groaning. Groaning was good. Docker lifted the camera as high as he could with his right hand and pushed hard at the wardrobe doors with his left. Nothing. He pressed again with the heel of his hand. Jammed. From what the woman was shouting, God must have suddenly arrived in the room.

He eased himself into a crouching position and, with as much force as he could, rammed his left shoulder into the door. It didn't budge, but the wardrobe did, falling across the room and landing with a crash. Docker found himself lying face down on the jammed door, wire coathangers in his hair and a sharp pain rising from where his holster cut into his side. Through the wardrobe's plywood back he could hear the woman's screams merged with the man's cursing. God would have been appalled.

As the hotel door banged shut, Docker twitched and his finger slipped. The camera flash flared in his face, blinding him. He rolled onto his back and kicked at the rear of the wardrobe. The plywood board flew into the air and he leapt up jack-in-the-box style, but the man and woman were gone – together with his dignity. He limped out of the room with only his camera, bruised ribs and a sore wrist.

Manhattan was waking up to a damp, mild day as Docker slouched along Broadway. He sighed, rubbed his wrist and reviewed the past hours. It was unlikely the millionaire's wife would pay for a photograph of Docker's startled face inside a wardrobe and, once again, he considered tossing his private investigator business cards into a trash can. Instead he decided on breakfast. Stopping at a newsstand on Mercer Street, he glanced down the ranks of papers and chose *The New York Times*.

Jonah's counter was lined with postal workers, packers and truck drivers. Sliding into a booth by the window, Docker looked out at two bums arguing in the middle of the narrow street until a truck honked them out of the way.

'Newspaperman?' the waitress asked.

He looked around to see the waitress admiring his camera. She was new, at least to this diner.

'No. Wedding photographer,' he said, moving the camera off the tabletop and putting it down near his feet.

She handed him a small cardboard menu and waited for him to light his Camel. 'A little early in the day for a wedding, isn't it?' she asked.

'I had to photograph a very eager couple who couldn't wait for a priest.'

Docker ordered breakfast, handed back the menu and propped his paper against the ketchup bottle. He saw that the British were celebrating the spring of 1948 by sending more troops to Palestine, and the Red Sox had beaten the Yankees 7 to 1. Wasn't there any good news?

The waitress returned with ham fried as hard as the neighbourhood cast iron and eggs just the way he liked them at this hour, over easy and definitely sunny-side down. He heard coffee being poured into his mug and thanked the waitress without looking up, cutting into the eggs with the side of his fork and reading the paper again.

As he reached for his coffee he sensed someone standing on the sidewalk watching him. He lifted his head slightly but whoever it was had disappeared. He went back to the newspaper, noting that Cary Grant was advertising metallic kitchens.

The quality of the air abruptly improved in the diner, the aroma of nightshift workers and fried fat replaced by something more fragrant – perhaps a hint of lemon from a warm pie or a perfume bottle.

Glancing up again, he saw a woman standing close to his booth – so close that her scent invaded his senses, throwing him off guard. She had blonde hair in a sleek pageboy cut, pressed down by a small navy-blue hat perfectly coordinated with her stylish suit.

'Mr Docker.'

It wasn't a question but he nodded anyway.

'May I sit down?' she said, doing so before he could reply. 'I have come to ask for your help.'

He could hear the trace of an accent. Possibly German, possibly not. Her eyes were china blue. Her outfit was classy enough to let you know she had dough but understated enough to signal she also had taste.

'I was going to your office when I thought I saw you through the window.'

'You would've had a long wait at the office. It's early.'

'I am very patient.'

There was something unsettling about this woman. How had she recognised him? He'd never seen her before. He felt exhausted. 'And why did you want to see me at . . . at . . .'

'I need you to find my father. He is missing.'

She opened her handbag and took out a stiff, white name card. Reading it, Docker's jaw tightened. He dropped the card on the table and pinned it in place with his fingernail, the angry pressure leaving a crescent dent in the cardboard.

'Of course you know the name,' she said.

'I *once* knew a man with that name,' Docker corrected her. He picked up the card and slipped it into his shirt pocket without looking at it again.

'It is the same man. My father is Dr Friedrich Kessler. He has gone missing in Berlin. I am Elsa Kessler.'

'Berlin,' Docker repeated. Suddenly he wished he'd walked out the door, gone to his apartment, poured an early drink and put on Billie Holiday as soon as he heard her accent. Now he was trapped in a diner with a congealed egg and a Saks mannequin look-alike who could only mean trouble.

'What was he doing back in Germany?' he asked, stopping himself from adding '*again*'. 'I'd have thought, after what he'd been through, the US government wouldn't let him out of its sights or out of the country. Last I'd heard your father was in his New Mexico bunker happily playing with his Bunsen burner and big pay cheque.'

'He *was* in New Mexico and he was happy. Perhaps he was happy because my mother wanted to stay in Manhattan.' The way she pronounced the island made it sound both exotic and erotic. 'Then my father heard that his mother was dying.'

This time Docker did say 'again'. Jesus, hadn't that old broad caused enough trouble?

Elsa's lips drew apart in what he feared would be a snarl, but instead she smiled. Although her eyes definitely said 'fuck you', she was playing at being gracious. Her self-control was exceptional. He tried not to be impressed.

Keeping her voice low and level, Elsa explained that her father had left New Mexico without informing his colleagues. He'd arrived in New York and booked himself on the only available European flight – a Pan American Clipper to Lisbon. From the overseas terminal at LaGuardia Airport, her father had called Elsa and told her that her grandmother had had a relapse and had only weeks to live. He didn't say how he knew, but he did say he would write.

He kept his promise about writing. Mail began arriving regularly with first a postcard from Lisbon saying he was catching a train north. Two days later there was a card from the Gare du Nord in Paris giving the number of the train he was catching to Berlin via Brussels. A week passed before she received a three-line note on hotel stationery saying he had arrived safely in Berlin and could be reached at the Askanischer Hof on Kurfürstendamm. There were no more letters and eventually, worried, she called the hotel and was told that her father hadn't been in his room for some time. No one had seen him leave.

Docker began to ask what the police had said, but she interrupted. 'The *Schutzpolizei* are not interested. They told me to contact the American authorities in the city.'

'And?'

'No one will help. I even tried his laboratory in New Mexico. I thought they would be worried about him going missing. After all –' She broke off as Docker put his forefinger to his lips, his eyes darting around the restaurant.

'He means a lot to America,' she continued.

'Leading the Nazi's heavy-water experiments to split the atom makes him a valuable commodity *anywhere* in the world,' Docker said in a low whisper.

She leaned her face towards his as if trying to catch his words. Docker avoided her gaze, pretending to take an interest in his plate. The lone egg was still there. She reached across and touched his forearm. It was a European gesture, not a sign of affection. 'I'd like to pay for you to go to Berlin and find him.'

He paused, thought about the next month's rent, calculated he probably had enough to cover it and said, 'I'm sorry, Fräulein. I can't help.'

'Why not?' She glanced at his clothes, his well past five o'clock shadow and his tousled hair. 'I will pay well. *Verstehen Sie?*'

'I'm very busy,' he said too quickly, aware that she knew it was a lie. 'Thanks for the offer, but . . .' He paused. Would it be simpler just to tell her the truth? That he'd be dead within 48 hours if he so much as stepped back into Berlin. Nothing elaborate, just a quick and brutal end with a bullet to the back of the head and perhaps an extra one out of spite.

He put some dollars under the lip of his plate, and picked up his hat, newspaper and camera, taking one last, hard look at her. There was something about her that worried him. Was she lying to him? If she wasn't and he walked away then, once again, he'd be letting her down. Months before he was meant to pick up a phone and call her. One damn phone call was all it would have taken. He still felt guilty but that wasn't going to affect his judgment.

After whispering *'Auf Wiedersehen'* he began backing out the door. This isn't my finest hour, he thought as the fast-closing door slapped his butt, propelling him out into the street.

Docker glanced back at her through the window as he walked towards the neighbouring building. She was clenching a napkin in her hand. He thought her lips formed the word *'Arschloch!'*

DREI

British Sector, Berlin, 1 June 1948

Even for an Englishman, June conjured up visions of pale blue sky, the odd white cloud for contrast, a warm breeze and the sound of birds. Beauchamp was definitely in the wrong city. In Berlin the locals only discussed the weather if it was sunny – and nobody was discussing the weather this morning.

He stood at his second-storey office window and looked down at the guardhouse, a damp sentry and a red and white striped boom gate. The oak tree next to the guard-house was glistening with rain. If he tilted his head he could read the English-language warning notice: *When snow and ice on steps use only at your own risk*. Beauchamp had wondered why the notice stayed up year round until he experienced his first chilly Berlin Spring day.

A neighbouring sign in large black lettering had also seemed unnecessary: *Lieferanten/Besucher Kraftfahrzeuge bitte in der Wache melden*. It ordered deliverymen and other visitors to report to the guardhouse. Given that there was an eight-foot-high steel-reinforced fence looped around the building housing the Royal Military Police headquarters, all arrivals had no choice but to be funnelled past the guardhouse. Beauchamp decided that the sign was there because the military enjoyed giving orders. He doubted the locals enjoyed taking them these days.

The Royal Military Police headquarters was near the Olympic Stadium and Beauchamp's office was part of the former Haus des Deutsch Sports, which was set off to one side of the 1936 stadium. The whole Olympics area was under the command of the British military but the only sport Beauchamp saw was on Saturdays when polo ponies were exercised on the Maifield at the rear of the stadium. He wasn't a polo enthusiast, however he enjoyed hearing the sound of hooves on grass and the crack of mallet on ball. He also liked to muse, in his official capacity, about the income sources of the officers who could afford such postwar luxuries. He was hard pressed surviving on his service pay and a small monthly stipend from his family.

Enough of that, he thought, bringing his mind back to the job. On a side table were plaster moulds of the tyre tracks and a selection of cigarette butts. Fortunately the used condoms were held elsewhere. The tracks and the butts had proven to be useful leads. The tracks indicated that whoever drove the killer's vehicle could afford new tyres. White was confident that a Volkswagen had been driven up to the building. It was a sound assumption given that there were few private cars in Berlin and, of those still running, over half were prewar Volkswagens. The butts confirmed that the prostitute's customers were mainly British soldiers. This left the puzzle of who had stubbed out the French cigarettes on the floor.

A soft cough at the door and an even softer 'sir' made Beauchamp turn. A young private was standing in the doorway, an envelope in his hand. Beauchamp took the envelope, read the enclosed note and rang for White. Minutes later he and White were descending the staircase to the ground floor.

'One of the prisoners in Spandau wants to talk to me. The note doesn't say which one,' said Beauchamp. 'This had never happened before. Why would a German prisoner contact the RMP?'

'We were scheduled to go to the Spandau morgue to inspect the body again,' said White. 'Possibly it's to do with the murder.'

'At least it'll save two trips to that bloody place.'

They left the administration building, crossing to where the Royal Military Police vehicles were parked. If nothing else, being a copper got you the best parking spaces. White gunned the engine and took off in the direction of Spandau.

The red brick Spandau Prison on Wilhelmstrasse was flanked by British Army barracks and surrounded by a high outer wall, which in turn was ringed by an electrified fence. There were six watch towers. Of the four occupying powers in Germany, it was Britain's turn to guard Spandau.

They waited at the guard post for their credentials to be checked. 'Look at the security,' said White. 'There must be a platoon guarding this place. What for? Seven Nazis and a morgue. Fucking ridiculous.'

The sergeant on duty asked Beauchamp to surrender his side-arm for safekeeping before taking him to a room split by a double grille.

A pale man in a drill uniform with the figure 5 stencilled on the jacket entered the other half of the room and closed the door behind him. He pulled up a chair and motioned for Beauchamp to sit. Beauchamp took a chair and pulled it close to the grille.

'I'll be back in 15 minutes, sir,' said the sergeant. His loud voice made Beauchamp start.

Beauchamp heard the door slam behind him. He couldn't stop staring at the man opposite. Hair parted on the right, rigid bearing, calm gaze and a weary smile – except for the uniform he looked less like a prisoner than a prison superintendent. In one of the last photographs Beauchamp had seen of Albert Speer, the Reich Minister for Armaments and War Production stood forlornly beside Admiral Karl Dönitz and General Alfred Jodl. The three men wore beautifully cut double-breasted overcoats, while the lone Tommy guarding them with a Bren gun was kitted out in an ill-fitting battle dress jacket.

Speer, head bowed, had looked beaten in the photograph. Now, one year into his 20-year imprisonment, he looked self-possessed and comfortable despite the grim prison surroundings.

'Welcome to Spandau, *Kapitän*.' Speer's voice was hospitable, almost as if Beauchamp was his guest.

'I can't imagine why you'd want to talk to me, Herr Speer.'

'Strictly speaking, you should address me by my number – "five". It is all part of the dehumanising process for we German prisoners. What do you think of my uniform?'

'I suggest you have a word to your tailor,' replied Beauchamp. 'It's a little tight in the shoulders.'

'Perhaps. But it came from the camps where my armaments workers –'

'Better known, I believe, as "slaves",' Beauchamp interjected.

'Let us agree that they were not there of their own free will. But, getting back to the uniform, it is the same as the ones worn in those armaments camps. It is just another example of the Four Powers' attempts to belittle us.'

'We've only got 13 minutes left, Herr Speer. Why did you want to see me?' Beauchamp asked coldly.

'You have an excellent reputation in Berlin – and not only within the British Army. You are said to be an extremely capable investigator, a man able to focus on the job at hand no matter what the distractions.'

Beauchamp was amused by the German's attempt at flattery. He'd read of Speer's legendary ability to win over opponents. Beauchamp decided to play the game. 'Distractions?' he queried.

'Despite pressure from your superiors, you recently solved a murder carried out by a British soldier. And, four months ago, you arranged the release of two civilians unjustly accused of profiteering in your sector. Again you went against the wishes of your superiors. It is also said that you are incorruptible. Of course, all that may mean is that nobody has ever offered you something you really want. Or perhaps you are a man of honour. But now, to the business at hand. I am advised that you are investigating the death of a man who is currently residing in our morgue. I can guide you towards someone who may be able to assist. In turn, I want you to arrange the return of a missing artefact.'

'I'm not in the lost and found business,' said Beauchamp.

'This item is of monumental importance to Berlin. If you can have it returned it will assist in making this city great again.'

'And what am I looking for?'

'The Cross of Christ,' said Speer.

Beauchamp looked at Speer as if the German's hair – what there was left of it – was on fire. 'With or without Christ on it?'

'You have moved from flippancy to blasphemy. In fact you will be seeking a small piece of the Cross.'

Impatient with Speer's ridiculous time wasting, Beauchamp checked his watch, noticing as he did so that Speer didn't wear one.

Speer saw Beauchamp's gesture but continued at the same leisurely pace. 'When it was the Soviets' turn to guard us some months ago, I had a visit from a very unpleasant man.'

Beauchamp raised an eyebrow. 'Unpleasant? *This* from a person who worked alongside Goebbels and Himmler.'

Speer ignored the comment. 'This visitor was Russian. I never learnt his name. He said there were rumours that I possessed a piece of the Cross of Christ, which I had once planned to place in the dome of the Great Hall in this city. I told him that I refused to discuss the matter because the hall was never built and, as far as I was concerned, it was no longer of any consequence what ideas I had all those years ago. The Russian became angry. He showed me a number of photographs of some architectural plans that appeared to be brilliant fakes. From what I could tell, they were faultless, right down to the forging of my signature. The plans were of a camp for Upper Silesian Jews. It was called Blechhammer.'

Beauchamp scratched his chin. 'And?'

'Blechhammer was in the Auschwitz region of Poland. Workers were sent there to assist in the construction of a chemical-products plant related to armaments manufacture. The camp was built in 1942 and three years later the workers were transferred to Buchenwald.'

'And they died.'

'Reportedly there and at Blechhammer. But I had no knowledge of the conditions in the camp. I had nothing to do with the camp. I certainly never designed it. I have only been to one camp – Mauthausen. The rooms were neat, there were flowers, and the detainees were well treated. I went home reassured. In fact I later incorporated them into my armaments production plans.'

Beauchamp held up a hand to stop the flow of words. 'So this visiting Russian claimed to have evidence that linked you to the concentration camps?'

'If the authorities had seen the forgeries there would have been a further trial and I would have been hanged within the month.'

'So you told the Russian where the Cross was?'

'Of course. I had no choice. I told him it was hidden in the wall of the courtyard at the Cecilienhof Palace in Potsdam. I personally bricked the relic in before the Soviets arrived.'

'Why would the Russian government want the Cross?'

'I'll come to that. The Russians certainly do not believe the Cross has any power while I, on the other hand, believe that it does. I'm not alone. Countless others down the centuries have also witnessed its power – in defence and in attack. The Emperor Heraclius embedded the Cross in a statue to guard the gates of Constantinople and later it was carried into battle by Richard the Lionheart against the Saracens. The Cross was also seen tied to King Henry's saddle as he went into battle at Agincourt. And then, nothing. It was not heard of again until the British Army took the Cross to Abyssinia where it disappeared during the battle of Magdala. It was fortunate our Italian friends found it again and gave it to the Führer.'

'Aren't you worried I might keep this piece of wood if I find it? It seems to have a lot of British ties.'

'Do you believe in the Cross's power?'

'No.'

'Then it is worthless to you. But this city – surrounded by the Communists – needs it now more than ever.'

'You seem awfully enthusiastic about what could be a piece of old tree.'

'For good reason. The lead aircraft in our initial attacks on Poland, Belgium, the Netherlands and France all carried the Cross. Then our Sixth SS Panzers swept forward with the Cross into what you called the Battle of the Bulge.'

'You lost that one.'

'Not at the beginning. But, sadly, the Führer insisted on being involved in every detail of the battle. It was a mistake. He interfered and so I did too. I took the Cross and hid it. I knew the war was nearly over.'

The door opened. 'Give us a few more minutes,' Beauchamp said to the guard before continuing. 'Herr Speer, I'm dealing with a murder case. I haven't got time to chase some unnamed Russian with a crucifixion complex.'

'I believe the murder and the Cross are linked.'

'Why?'

'Berlin has an underworld that thrives on the black market. Goods are traded, lives are traded and so are secrets. As I said, the Russians are not interested in the power of the Cross, but they are interested in the power of secrets. One can be exchanged for the other.'

'Where do you and I fit in?'

'If you promise to bring the Cross home then I will, as I said, guide you in your investigation.'

Beauchamp was intrigued but said nothing.

Speer appeared to take the brief silence as a rejection. 'Despite my situation, I am not a patient man. If you do not assist me, I will seek help from others. I cannot afford to waste time. Do I have your word that you will bring the Cross home?'

Pragmatism was the only answer, Beauchamp decided. If Faust was willing to make a pact with the devil, why not an RMP officer? Drawing in his breath, he said, 'I'll do my best. Now, how can you help me?'

'I can give you only one name.'

'Which is?'

'Amistead.'

Pushing back his chair, Beauchamp stood up. Speer rose quickly, as if to take a salute. Beauchamp simply nodded. 'I hope that name is worth the deal we've done.'

'Remember your promise, *Kapitän*. The future of Berlin depends on you.'

VIER

A phone rang in another world. Docker could hear it but he preferred to stay where he was, in a peaceful, soft, darkened place.

The insistent sound of the phone penetrated the kapok of his pillow. He yanked the receiver off its cradle. 'Ah hah?'

'Is that you, Mr Docker?' asked a polite male voice.

'I think so.'

'My name is Andrew Laurent. Do you think you'll be coming into your office today? I've been waiting some time. I'd like to talk business with you.'

Business? He sat up. 'What's the time?' At least it sounded more professional than 'What day is it?'

'Exactly four o'clock.'

'Give me 10 minutes, Mr Laurent.'

Docker washed his face, then crossed to his apartment window and wrenched it open.

Across the street, a middle-aged man in a badly cut, heavy woollen suit mooched along the sidewalk. Docker was certain the man had only begun to shuffle away when the window creaked.

Docker leant partly out of the window and saw the man was moving south towards Broome with the studied pace of someone trying to appear innocent. There was no time to think about who he might be, however, as Docker rushed out the door and headed to his office.

He guessed that Laurent was the natty party sitting stiffly on the narrow bench pressed against the wall on the landing outside his office. Laurent looked like he'd been ironed into his suit. His pocket handkerchief had more silk in it than Docker's entire wardrobe.

The visitor delivered a double handshake – his right hand gripping Docker's tightly while his left hand cupped Docker's elbow. Docker felt as if he was about to be sold something. Something he didn't need.

Inside the office, Docker indicated two mismatched visitors' chairs and sat down in his own chipped captain's chair, watching as Laurent took in a steel desk fan, an outdated phone and a ceramic ashtray with Edison Hotel markings. The only human touch came from faint piano music seeping in through the thin wall – Gershwin's 'The Man I Love' courtesy of the music teacher in room 202.

Laurent opened by offering his profuse thanks to Docker for coming to the office so quickly. It was getting late and Docker must be very busy.

Docker shrugged slightly. 'We're both busy men.' His

remark took Docker back to his morning lie to Elsa Kessler.

'Are you a religious man, Mr Docker?' asked Laurent.

'It depends on how much trouble I'm in.'

'In your line of business you must be praying all the time. I certainly am in mine.'

'And what business is that, Mr Laurent?'

Laurent looked momentarily surprised, not by the bluntness of the question but by the fact that Docker didn't know. 'I'm an antiques dealer,' he said, touching the knot of his tie. 'Antiquities mainly, not the usual bric-a-brac. I've just received a shipment of extraordinary Roman glass and busts plus a collection of early Byzantine icons.' He glanced around Docker's dowdy office and sighed as if he couldn't imagine any of the items displayed there.

'Mr Laurent,' Docker broke in. 'The reason you interrupted my afternoon to come to the office is . . . ?'

'The Cross of Christ,' said Laurent, watching for Docker's reaction. 'Well, actually a small piece of the original Cross. It's worth a fortune.'

Docker's mouth twitched into a small smile.

Noting the sceptical reaction, Laurent pulled a steel cigar tube from his inside coat pocket. He fumbled in another pocket and found a cigar cutter and a gold lighter with milled casing. 'Mr Docker, what do you know about the history of crucifixion?' he asked, aligning the three objects on the desktop in the shape of a cross.

'Very little,' admitted Docker.

'The first thing to remember is that the Romans saw

nothing heroic or mystical about crucifixion. It was Christ's followers who eventually took the shape of the cross as a symbol of their faith. But the actual Cross – the True Cross – may not have been as modern Christians imagine it. The Cross may have been in the shape of a capital 'T' or even just a simple pole. The only thing that is certain is that it was made of wood. There are countless fragments of wood purporting to come from the True Cross scattered across Europe in cathedrals, abbeys and private collections.'

Docker was beginning to fidget. He pushed his chair back to stretch his legs and pulled out a cigarette.

Laurent appeared a little irritated. 'Surely you're interested in crosses, Mr Docker?'

'Only double ones,' replied Docker. He nodded at Laurent's items on the desk. 'I don't want to disturb the pretty pattern, but can I have a light?'

Laurent flicked the wheel on his lighter and leant across the desk to Docker. 'You should try cigars, they're more satisfying.'

With that, he clipped the end off a Montecristo and lit it. The smoke cloud was worthy of Dresden. 'The good news is that I know a country where there's a reliquary holding the real McCoy.'

'Palestine?'

'No.'

'The US?'

'Right on the money, Mr Docker. Now I want to buy that treasure.'

32

'What's stopping you?'

'Only one small detail. I don't know precisely who owns the Cross.'

'And you'd like me to find the owner?'

'That's right. And I want you to negotiate a deal for both the reliquary that holds the Cross and the Cross itself.'

'This sounds like *your* type of work. I know nothing about buying antiques.'

'Under normal circumstances I'd handle it,' said Laurent, and he paused again for effect before drawing on his cigar and blowing smoke at the ceiling light. 'Unfortunately, the current owner didn't go through legitimate channels to get the Cross. You're definitely the man for the job, and you're said to be honest. Wouldn't you agree?'

'I'd never trust any man who described himself as honest.'

'Nevertheless,' said Laurent, 'others see you as someone who can be trusted.'

'Who are these *others*?' Docker looked Laurent up and down. 'And how'd I know anyone that you'd know?'

'I think you're being too modest. There are a variety of people who speak highly of you, including some who've told me that you were once stationed in Germany.'

Docker tensed. 'What's that got to do with it?'

'I'm told by my contacts that you were in the military police in Berlin. When I heard that, I knew you were the man for me. The German connection will be useful. After all, we're talking about the spoils of war.'

Docker drew in air with a snort. 'Nazi treasure.'

Laurent waved his cigar. 'I take your point. I wouldn't waste your time or mine on fool's gold. However, it'd be hard to deny this isn't treasure and the last owner wasn't a Nazi. Do you know of Mr Albert Speer?'

'I saw what was left of his work in Berlin.'

'He's a great architect if you like your public buildings big and boorish. Speer had one such building in mind, a Great Hall topped by a dome so massive that clouds would form beneath its ceiling. He planned to build the Great Hall near the Reichstag and symbolically, or perhaps whimsically, decided that a piece of the Cross should sit atop the dome. It was to have been the world's most powerful good luck charm.'

'Where'd the Germans get the Cross from?'

'When it comes to the Cross, nothing is ever straightforward,' said Laurent. 'The relic bounced around the Middle East and Europe before disappearing in North Africa. However, in 1920 two missionaries browsing in an Addis Ababa souk spotted the reliquary it was kept in. The Cross was still inside. For 30 silver thalers – an ironic price in the circumstances – they struck a bargain. They were preparing to head for the Red Sea when they were arrested for trafficking in antiquities. Their purchase was placed in the Coptic cathedral in Addis Ababa, from where it was souvenired by the all-conquering Italian Army in 1936. The Italians took it to Rome and left it with the Vatican for safekeeping. Three years later, Mussolini presented the Cross to Hitler as a gift.'

'How much is it worth?'

'I'd estimate it's worth up to half a million dollars.'

'Christ!'

'Precisely.'

Laurent took out a long leather wallet and withdrew a neatly folded slip of paper and five $100 bills. 'It's a down payment for fees and expenses. Both have to be accounted for in writing.'

Docker noted that Laurent allowed his charm to slip a little once he placed the cash on the table. He also spotted that, when Laurent relaxed, the Claude Rains delivery gave way to something less refined.

The slip of paper contained details of a trans-Atlantic Pan American Clipper that had arrived at LaGuardia.

'My guess,' said Laurent with the firmness of a man who didn't make guesses, 'is that the relic was tucked in the baggage of an actress named Bridgette Hunter who has ties with a New York fine arts and antiques dealer called Clive Gaffney. But there's no sign of Gaffney having accompanied her to Europe.'

Docker picked up the paper and left the money on the desk. He looked the paper over and then drummed his fingers on the desktop. 'Anything else, aside from the two names? Who'd Miss Hunter meet with in Europe?'

Laurent shook his head. 'Unfortunately, I don't know the answer to that.'

Docker reached for the money, asking himself: Who am I to get uppity about accepting a job? Anyone who spent the night in a hotel closet had no call to sneer at a case involving the Cross of Christ and a pile of nice crisp $100 bills. A thin pile, but a pile all the same. Docker put the money into his wallet and asked Laurent if he knew where Miss Hunter and Gaffney were now.

'Forget the woman for the moment. I'm still trying to find out where she is. The person to start with is Gaffney. He's got an office on East 86th. But be wary of him.'

'How wary?'

'I suggest you carry a gun.'

FÜNF

The attendant already had the body on a trolley by the time Beauchamp and White entered the morgue at Spandau. The body had lost the defiled appearance it had on the first day Beauchamp saw it and seemed to have regained some semblance of dignity. Beauchamp leant forward and forced back the dead man's lips to inspect his teeth. 'As I said before, local dental work. Not particularly impressive. The Americans do these things so much better.'

'Perhaps the Krauts were fighting for better dental care,' said the attendant, only adding 'sir' when he saw Beauchamp's raised eyebrow.

'Where're his clothes?' Beauchamp asked.

The attendant bent down and lifted a wicker basket off the floor. He placed it next to the body.

As Beauchamp worked his way through the clothes, he tried to ignore the sweet, ripe smell rising from the nearby corpse. He lifted the victim's jacket up and admired the cut. On the inside right-hand pocket he noted a barely visible cloth tag with *W288R* stitched in gold thread.

'Jesus wept. I'm an idiot,' he murmured before tossing the coat into the basket and snatching up a shoe. On the inside of the leather tongue there was also a mix of figures and letters. He threw the shoe the length of the morgue room and White caught it.

'Bespoke tailoring,' Beauchamp said, waving the coat. 'There are personal codes from the maker sewn into the clothing. It's the same with the shoes. Get on to Kilgour French Stanbury in London and Johnston & Murphy, wherever the hell they are in the United States. Quote the codes to them and find out who this customer was.'

As soon as White returned to headquarters, he began making the calls. He had his answers within 24 hours, first from London and then from Nashville, Tennessee. The customer who'd bought the suits and the shoes was Dr Friedrich Kessler. In both cases the address given was on East 68th Street, New York City. The corpse finally had a name but Beauchamp still had no inkling as to Kessler's background. An industrialist? A diplomat? A spy? German, most likely. But what was Kessler doing living in America, having his tailoring done in England and dying in Germany?

Beauchamp asked White to follow up with the US authorities in Berlin and precisely two hours after White made the phone call, military policemen in a US Army ambulance appeared at the Spandau morgue with papers to claim Kessler's body. The morgue attendant contacted Beauchamp.

'Not a chance,' Beauchamp snapped into the phone. 'Leave Herr Kessler where he is.'

'The MPs are fairly insistent,' said the morgue attendant nervously. 'They want the body.'

'Give me half an hour,' said Beauchamp, thumping down the phone. It was far too early in the investigation to release Kessler's body, but he knew he needed support. He went immediately to his commanding officer, Major Ashley Cooper-Wright.

Cooper-Wright's response was blunt: 'For God's sake, why the hell should we keep the bloody body? Have the Americans given you any information about the victim?'

'None, sir. We've only just alerted them to the fact he had a US address. Now they want to scoop up the body. I can't imagine why they won't tell us about Kessler's background. It's very frustrating.'

'That's a policeman's lot, captain,' said Cooper-Wright. He straightened in his chair. 'Give the body to them immediately.'

'When you say "immediately", sir, do you mean –' Beauchamp began.

'Now, captain!' Cooper-Wright shouted before adding in a quieter tone, 'I also suggest you hand the entire case over to the Yanks. It's one of their citizens, let them worry about it.'

With the issue solved, the major returned to dunking his biscuit in his milky tea.

Beauchamp repeated the conversation to White, stressing the word *'suggest'*. 'It wasn't an order. As far as I'm concerned we're still responsible for finding out who killed Kessler. We've got his name and, for what it's worth, Speer's tip-off about Amistead.'

'What should we tell the morgue?'

'Let the Americans have the body. It's getting a bit pongy anyway.'

'And Amistead?'

'I think we should pay him a visit.'

There was a glimmer of sunlight through the office window. With a small smile, Beauchamp crossed the room and looked out, thinking. The killers had driven up to the abandoned hotel in a car with new tyres. You didn't have to be Richard Hannay to realise only a few privileged civilians could afford such luxuries in Berlin. If you had money in this city and were ostentatious enough to spend it, then you were either in the black market or buying from it. Either way, you dealt with Alaine Amistead. He was the most powerful of the city's *Schieber*, the large-scale black-market operators. The problem was that Amistead lived in Berlin's US sector. In theory, the partition of the city in 1945 wasn't a major impediment to the Western Allies' military police forces operating across sectors. In practice, Britain, France and the US took a parochial approach to their slabs of urban territory and actively discouraged what they saw as competitive police activity. Just raising the idea of a visit to the US sector was enough to get White looking anxious.

Beauchamp remained breezy. 'We're allies. You and I will just be taking a short drive into the zone for a brief chat with someone who does business all over the city. Who could complain about that?'

White started to protest but Beauchamp reassured him. Entering the US sector on official business wouldn't be a problem. The British, French and Americans had agreed to bring their three sectors in Germany under the banner 'Trizonia'. 'A suitably Ruritanian moniker,' Beauchamp said when he'd first heard the name. This Allied cooperation also extended to the western sectors of Berlin. Surely the Yanks couldn't kick up a fuss if he and White did a little low-key snooping?

By mid-morning, they were heading towards Amistead's home. A frustrated White sat at the wheel grumbling about the traffic. He swung the Jeep around a pile of debris spilling out onto Grunewaldstrasse, but the vehicle was soon hemmed in by a number of trucks driven by *Trümmerfrauen* – rubble women. These *Frauen* were paid to haul rubble from bombed-out buildings and transport it out of the city centre.

White turned into a side street to avoid the jam, mumbling that he was sure the trucks were in fact delivering rubble *into* Berlin. He put his foot on the accelerator as Beauchamp flipped open his notebook. Beauchamp needed to get the case in order. He wasn't puzzled by the fact that the corpse's fingerprints weren't on file. In chaotic postwar Germany, numerous files had been lost, most of them deliberately. Beauchamp was, however, baffled that no one had reported the dead man missing. He corrected himself: no one had reported to the *British* authorities that the man had disappeared. The Yanks, however, must have known.

Through the Jeep's windscreen, Beauchamp caught sight of strings of small flags outside a line of dreary shops. The Union Jack, the Tricolore and the Stars and Stripes caught what breeze there was. Beauchamp knew the locals here appreciated the occupying forces on a purely commercial level, unlike shopkeepers in the Russian sector. He couldn't picture Germans in the East hanging out flags for the Soviets.

Turning to White, he said mischievously, 'What do you think our chances are of getting away with a quick visit to the Russian sector as well as the US one?' He only had to wait a second for the reaction.

'Fucking hell!' shouted White, knuckles blanching on the steering wheel. 'The Ruskies are a right pain in the arse at any time. If we go snooping around their sector without notifying them, they'll have a fit. If we aren't arrested, they'll dump us in the shit with the major.'

'Just kidding,' said Beauchamp, rather pleased to have lit the corporal's fuse. The Royal Military Police were wary of the MGB – the Russian Secret Service – and the feeling was mutual. The MGB had orchestrated a recent spate of street kidnappings, which had the dual effect of removing German citizens perceived to be pro-Western while terror-ising the remainder of the population.

Berliners in the East had every reason to be scared, and the RMP had decided to stay clear of the Russians. Even at

Potsdamer Platz, where the zones intersected, the RMP avoided upsetting their Russian counterparts.

The Russians, however, weren't nearly as well mannered and had been playing their disruptive games for months. In April a British Viking civilian passenger aircraft had been intercepted by a Soviet Yak fighter about two miles from touchdown at Gatow airfield in the British zone. First the Yak had buzzed the Viking, then banked, rolled and collided with the Viking, ripping off its wing. Both planes went down, with the Yak crashing in the British sector and the Viking falling on the Russian side. When the Russians refused to hand back the bodies of the 14 people who had been aboard the Viking, the British declined to return the Soviet pilot's body. Beauchamp had been part of the negotiating team. Or 'non-negotiating team', as he'd dubbed it.

April had been a difficult month. A few days prior to the Viking crash, the Russians had temporarily stopped outgoing freight trains to Munich and Hamburg. A team working out of the RMP's headquarters was putting armed guards on locomotives to attempt to stop the Russians commandeering western sector trains.

Guarding trains wasn't Beauchamp's line of work. He liked the flexibility of criminal investigation, which involved worse hours but more freedom.

By the time Beauchamp and White reached the US zone, the sun was out and the pavements on either side of the road looked relatively clean. When Beauchamp saw the first of the ice-cream shops that had sprung up in the American sector, he said to White, 'Too good to pass by.'

White nodded, turned the wheel and the Jeep edged alongside the kerb. Beauchamp was first in the shop door, hand in trouser pocket reaching for his money. When wartime rationing forced the banning of ice-cream making in Britain after 1942, Beauchamp had been miffed. Now, six years later, he took every limited opportunity to enjoy it.

'Is this allowed in work hours?' asked White as they slipped back into the vehicle with their ice-cream cones.

'We've been busy interrogating a reliable source,' Beauchamp quipped.

'You only asked him if he had chocolate.'

'It was a legitimate question. Should a senior officer ever stop me and ask about ice-cream flavour availability, I'll have the answer.'

They drove on, the silence broken occasionally by Beauchamp's sighs of delight.

Beauchamp and White enjoyed working together although they didn't share too many interests. When White had first been assigned to Beauchamp they'd had little to say after the first few minutes, then somehow the conversation turned to food. Eating had become a topic they could safely fall back on to escape the monotony and horror of police work.

White drove down increasingly suburban streets. Only a few of the trees had been cut down for firewood and there were enough newly sprouted linden leaves to give the area a sense of calm.

A woman pushed a pram down a cracked footpath. The reassuring familiarity of the scene was slightly spoilt for

Beauchamp by the pram being piled with pieces of broken furniture. On the same footpath, an elderly organ grinder with a frog-like mouth and a once dapper suit steered his contraption in the opposite direction, politely stepping aside to allow the woman to pass.

Guarded by two men, the black iron gates at the entrance to Amistead's home in Schöneberg were impressive. As the Jeep turned in, one of the guards moved quickly to the driver's side and tapped on the window. White slid the window down so that Beauchamp could lean across to explain they'd come to speak with Amistead.

The man put one hand on the Jeep door handle while he spoke into a walkie-talkie. After listening to the returning crackle he smiled and said, 'Herr Amistead would like to know if this is a social visit or a police matter.'

'We're here to discuss a murder,' said Beauchamp.

The answer was relayed in German, and Beauchamp heard a one-word reply in French: '*D'accord*'. The man stepped back, waving for the gates to be opened. Beauchamp calculated that if he returned uninvited and the gates were locked, he'd need more than a Jeep to crash through.

They were guided by a man in a waistcoat and striped trousers into a small entrance hall and then along a wide corridor lined with a selection of pricey but mismatched furniture – here a mahogany bureau, there a marble-topped console table. Beauchamp paused for a moment and studied the furniture. No doubt Amistead would claim the items were bought legitimately and he'd have the receipts to prove it.

They were taken into a room panelled in dark wood that smelt of furniture polish. It was the most welcoming thing about the house.

Beauchamp looked away from the furniture to White who was attempting to look taller than his stocky five foot nine. One hand hovered near his holster while the other toyed nervously with his lanyard. Beauchamp signalled to him to relax. There was little chance of violence in this expensively decorated room. The pile of the carpet was too thick and too well tended for the owner to want it scuffed or stained.

Their guide spoke quietly into a telephone. Yet another man, this one dressed as a valet, appeared a minute later. The valet asked Beauchamp and White if they would mind leaving their weapons with the guard.

Beauchamp gave a short laugh. 'Not a chance,' he said, heading off in the direction the valet had come from. White took his cue and followed. The valet didn't appear ready for a confrontation and caught up with them at a doorway. '*Kommen Sie mit mir, bitte,*' he said, opening the door and gesturing to them to follow.

This time they were led into a large room painted a pale yellow. The walls were covered with artworks.

Beauchamp brightened suddenly. Ice-cream wasn't the only thing rationed in Britain during the war. From 1939 on, London galleries moved their artworks to safety, leaving amateur enthusiasts such as Beauchamp with empty Saturday afternoons. In place of galleries, Beauchamp had taken to roaming antique shops admiring furniture he couldn't afford. Now he had a chance to experience art again. He tapped White on the forearm. 'Now this is interesting,' he said.

He began to examine the paintings. Manet, Sisley, Cassatt, Degas. Beauchamp was certain of the artists and their styles but he didn't recognise the majority of the paintings. Only a few were signed. Almost pressing his nose against the canvas, Beauchamp admired a Kirchner with its trademark sinister dark lines and anonymous faces.

A smooth, French-accented voice behind him asked, 'Is it to your taste, *capitaine?*'

'Yes,' Beauchamp replied, continuing to study the brushstrokes.

'This is the ideal city in which to hang one of Kirchner's works.' Beauchamp straightened as the Frenchman moved to his side and grasped his hand in a firm handshake. His smile seemed sincere. Amistead was just below medium height, with pale skin and a thickening waistline. His cream shirt and pale grey slacks were cut with enough flair to disguise most of his visible faults. A paisley patterned cravat covered his second chin. The look was that of a successful Parisienne stockbroker.

'The Expressionists were infatuated with Berlin, particularly with its gangsters and whores,' Amistead concluded.

Beauchamp asked if the painting was genuine.

'*C'est vrai, capitaine.* You are right, of course. It is a fake. Quite a few in my collection are forgeries, although many of the works are genuine. The trick is to spot the phoney from the real thing.'

'It's illegal to pass off a forgery as the genuine article whether it's currency like the Reichsmark or a work of art,' said White with the slow intonation of a beat copper who'd caught a butcher selling horsemeat.

It was the Frenchman's turn to take the high ground. 'But in this case I am not selling the paintings. They are for my amusement only. I must say your comment about the Reichsmark was perceptive, *caporal*. The artist who created this painting was once a forger. *Malheureusement*, with the value of the Reichsmark now it is more profitable for him to create copies for people such as myself.' He offered his hand to White. 'I am Alaine Amistead.'

Beauchamp watched as White took Amistead's hand and stared down at it. There was an awkward pause in the conversation which Beauchamp filled. 'Captain Beauchamp, Corporal White. We've come about a body.'

'I cannot help you, *capitaine*. I am a businessman and I deal in most things, but not dead bodies.'

'Really,' said Beauchamp, thinking: What if they still have pulses? According to Beauchamp's informants, Amistead ran a stable of whores in Charlottenburg. Still, today wasn't the day for questions about pimping. 'The body we're interested in was chauffeured to where it was dumped. In any other city that mightn't be so important, but here it indicates that the killers had access to private transportation, in this case a Volkswagen. And going by the tracks they left, the killers had something even rarer still – new tyres.'

'I do not own such a car. After all a Volkswagen is not

élégant. If, however, the people you are seeking had the good taste to be driving a Mercedes 170 –'

Beauchamp was impatient. 'I understand. But I hear you're a handy man to know if you need a spare car part.'

'As I said, I am a businessman. There is nothing illegal about car parts, *n'est-ce pas?*'

'That depends. I also hear that if I was looking for scarce medicines or a slightly used woman, you'd be the man to come to.'

'*Capitaine*, you are out of your league and your terri-tory,' said Amistead. 'This is the American zone. My business is not your business.' The smile came back. 'I think we should discuss anything further over coffee.'

With a nod the valet left the room and Amistead eased himself into an upholstered chair.

'You appear to be a man of taste,' he said to Beauchamp. 'What do you think of this?' He slapped the chair arms.

Beauchamp cocked his head and, with the confidence of a Saturday afternoon browser, took a guess: 'It's a copy in the style of a Louis XV fauteuil.'

Amistead studied Beauchamp for a few seconds before asking softly, 'A copy? Should I take a policeman's word or that of the person who sold it to me?'

Before Beauchamp could reply, Amistead crossed the room to another chair. 'And this one?'

'Another copy, passing itself off as a George III wing armchair,' said Beauchamp. 'But please,' he added, 'don't take my word for it.'

'I won't,' said Amistead.

Beauchamp was confused – one moment the Frenchman was agreeing his art was faked, the next he was defending the integrity of his furniture. Perhaps he was lying about the first and just plain conceited about the second. Beauchamp was about to return to the paintings when an elderly woman in black and white entered with the coffee. As Amistead watched, Beauchamp slowly savoured the flavour of the arabica beans. It'd been months since he'd tasted coffee that hadn't been augmented with chicory.

As Beauchamp and White refilled their cups, Amistead adopted a softer tone. 'Who was the victim?'

'Friedrich Kessler,' replied Beauchamp. 'An American citizen but possibly German-born. Do you know him?'

'No.' Amistead finally poured himself a cup of coffee. 'Who is he?'

'That's a mystery – for the moment,' said Beauchamp.

'How did he die?'

'A bullet to the head. It appears he was tortured over a number of hours – perhaps days – before being killed. His body was left in a hotel near the Landwehrkanal.' Beauchamp put down his cup. 'You mentioned that you don't own a Volkswagen. What about a Walther P38?'

'Is that a car?'

Beauchamp maintained a level tone. 'No, it's a gun. Kessler was *shot* with a Walther P38.'

'I am a Frenchman living in the American zone, with the British to the west and the Russians to the east. With so many armies protecting me, why would I need a gun?'

Beauchamp wasn't going to get far with Amistead

playing a dead bat to every question. He would have to do some more digging before talking to Amistead again. Settling back in his chair, he concentrated on the rich coffee, trying to make the cup last. It reminded him of his first trip to Paris before the war. He'd just left university, had some money and was staying in an irresistible city. Today his values were so compromised he was willing to listen to a crook babble on for a while if it meant a decent cup of coffee. He was disappointed that there was no offer of a final cup. Amistead reached for a small brass bell and tinkled it. The valet came in and the two Englishmen left without shaking Amistead's hand.

As White gunned his engine and nosed the Jeep down the driveway, Beauchamp wondered how long it would take before Amistead's slow fuse finally set off a Gallic explosion. Beauchamp had noted how Amistead's fingernails had pressed hard into his palms as the policemen lingered over their coffee. Despite feigning hospitality, Amistead had wanted them out of that house – fast. Guilty as sin, thought Beauchamp, but which sin? At this stage of the investigation, it seemed an illogical step to link a crook who specialised in contraband and pimping with the torture and death of an American citizen.

Beauchamp was frustrated that the British knew so little about Kessler other than his new nationality. Why had the Americans been in such a hurry to secure the body and take it from Spandau? There were no files that tied Kessler to the Nazis, the Americans or the black market but, like the man's missing fingerprints, Beauchamp wouldn't be surprised if Kessler's life had been wiped from the joint Allied records. It was so easy to make a man disappear; just open a filing cabinet, lift out a manila folder and light a match. In the past, Beauchamp had done it himself to keep an informant from being collared for some mundane crime by the *Schutzpolizei*.

His thoughts were interrupted by White taking a corner a little too quickly. Beauchamp looked up. The northern part of the sky was dark with approaching rain as they headed back towards the British zone. In full sarcastic flight, White mimicked the Frenchman's accent. 'Walther P38? Ees zat a car?' Then he added the only French word he was confident of, '*Merde*'.

'He wasn't telling the truth about a lot of things,' agreed Beauchamp. 'That includes the paintings. He's a man who values rare objects. That business about forgeries was just a red herring. I'd say the majority of the art and the furnishings were real and almost certainly looted during the war.'

The traffic was thinning out, and Beauchamp leant back in his seat, allowing himself the luxury of relaxing and thinking about the officers' mess dinner that evening. Shepherd's pie.

A moment later Beauchamp was flung sideways, his shoulder thumping against the window when White swung the steering wheel hard right. The vehicle bounced off the kerb as White tried to avoid hitting another Jeep that had cut in front of them and was now screeching to a halt.

Fünf

Two US military policemen jumped out and ran towards the Englishmen, the lead MP shouting: 'Out, out! Get the fuck out of the car!'

SECHS

'When you telephoned you said you were involved in collecting, Mr Docker. What's your main passion? Paintings? I have a stunning Cézanne available immediately or, if you prefer something with extra bite, I'll have a Braques arriving within the month.'

Docker had been expecting a flamboyant person with a substantial belly. Gaffney was a tall, thin, freckled, copper-haired man with a damp but firm handshake. Docker judged that Gaffney's unctuous manner was designed to ingratiate him with clients – the Uriah Heep of the Upper East Side.

'I'm a wood man, myself,' replied Docker.

'Excellent. I have a pendant mask from the kingdom of Benin.'

'I'm looking for something a little older. Something men would go to war over.'

'Such as?' asked Gaffney, his eyes narrowing.

'The Cross of Christ,' said Docker.

Gaffney opened his mouth as if to say something, then snapped it shut and reached across to a silver box to pinch out a cigarette. 'I suggest you try the Church of the Holy Trinity. It's two blocks north.'

'Thanks,' said Docker, 'I'd heard you're good at geography. In fact, I'd heard you can get anything from anywhere.'

'Anywhere,' Gaffney agreed with a hint of pride, leaning back in his chair and letting the cigarette smoke stream into the air. It was a pose he obviously enjoyed – there was a brown smudge on the ceiling where the smoke had drifted up over the years. 'Who told you about me?'

'Someone in the trade,' Docker replied.

'Without being rude, Mr Docker, you don't look like someone who even knows a collector. The people I usually deal with aren't quite as . . .' Gaffney appeared to hunt for a word that was the least likely to prompt his visitor to swing a punch at him, 'athletic.'

'I'll take that as a compliment,' said Docker. 'Getting back to the item in question, do you know where I can find it?'

'Possibly. Are you aware there is no longer *one* Cross?' Not waiting for an answer, Gaffney went on. 'It was broken up. If there are any remaining pieces they're rare. Very rare. Genuine collectors are obsessive about a relic's provenance. In the case of the Cross that provenance must be impeccable and, after so much time, how can one be sure which is the genuine article and which is a fake, albeit a fake that might be centuries old?'

Docker was about to say he didn't think people actually said 'albeit' any more but decided against it.

'How much are you willing to pay for such a treasure?' Gaffney asked.

'That depends on how valuable it is.'

Gaffney's nostrils splayed as he sneered, 'Ah, I see you're a philosopher.'

'Put it this way, I'll pay the market price plus a premium.'

'In that case, I may have an idea where to start.'

Showing Docker to the door, Gaffney was solicitous. 'I'll pick you up at 11 in the morning. You're going to enjoy tomorrow.'

Gaffney picked up Docker on the corner of Prince and Mercera. He was driving a new Ford Sportsman De Luxe with the hood down. They drove north through Manhattan.

The car swung away from the Connecticut coastal road and headed towards the wooded hills. In the passenger seat, Docker was attempting to keep his hat on. He felt uncomfortable with the muggy air pulling at him. Occasionally a rivulet of sweat rolled down his body and pooled on the waistband of his trousers. A few seconds later the sweat evaporated. Even in shirtsleeves he was too hot. Fuck the great Connecticut outdoors, he thought. His only comfort was knowing that his Smith & Wesson .38 was in the pocket of his jacket, now flung across the back seat.

Docker felt himself tilt sharply sideways as Gaffney

suddenly took a forest road. He swung the powerful car up a winding section that made Docker slightly bilious. At least it was cooler, with the trees shading most of the road. They drove higher and the mugginess started to give way to something refreshingly like . . . like . . . Docker couldn't quite place it. He sniffed.

'Fresh air,' Gaffney said, as if reading his passenger's mind.

Gaffney slowed on the forest road and turned up a long driveway.

They drew to a halt outside an imposing dark grey Gothic Revival house, its steep gable roof trimmed with fussy, light grey vergeboards. The effect was of an evil gingerbread mansion. The house sat with its back to a small cliff.

Docker found the brooding house and the isolation disconcerting, but Gaffney appeared oblivious to the wary look on his face. He drummed his palms on the steering wheel in delight. 'I get out here every few weeks but the place still excites me. My client has a plantation in Cuba but rarely leaves this property these days.'

'Really?' said Docker, forcing himself out of the car. In a centre window on the top floor, a curtain moved. 'Someone knows we're here.'

'Don't worry, we'll get a warm welcome.'

Docker weighed the tone of Gaffney's voice to assess the level of irony. There wasn't any and he started to calm down a little. Following Gaffney, he headed towards the house, patting the gun in his jacket pocket for reassurance.

As they reached the steps the front door creaked open and a young man in a plaid shirt and carefully pressed flannel trousers stepped into the sunlight. The casual clothes made Docker feel over-dressed.

The man smiled at Docker. 'Welcome, my name is Willi Rühmann,' he said in a voice that was very low, hesitant and accented. 'Randolph is in the garden.'

Rühmann nodded at Gaffney. 'Good to see you, as always.'

'Do you two work together?' Docker asked Gaffney.

'Yes. Willi is a . . .' he hesitated for a second, 'business acquaintance. He acts as a negotiator for some very interesting contacts. Don't you Willi?'

'That is correct – I work mainly in Europe,' said Rühmann so softly that the breeze almost carried away his words.

'*Ich habe es leider nicht verstanden,*' Docker said casually.

'Your German is sound – for a foreigner,' said Rühmann, who immediately turned away and walked into the house.

Gaffney touched Docker's elbow. 'What did you say?'

'I told him that unfortunately I hadn't heard a word he'd said.'

'Showing off your German?'

'No, just trying to be friendly.'

'Friendly.' Gaffney repeated the word as if it were the first time he'd come across it.

They followed Rühmann inside and Gaffney began rubbing his hands with excitement as he walked past walls dotted with mounted elk horns, feathered head-dresses and crossed muskets. 'Wait 'til you see the view!' he said excitedly.

Rühmann led them to French doors that opened onto a wide terrace beyond which soft green lawn ran several hundred yards to the lip of the valley.

'Now isn't that breathtaking?' said Gaffney.

To Docker it was all too stagey, too much like a *Vacation in Scenic Connecticut* pamphlet. Nevertheless he played the game, whistling his appreciation.

On the other side of the lawn, a bald man dressed in sporting whites was notching an arrow into a bow. He pulled back the bowstring, aimed at a butt near the cliff edge and released the arrow. It arced slightly before whacking into the butt's bullseye.

Gaffney clapped his hands in polite applause. The bald man turned, smiled and mouthed something unintelligible, beckoning them over. The two men went down a wide set of steps and onto the lawn, with Rühmann following a few paces behind.

His previous nerves now abated, Docker revelled in the spring of the turf beneath his feet. He'd spent his life in big cities, loving the excitement and the press of the crowds on the sidewalks. But, hell, this grass was something else. It felt alive.

'Welcome,' the bald man said, propping his bow in a rack before walking towards Docker, his hand out-stretched. The slight flabbiness beneath his jawline and his liver-spotted hands marked him out as over 60; he strode forward with an athlete's gait and pumped Gaffney's hand.

'Randolph Morton,' he said, putting the emphasis on

'Randolph'. Docker responded with 'John Docker', stressing the surname instead.

'Delighted you could come, John,' said Morton, ignoring
the hint. 'Would you care to try your luck?' he asked,
gesturing towards the bow in the rack.

Docker walked across to the rack and lifted out the
nearest of three wooden bows. It was heavier than he had
imagined and he felt awkward holding it. After jerking at
the bowstring, he was gently scolded by Morton, who
insisted he draw the string taut in one fluid movement.
Docker felt the bow swing down as he shot the arrow
forward. He watched as the feathered tail sailed gracefully
over the top of the target and caught an updraft from the
cliff face. It continued to arc until it dropped out of sight.

Docker quickly handed back the bow to Morton. 'Sorry
about the arrow,' he said. 'I hope nobody's hiking down
there.'

'In some places it's a sheer drop of 200 feet onto the
rocks. Only folks who live around here would go down
there. People like me. I always take a walk before dinner,
don't I, Clive?' He looked at Gaffney.

Gaffney simply nodded.

Turning his attention back to Docker, Morton put an
arm around his shoulder. 'But first, let's have a drink.' With
Rühmann a few steps behind, the group headed for the
house.

Docker could just see the outline of a young woman in
the doorway that led onto the terrace. As he shaded his eyes
to study her, she pulled back into the room behind her.

'You'll be meeting Bridgette over drinks,' said Morton, taking it all in. His arm still around Docker's shoulder, he added, 'I'm told, John, that you're a collector.'

Docker kept staring at the empty doorway. So *that* was the Bridgette mentioned by Laurent. 'Let's say I'm interested in rare objects,' he said.

In response, Morton's hand squeezed Docker's shoulder. It hurt. Docker couldn't tell if the gesture was an overly friendly one or a sign of what was to come.

SIEBEN

Beauchamp tried to block out the organ grinder's music that rose from the corner across from the US military police headquarters. Looking through the window, he could see a white-haired, bespectacled man, neatly dressed in a long-coated, three-piece suit, standing proudly alongside a hand-cranked organ. The elderly man was playing the second movement of Brahms' German Requiem. The music was an unpleasant intrusion in an unpleasant day. Even from a distance, Beauchamp could see the instrument sat on a specially made carriage, like a giant baby pram. Suddenly the man stopped grinding and stepped back, glancing down at his dusty black shoes before running the toe caps over the back of each trouser leg.

Beauchamp had seen the man before, in the street near Amistead's house. The organ grinder appeared to be preparing for another performance. Beauchamp swore under his breath. He hated the sad monotony of the manufactured music, with its mournful tones reminding him of overcast days, desolate town squares and discarded newspapers blowing against his ankles. Beauchamp liked his music flowing from a wireless as he sat in comfort with a cigarette and a gin and tonic.

As the elderly man began to crank the handle, Beauchamp turned away from the window. He tapped out two cigarettes from his Chesterfield packet and offered one to White. The men smoked in silence, watching the tall door that dominated the room. The door had been shut for nearly an hour, leaving Beauchamp and White to choose between sitting in the ornate chairs or standing by the window.

Staying calm was the key, Beauchamp knew. He tried to focus on the positives. Both men still had their side-arms, although White had been forced to surrender the key to the RMP Jeep. The Americans had also given them coffee – not up to Amistead's standard but welcome nonetheless – and a tin ashtray.

Beauchamp quickly ran out of positives as the door swung open and a US captain strode in and took centre stage in the room, resting his clenched fists on his hips.

'I had a hunch that one day you Limey cops would come barging into my neighbourhood,' the US captain shouted without bothering to greet the two Englishmen. 'Who the fuck do you think you are?'

'Allies?' suggested Beauchamp.

'Don't get smart with me.'

'Obviously there's been a misunderstanding, and I'd like to apologise,' said Beauchamp.

'Way too late for that.'

'We are investigating a murder.' Beauchamp tried not to sound defensive.

'*Were* investigating. *Were*,' came a voice from the doorway.

Beauchamp tried to peer past the US captain to see who the newcomer was.

The man entered the room, immediately positioning himself between the Englishmen and the window. Although the light behind cast shadows over the man's features, Beauchamp could see that he was in civilian clothes and had the bearing of someone more comfortable in uniform.

'You're off the case,' he said, stepping forward so that he was only a few feet in front of Beauchamp. The overhead light now picked out more of his features but Beauchamp still didn't recognise him. The man's crew-cut hair was going grey and his face was lined. He didn't look happy. He didn't *sound* happy. 'Got that?' he snapped.

'I understand what you're saying, but I have to disagree.'

'So, you disagree,' the man said with a hard American edge to his voice. As if on cue, two white-helmeted US military police came into the room to take up positions in front of the doorway.

Ignoring the MPs, Beauchamp maintained such a reasonable manner that he could almost hear the Americans' teeth grinding. 'It all seems quite straight-forward – or at least the logistics are clear-cut. The body of Dr Friedrich Kessler was found in the British sector by a British solider, therefore this is our case. But we are asking for your help. We still don't have any background on Kessler. You've taken the body and given us nothing in return.'

'You have our thanks,' said the man in civilian clothes, lighting a cigarette and adopting a more patient tone. 'In regards to logistics, we see it another way. The body may have been *dumped* in the British zone, but it's damn likely the murder took place in *this* sector. From the preliminary report sent to us by your superior officer . . .' He paused to let the statement sink in before continuing, 'It's obvious the victim, an American citizen, wasn't killed at the hotel where he was found. So, my money's on him being bumped off in our neighbourhood.' He blew streams of cigarette smoke out of his nostrils, giving him the appearance of a cartoon bull in an animated film. 'I'm saying this for the very last time,' he went on. 'This is definitely our case. We can either make this easy for everyone or we can file a formal complaint against you and the corporal for carrying out an investigation here without permission. Which is it to be?'

Beauchamp heard the question but didn't respond. He could only think of that bloody major, Cooper-Wright. The major must have been so determined to get the Kessler case off his books that he'd given the Yanks a copy of Beauchamp's report. He could imagine the reasons behind Cooper-Wright's narrow thinking, but why were the Americans being so uncooperative and evasive? Up until now, Beauchamp's main interest in finding Kessler's killers has been professional; the Americans' antagonism and

Cooper-Wright's mischief-making were turning it personal.

Beauchamp shrugged. 'Fine. Have it your way.' Turning to White, he said, 'Corporal, it's time to leave. We wouldn't want to monopolise these important men's time. They've got murderers to catch.'

Beauchamp and White got up. The US captain took a step forward as if to push Beauchamp back in his seat but Beauchamp's anonymous inquisitor put a hand on the US captain's elbow to stop him. He looked at the Englishmen and nodded towards the door. 'Scram.'

Beauchamp and White followed him out the door, with the captain and the MPs bunched behind them. As the group descended a broad circular staircase, a young woman stepped out of an office near one of the higher landings. Beauchamp's eyes widened. Good ice-cream and beautiful women – the Yanks had it all.

The woman stopped, put two hands on the marble railing and, ignoring the others in the group, called down to the anonymous man. 'Major Oswald!' She had a soft German accent. 'I thought of something else that might help you.'

Oswald looked up at her and clenched his jaw.

'Major Oswald? Sir, we didn't get to meet formally,' said Beauchamp and saluted the American.

'Fuck you,' whispered Oswald before looking back up to the woman. There was a note of frustration in his voice. 'Thank you, Miss Kessler. I appreciate it. I'll see you when I return.'

Oswald turned to go but the woman was already clipping down the stairs. As she came abreast of Beauchamp, he smelt a cologne that triggered heady memories of weekends in London.

She spoke only to Oswald and continued to ignore the other men. 'I have just remembered one more thing. My father said he was attempting to find . . .' She paused as if trying to think of the appropriate word, 'Special medicine for *Oma.*'

'*Oma?*' queried Oswald.

'Grandma,' Beauchamp cut in.

'I thought I asked you to keep quiet,' Oswald snapped.

'And when you say "special", Fräulein,' Beauchamp said to the woman, 'I assume you mean "black market".'

Beauchamp watched her face as she nodded first at him and then at Oswald. That's a determined jawline, he decided. Good taste in shoes and cologne plus an excellent bone structure. He judged that it would take more than chocolates and stockings to catch this Fräulein's attention.

'I'll just see these two visitors to the door,' said Oswald, clearly edgy.

'Don't bother, sir. You've been too kind already,' said Beauchamp and turned to the woman again to introduce himself.

'Elsa Kessler,' she said in response, then caught Beauchamp by surprise by offering her hand. Englishwomen rarely shook hands. Was it a show of strength, an indication she wasn't concerned about being surrounded by all these men? There was little emotion in her face as she looked at Beauchamp. He'd been hoping for more.

Oswald tried to break in, but Elsa was already speaking. 'Are you helping the major find my father's killers?'

'I hope so.'

Oswald stepped between the pair. 'Captain Boo-chump has to leave now.'

Beauchamp decided it wasn't time to argue about the pronunciation of his name. He looked back at Elsa as he was bustled down the stairs.

As he neared the bottom, Beauchamp glanced across to the adjacent street corner where out in the afternoon sunlight the elderly man continued to crank the organ handle. Was it a coincidence he had also been outside Amistead's?

The Englishman felt a push in the small of his back as the US captain nudged him down the final step. Beauchamp swung around. 'Thanks for the hospitality,' he said, smiling at the captain.

'You're welcome,' the captain replied stone-faced, then, turning to one of the MPs, he said, 'You have my permission to shoot this asshole if he returns.'

As their Jeep pulled away, Beauchamp said to White, 'Don't look, but just back there is an old chap I saw near Amistead's. Once you get out of sight, pull over.'

'What about Major Oswald and his pals?'

'Don't worry, they think they've put the fear of God into us.'

'They have,' mumbled White as he slowed and then stopped in a side street.

Beauchamp leapt from the vehicle and jogged to the corner of the main road. In the distance he could see the backs of the Americans as they filed into the building. The elderly man waited a minute before he began packing up. He draped a clean but moth-eaten cover over the musical instrument before slowly wheeling it down the street towards Beauchamp.

Beauchamp ran back to White. 'Right, we'll have to go,' he said. 'We can't tail some organ grinder when he's on foot and we're in a Jeep and in uniform.'

Near the border of the Kreuzberg and Tiergarten boroughs, White eased his foot off the accelerator. 'Talk about stroppy. For a second there I thought we'd be in a Yank jail tonight. I wonder if they serve hamburgers.'

'Good point, corporal. Perhaps we should turn around and go back.'

The day, however, had taken the edge off both their appetites. They were used to doing the quizzing, playing the interrogation game, being in control. They'd had a sharpish lesson in humility. The ice-cream shops in the US zone had lost their appeal and, as they passed the US military's sprawling PX facility on the right-hand side of the road, neither man was eager to stop.

'I'm not getting shot for a Hershey bar,' White said when the building was out of sight. 'So it's off to the NAAFI for me.'

Berlin had made an effort to look smart that morning, but scruffiness was back in vogue by late afternoon. Beauchamp idly watched the streetscape through the smudged windscreen. The city seemed bleak and down-trodden. Nearly every building had suffered from the Allied bombing, the Russian assault or the German defence. If a wall was still standing it had irregular patterns of machine-gun fire stitched up the side. If a wall was in rubble, swarms of labourers – men, women and the occasional adolescent – would struggle atop mounds of unidentifiable concrete to create some sense of order. To Beauchamp it appeared an impossible task.

As they neared the British sector, the scenery remained dreary. Loose electrical wiring hung from street poles, scraps of metal and charred rubber had been swept off roadways and left lying in gutters, tatty notices in English or German – it was impossible to tell – were plastered on most doorways.

One magnificent church appeared to stand relatively unharmed until Beauchamp noticed the windows had been blown out and the clock stood permanently at 11.34. A man in a dirty suit sat in the square in front of the church, staring intently at nothing. Two mules harnessed to an ancient cart waited passively by a street lamp. It might have seemed picturesque this morning, now it was depressing.

White had been driving with his hands clenching the steering wheel but once they crossed into the Tiergarten, he relaxed. 'Shall I check where that Kessler girl lives?'

'Okay, and see what else you can find out about her,' said Beauchamp. 'I doubt she lives here permanently, she's too smartly turned out for a Berliner.'

'Like father, like daughter.'

A Red Cap at an intersection flung up a white gauntlet to halt the Jeep. Beauchamp watched a stream of trucks move slowly across the road. Most of the junior RMP ranks were on point duty across the sector, trying to sort out the chaotic flow of convoys carrying fuel, food and machine parts. The convoys had increased in recent weeks as the petty, disruptive behaviour of the Soviets induced a defensive mentality amongst the Western powers.

Beauchamp was braced for more trouble from the Soviets. Just days earlier he and his senior RMP colleagues had been given a secret briefing at York House, one of Britain's headquarters in Berlin. Beauchamp had been advised that the Allies were about to introduce a new currency into western Germany and the western sectors of Berlin, and the Kremlin would see the move as a provocative act. By controlling the production, distribution and value of the the Reichsmark's replacement – the Deutsche Mark – the Allies would have control of Germany's currency, leaving the Russians sidelined.

The Royal Military Police's task was to safeguard the banks and ensure the smooth introduction of the currency. Beauchamp hadn't been given a date, just an indication it would be 'before the end of June'.

He'd learnt that two tons of the new Deutsche Marks, each bill stamped with a B for Berlin, were locked in a special cage in York House. From a set day, people of the western zones could exchange their Reichsmarks for

Deutsche Marks. The announcement could spark riots, or the Germans might calmly accept the changes.

Beauchamp had been advised that there would be a two-stage process. At first, German citizens would receive only enough of the new money for their current needs and then, at a later date, they could exchange the remainder of their Reichsmarks. The plan was to stop criminals parcelling out chunks of cash to front men who would claim the money was theirs. The briefing officer had said that anyone who hoarded large amounts of cash earned *heimlich, still und leise* – on the sly – would eventually have to declare it, or be left with worthless paper.

What surprised Beauchamp was the naïvety of those behind the secret briefing. They were confident that neither the Kremlin nor Germany's criminal element had any detailed knowledge of the plans for the Deutsche Mark.

By the time the Jeep drew up outside RMP headquarters, Beauchamp had given White the names of two lance corporals who might be available to assist him with tracking down the details of the girl and her grandmother and, if they were lucky, her father's movements. He also gave White a deadline – three days.

He took the stairs to his office two at a time. Despite being patronised by a black marketeer, nabbed by MPs, given the bum's rush from the US zone and losing his taste for ice-cream, he felt the day hadn't been a total loss, until a voice boomed, 'Captain! For Christ's sake, get in here!'

Beauchamp paused at the open door of his commanding officer. Seemingly trapped behind his desk by his bulging stomach, Major Ashley Cooper-Wright was apoplectic. His broad face was mauve with rage and even the small, very neat moustache bristling beneath the major's nose appeared angry.

'Are you out of your fucking mind, captain?'

'I wouldn't have thought so, sir.'

'That's where I beg to differ. For God's sake, this city isn't some English village. You can't wander anywhere you like. Our allies don't want to see two Red Caps carrying out investigations in their sectors.'

'I take *full* responsibility for going into the US zone on a case.'

'So you should.' The major sucked in air as if trying to calm himself. 'Why wasn't I informed that you were carrying out investigations in another zone?'

Beauchamp's first reaction was to go on the offensive. 'I'd like to know –' Then he stopped himself. He was about to demand to know why Cooper-Wright had passed a confidential file to the American military police without first advising the RMP team running the investigation.

'Like to know what?' Cooper-Wright clearly resented Beauchamp's tone.

It was tactical retreat time, Beauchamp decided. 'I was about to say that I would like to know why the Americans were so edgy. But, leaving that aside, I can assure you we did precisely as you ordered, sir. We allowed the Americans to take the body. But we were keen to tie up a few loose ends – such as trying to get more information on Dr Kessler's background. And we wanted to know why the killers chose our sector to ditch the body. The Yanks were less than helpful.'

'I don't blame them,' Cooper-Wright snapped. 'Bloody hell, captain, don't you know how busy we are? This is no time to miss the big picture by concentrating on some pissy little murder. Stick to your own patch, you've got enough to do.'

Beauchamp saluted and left. As he walked down the corridor it occurred to him that he hadn't told Cooper-Wright about Miss Kessler. Still, there was no need to bother the major with details.

When Beauchamp reached his office, White was depositing several stiff cardboard folders into the captain's already full in-tray.

'I imagine we're in the shit. Do we continue, sir?' asked White.

'Yes,' said Beauchamp, his lips drawn back in a forced smile. It was hard to appear confident with your commanding officer's boot protruding from your backside.

ACHT

Taking the proffered glass of Glenmorangie, Docker waved it under his nose, savouring the aroma. He could detect hints of vanilla and cinnamon, and was reminded of his first taste of this whisky in Berlin. Paranoia prompted him to put the glass down on the stone balustrade that wrapped around most of the terraced area. Berlin was stalking him. Everything in his life appeared to be linked to the city. Was it possible that this assignment from Laurent was an elaborate charade to lure him into the sticks so that Morton or maybe Gaffney or Rühmann could ice him? Were these men linked to what had happened in Germany? He moved closer to where Morton had poured the drink, trying to judge if the host had time to slip him a Mickey Finn.

The other men were ignoring Docker and enjoying their early evening drinks. Morton, playing the ebullient host, stood near a table dotted with liquor bottles, mixers and an ice bucket.

Walking back to where he'd left his glass, Docker picked it up and, with one clean movement, tipped its contents into the rose bushes below. For a man who enjoyed whisky, it was heartbreaking watching the light, sweet malt splashing onto the flowers.

He rejoined the group with the empty glass, and was caught off guard when Morton whisked the glass away and immediately refilled it.

'As I said earlier, you're a man after my own tastes,' Morton said. 'Except you take your whisky neat.'

'Unsullied,' agreed Docker, relieved that this time he'd actually seen the drink being poured. As he leant forward to pick up the glass, Docker saw from the corner of his eye a movement in the doorway onto the terrace. The woman he had glimpsed previously was making her entrance.

'Let me introduce Bridgette Hunter,' said Morton. 'Bridgette, this is John Docker. John's a specialist in antiquities. John, Bridgette's an actress.'

A striking brunette, she was tall, almost too tall for Morton. She was sharply dressed in jodhpurs, a pink polka dot shirt and matching scarf, and high riding boots. Docker knew very little about riding, but even to his inexperienced eye it seemed likely she'd never been near a horse, let alone mounted one. Bad luck for the horse.

'Broadway or the movies?' he asked.

'Broadway,' she said after a couple of beats.

'Anything I might know?'

'I had a small part in *The Heiress* with Basil Rathbone. He got a Tony award. Did you see the play?'

Should he lie? It appeared safer to say 'No'.

'Don't you like the theatre?' she asked, clearly unim-
pressed by his candour.

'I'm more of a movie man. *But*, if you're in anything at
the moment...' His voice trailed away before he said
more confidently, 'Are you performing?'

'Every day,' she said. There was a brief pause, as if she
thought better of her answer. 'Actually, the truth is that I'm
between roles, and I've been helping Randolph with –'

Morton cut her off by steering her over to where the
small bar was set up. 'The usual?' he asked, and began
mixing a drink before she could reply.

Morton combined bourbon, vermouth and bitters with
ice cubes – here was a woman who drank Manhattans.
Waiting until she'd taken her first taste of the cocktail,
Docker moved closer. 'You were about to say something
about helping Randolph?' he prompted.

Before Morton could stop her, Bridgette began talking.
'I like to travel and Randolph doesn't mind indulging my
whims. So if I can travel and get paid for it, then what
could be more ideal?'

'What could be more ideal is for you to stop discussing
our business in front of John,' said Morton, clearly annoyed.

'Darling, I'm certain Mr Docker is fascinated,' said
Bridgette with a smile that did nothing to soothe Morton
who walked off to talk to Rühmann.

Bridgette screwed a cigarette into a long holder and
waited for Gaffney to light it before he went over to join
the others. After a brief puff, Bridgette smiled at Docker.

'Have you always been an actress?' Docker asked, mesmerised by Bridgette's cocktail shaker mix of savvy, sensuality and sophistication.

'I studied at NYU's Institute of Fine Arts,' she replied. 'But acting is far more exciting than art history.'

Docker was accustomed to seeing down-at-heel actors traipsing Broadway's theatre district, grimly going from one audition to another. 'I can't imagine there's much money in acting.'

'That's why helping Randolph is *so* handy,' said Bridgette, her voice as bright as her eyes.

Helping? wondered Docker. At what? He could imagine how the soft-spoken Rühmann, the dealer Gaffney and the millionaire Morton might eventually lead him to the Berlin Cross, but where did Bridgette fit in? Unless she too was involved in spinning what was becoming, in Docker's worried mind, a spider's web.

As Bridgette talked she started slowly walking away, deliberately leading Docker out of earshot of the three men. Once they were clear of the others, she pointed up at a heavy white cloud lit underneath by the rays of the setting sun. 'It looks like an illustrated Bible cloud,' she said.

Docker was about to reply when, without warning, he felt her fingers clench his forearm. 'I want you to get me away from here,' she whispered.

His reaction was to try to pull free but her fingers dug into his flesh. 'Away?' was all he could say.

'They're going to kill me, I know they are,' she said, then abruptly released his arm. 'Well, if you won't help me –'

She didn't finish the sentence. Morton had turned to look at them and jerked his head in the direction of the valley. Hooking her arm through Docker's, she led him to the men. 'I hadn't realised John was so keen on nature. He tells me that cloud's a cumulus nimbus.'

'I'll remember that,' said Morton, finishing his drink and bringing the glass down a little too hard on the table. 'Now it's time for a pre-dinner stroll.' Without waiting, he turned and set off. The four others put down their drinks and followed him, as he marched across the lawn towards the cliff walk.

The group reached a narrow track carved out of the cliff face. In single file they made their way along the pathway.

Docker wondered if this was the time to mention he was afraid of heights. With Bridgette looking so confident – not to mention beautiful – he decided against it, but as the path became narrower, Docker decided to drop his Johnny Appleseed bravura. He and the countryside just didn't mix. He called ahead to Morton, 'Are you certain this is safe?'

Morton sounded peeved. 'Completely.'

Docker's heart was thumping and his throat was dry. 'I'll stop here for a minute to admire the view,' he said with a strained voice. 'I'll catch you up.'

Without pausing, Morton raised a hand to signal okay.

Shakily lighting a cigarette, Docker watched Bridgette, Rühmann and Gaffney follow Morton along the track which after 20 yards turned sharply around a bend, taking the four out of sight.

A split second later there was a woman's scream.

Docker ran along the track and rounded the corner, nearly colliding with Gaffney coming the other way. The art dealer was out of breath. 'Come quick, Bridgette's fallen!' Turning, Gaffney trotted ahead.

Further along the track, Rühmann was on his hands and knees peering down the almost vertical drop. Standing behind, Morton was also craning to see.

From his vantage point, Docker could just make out polka dots, the shine of leather boots and perhaps pale skin.

Within seconds he reached Morton. Looking over the edge of the path, he saw the drop was almost sheer to the treetops, except for a few shrubs growing out of the side of the cliff face.

Gaffney shouted, 'Bridgette! Can you hear me?' There was no answer. Tapping Docker on the shoulder, Gaffney said, 'I'm going down after her. If I get stuck and can't reach her, I want you to try.'

Docker looked into Gaffney's eyes. He seemed too eager to be the hero and too calculating to be trusted. 'No, I'll go,' snapped Docker. Blocking the terror from his mind, he got down on his knees and squirmed around to face the three men.

He dangled one foot over the edge. Eventually he felt rock, and tested to see if it would hold his weight. It did, so he lowered his other foot onto it. Refusing to look down, he felt for the next foothold.

Acid drops of sweat dribbled into Docker's eyes as he

made his way foot by foot down the cliff face. Holding onto a thin outcrop of rock, he brushed his face against his sleeve and had a brief rest. He realised that dusk was slowly cloaking the ravine. Finding another foothold, he was beginning to put pressure on it when he heard a whisper.

'Get off my fucking arm,' Bridgette hissed. Then came a quick, belated, 'Please.'

Docker looked down, shocked that Bridgette was immediately below him. She was sprawled in a small tree that grew at right angles to the cliff face. The valley floor was less distinct. He felt a spasm in his stomach and forced himself to turn his face back up to the sky. Then he took a breath and bowed his head again, squinting down into the darkness.

'Can you move?' he whispered, unsure of why he was keeping his voice low.

'No. My legs are caught in the tree.'

Docker waved his right foot around until he felt the trunk of a small tree or a bush – he couldn't see in the gloom. Heart racing, sweat saturating his shirt and trouser legs, he put his weight on it and felt the roots pulling themselves free of the sandy soil. He felt for another foothold, and slid lower until his face was inches from hers.

Holding onto a branch with one hand, he hooked his left foot into the branches wrapped around her legs then heaved. 'Now, move your legs,' said Docker.

Kicking one leg free, she swung it in mid-air. The other leg flopped sideways but was clear of the branches. 'I think it's broken,' she said with no hint that this was anything other than a minor inconvenience.

'Put your arms around my neck and I'll try to lift you up,' he said.

For a terrifying second they both teetered forward, but his grip held. He hoisted himself around to face the cliff and began to climb. Twilight was almost gone by the time his adrenaline finally got them both up near the path. A few feet from the track he sensed another presence but there was no way he could escape. It was Morton, lying on the path with his legs held by Gaffney, and reaching down with both hands to grasp Bridgette.

Docker was reluctant to let her go, fearing what Morton might do, but he was too weakened by the climb to hold her for more than a second. Pulling her up onto the path, Morton immediately reached back to help Docker.

'Our hero,' Morton said without a trace of sarcasm as Docker lay next to Bridgette on the track with the three men standing above them. Docker sat up and felt the muscles in his arms and legs immediately begin to ache. Staggering to his feet, he faced the men. 'What the hell happened?' he demanded.

Morton held up a reassuring hand. 'John, John, it was an accident.'

Docker was unconvinced, his anger replacing the relief he felt at being back on the pathway. 'Answer me. How did she fall?'

'As I said, it was an accident. One minute she was chatting to Willi, the next she was gone.'

Bridgette glared at Morton. 'Don't discuss me as if I'm not here.'

It was the first time Docker had heard Bridgette get angry with her, her . . . he tried to think of the least offensive word . . . employer, guardian. No, he knew he was kidding himself. There was another way to phrase their relationship, but Docker didn't want to even consider it.

Bridgette cut off Docker's thoughts. 'Someone pushed me!' she said.

'Who?' asked Docker, looking at the three men.

'I don't know,' she confessed, 'but I'm sure I felt a hand.'

'Don't be ridiculous,' scolded Morton.

Realising that a dark trail in the woods was not the place to discuss the matter, Docker said to the others, 'I think her leg's broken. We'll have to carry her.'

Bending low, Rühmann hooked Bridgette's left arm over his shoulders and quickly lifted her upright. Morton came forward to help. Docker could see Bridgette pull back, dragging the young man sideways. 'I'll take her other arm,' said Docker.

Morton moved aside and said without rancour, 'Let's get back to the house. I'll call a doctor.'

Bridgette's cheek was inches away from Docker's. Turning her head slightly, she whispered, 'And I'll thank you later.'

As they shuffled back towards the house, Docker weighed every word she'd said. How much emphasis had she put on 'thank' and on 'later'? Here was a woman with twigs in her hair, dirt on her face and possibly a broken leg, yet she could still be mysterious and flirtatious. And, he decided, if he didn't stay with her she could soon be dead.

NEUN

It was late and there was barely a sound in the corridors of the Royal Military Police headquarters. Under the strong light of the desk lamp, Beauchamp looked tired and distracted. He fiddled with a pencil, then set it aside to pick up a fountain pen before laying it parallel with the discarded pencil on the desktop.

Paperwork wasn't his strong suit, he admitted to himself, sighing as he noticed his in-tray was stacked high with roneoed documents and other Armed Forces flotsam while his out-tray held the one report he'd managed to write in the past two hours. He drew in a long breath before snatching up his pen and beginning to jot down his thoughts on the Kessler case.

His annotations were sketchy reminders of the problems he faced: he had a tortured body which had been snatched away by the Americans, a former Nazi architect obsessed with a crucifix, a smarmy black marketeer with excellent taste in art, an egregiously mannered US major out to shanghai the murder case, a gorgeous woman whose father had been murdered and, finally, one very pissed off English major who was probably fuming over a glass of officers-mess port while Beauchamp worked. He'd made a commitment to Speer to return the Cross to its home but, as far as Beauchamp was concerned, all he'd got out of the architect was a name, and, so far, that had led him nowhere. If Speer failed to deliver then Beauchamp wasn't going to keep his side of the bargain.

Beauchamp diplomatically left Majors Oswald and Cooper-Wright out of his case notes, but he made a point of outlining his meeting with Albert Speer. He was convinced that Speer was no more than a bit player in this drama, but he had little doubt about Amistead, who deserved more critical attention. Once again Beauchamp asked himself what the connection between the Frenchman and the dead American could be. He paused in his writing before going back and correcting his jottings to read: 'dead German American'. How infuriating. Was it sheer bloody-mindedness that kept the Yanks from telling the British just who Kessler was? Beauchamp had already made discreet inquiries amongst senior RMP colleagues across Germany, but no one had any information on *Herr Doktor*. His past had been erased.

White's efforts to track down more information on Elsa Kessler had delivered only a few fragments of information. Finding her hotel was the easy part, but the hotel manager could give White little except the fact that Elsa travelled on a US passport, had checked in to the Berlin hotel only a few days prior and had a New York street address – not surprisingly, the same one the RMP had received from Kessler's tailors. Elsa wasn't in the hotel when White visited, and that left the corporal with little to do but ask about her in a neighbouring restaurant mentioned by the hotel manager. The restaurant's maître d recognised Elsa's description, made a compliment about her looks and said she had dined alone. The woman was as mysterious as her father. When White had finally returned to headquarters, his mood was as downbeat as Beauchamp's.

Beauchamp's notes only highlighted the fact that he was missing too many parts of the puzzle. Wearily he lowered his pen just as White tapped jauntily on the doorjamb.

'Someone to see you,' said the corporal.

Beauchamp looked up from his desk, noting that a mischievous smile was transforming White's usually earnest face.

'Who is it?' Beauchamp asked, finding himself whispering.

'Elsa Kessler,' White whispered back.

Beauchamp shot up so quickly White had to take a step away.

'I thought your job was to find her,' said Beauchamp.

'Looks like she found us.' White turned on his heels to collect the visitor.

Minutes later, Elsa stormed into Beauchamp's office, stopped abruptly and stared haughtily down at him. 'Your man has been asking about me all around Berlin. I thought I would save you the trouble of tracking me down.'

Beauchamp blushed, putting paid to any notion of feigning innocence. He apologised and admitted the RMP had indeed been asking questions about her.

'I am just surprised you did not ask the American military police for my details, Captain Beauchamp.' It came out *Beeeesham*.

'Politics. This is a very political city.'

'I know, I was born here,' Elsa started, then stopped.

Beauchamp could see that she was deciding whether to continue and he offered her a cigarette. She looked at the brand before accepting it. 'Since I have been back, the American authorities have been helpful but . . .' Elsa drew on the cigarette and sat down, 'I do not trust that Major Oswald. I know he is holding something back from me. I am certain he knows who killed my father.'

'Really?' said Beauchamp, trying to get the right level of surprise in his voice to draw her out.

'That is why I need your help,' she said, for the first time becoming agitated. She sucked in more cigarette smoke.

'You mentioned that you were born here?' began Beauchamp, hoping to calm her.

'I left in 1936 and went with my mother to the United States. My father and grandmother stayed in Germany.'

'Why didn't they travel with you?'

'Politics. Personal politics,' she said flatly. 'My mother and father did not get along. She wanted to get away from this country and he wanted to stay and ingratiate himself with the Nazis.'

Beauchamp picked up his pen and started writing.

'My father became well known in his field.' There was no pride in her voice as she halted.

Beauchamp wanted to know what that field was but decided the only way to draw her out was to remain silent. He kept making notes, waiting for her to restart.

She watched the nib of his pen as it moved over the page. After a long pause she continued. 'My father was what is now called an atomic scientist. In those days he was called a fission specialist, working with the Nazis to develop an atomic bomb. He was a leader in his field. He was also what the Americans call a "mama's boy". My grandmother was very important to him. Too important, perhaps.' She sounded more wistful than bitter.

'Did your mother want to get out of Germany because of the Nazis?' Beauchamp asked.

Elsa was surprised. '*Meine Mutter?* She did not care about the Nazis. She was only interested in finding a place in the world where she could shop during daylight and dance after dusk. New York, to her, was heaven.'

'And your father?'

'He was not interested in what the Nazis did. If someone paid him to play with heavy water, he was happy. He had two loves – money and his work, even if his work could kill hundreds of thousands.' She looked up at Beauchamp now. 'Do you think that is immoral?'

'Possibly *amoral*,' he replied.

'When he surrendered to the Americans, they were as pragmatic as he was,' Elsa said. 'They offered him his own laboratory in New Mexico, well away from my mother.

They also offered to make my grandmother a US citizen. My father pleaded with her to accept but she refused. She said she did not survive the Allied invasion in order to desert the city she loved.'

Elsa looked intently at Beauchamp as if judging whether she had his attention. She did. Elsa shifted slightly in her chair, glanced down at her hands and continued. 'My father settled into his laboratory in New Mexico and started a new life that included, I believe, a mistress. Whether *that* woman had been provided by the US government along with the laboratory, I don't know. But my father was handsomely paid and was always beautifully . . .' she sought the word, 'groomed. He would use my New York address when ordering clothes.' Now there was a hint of pride in her voice. 'He could dance well and he enjoyed being with women. Except, unfortunately, my mother. Whenever he came to New York he avoided her by staying in a hotel. A year after the war ended he received a message at his hotel saying that my *Oma* had had a heart attack. He told me about the message and left immediately for Germany. I received a few notes from him, then nothing. He disappeared within days of arriving in Berlin.'

'I'm confused,' said Beauchamp. 'You mean he disappeared in '46 and again this year?'

'That is right,' she replied, but her tone said, 'Do not interrupt.'

'Tell me about the '46 disappearance,' said Beauchamp, keeping his voice low and soothing.

Elsa crushed out her half-smoked cigarette and began a

tale that surprised him not so much for its content – for police work had long since destroyed his faith in his fellow man – but for the fact that none of it was on record. Although he hadn't been in Berlin in 1946, what he was hearing should surely have been on file somewhere.

Elsa explained that when she failed to hear from her father, she contacted her grandmother's hospital in the US sector. She was told that her father had made only one visit to the hospital, and her grandmother had been distraught when he failed to appear the following day. To calm the elderly woman, the hospital contacted the US authorities. They were unable to help. Elsa had the same problem when she contacted the US MP headquarters in Berlin. She said that it was frustrating to sit in New York, having to rely on unhelpful policemen across the Atlantic. She knew something had happened to her father and was certain he'd been abducted. It was obvious that most nations would want the atomic fission secrets locked in his brain.

Late one night she received a phone call from an unidentified man who said her father was safe and that a US military policeman called Lieutenant John Docker was now involved in the matter and would be in touch with her soon. Although Docker never contacted her, she did receive an apologetic call from another MP even later that night asking her to stay by the phone. Within hours, her father rang. He said he was at Rhein-Main and was flying out of Germany shortly. He sounded frightened and at one stage used the word *gerettet*, German for 'rescued'. When she'd queried him he'd refused to discuss the matter and hung up. A week went by before he finally called from his New Mexico laboratory. He steadfastly refused to discuss the trip, his disappearance or even his mother.

The pressure of Beauchamp's hand on the pen splayed out the tip of his nib. He repeated the name 'Lieutenant John Docker', then turned to White. 'Was he one of the Yanks we ran into?'

'No, it could not have been,' Elsa interrupted. 'He has left the service.'

White's disbelieving voice came out of the gloom. 'So, let me get this straight. Your father disappeared in December 1946 and reappeared in New Mexico after being "rescued". Then he disappeared again last month and we find him dead a few weeks later.'

'That is blunt, corporal, but correct,' agreed Elsa, her voice cold.

Beauchamp shot White a look of frustration before turning his attention back to Elsa, but she'd obviously had enough. Suddenly standing, she asked, 'I have told you all I know, may I leave now?'

'Of course.' Beauchamp shook her hand. It was cool. His, he knew, was clammy. 'Corporal White will see you out.'

'I can find my own way, *danke schön*.'

Beauchamp hesitated. He wanted to point out that this was a military police headquarters and visitors didn't wander the corridors unescorted. Instead he opted for a polite, '*Gute nacht*, Fräulein.'

After she left, he re-read his notes and wondered if any or all of her story was true. If Kessler had been kidnapped almost two years ago – and the Americans had been forced to rescue him – then perhaps the kidnappers had orchestrated another opportunity to snatch him this year. Or had the Yanks got fed up with Kessler and killed him, disguising the murder by ostentatiously torturing the victim? Is that how Major Oswald got involved and why the body was taken so swiftly from the Spandau morgue? Or was it an entirely new group, somehow associated with Amistead, who snatched Kessler and killed him?

Whatever the scenario, Elsa Kessler's father had supposedly disappeared on two occasions. He thought of the Oscar Wilde quote that losing one parent was a misfortune, but losing both looked like carelessness. Fräulein Kessler had managed to lose her father twice – and she didn't look like the careless type at all.

ZEHN

Morton pushed open the double doors of the library and waved Docker through. Docker was unhappy about leaving Bridgette alone in her room but the grumpy local doctor, who was clearly annoyed at being called away from his pre-dinner martini, had been insistent that he examine her in private. Rühmann and Gaffney had withdrawn to their rooms, leaving Docker alone with Morton. He felt uncomfortable having those two no goods out of his sight, and to distract himself he inspected the library.

A large landscape painting of a sugarcane field almost filled one wall. On the other walls there were bookshelves filled with rows and rows of books seemingly arranged by size rather than content. *The Dictionary of Christianity* cheek by jowl with *The Lady in the Lake*.

Docker took down the dictionary.

'Are you a religious man, John?' Morton asked.

'In this case,' said Docker, 'I was interested in seeing what was under "C" for "cross".'

'Is that really what you're looking for?'

'I'm looking for the real thing, and Gaffney is pretty damn confident that you're the man to do business with.'

'I can assure you I don't collect simply out of passion, I also collect for profit,' said Morton as he poured two whiskies.

Morton handed Docker a glass and settled into an armchair, taking out a robusto cigar from a wooden humidor on a side table. 'You'll like this,' he said, waving his cigar in the air. 'It's got a Connecticut shade wrapper.'

'I've had enough of Connecticut for one day,' said Docker, staring into the bottom of his whisky glass.

Morton looked as if he was about to react to Docker's snappiness, then a smile returned and he asked, 'Would you like to stay the night? We can lend you a toothbrush and razor. Clive can take you back to Manhattan in the morning.'

Docker nodded his thanks, relieved he'd be able to keep an eye on Bridgette.

'Good. Now, tell me the truth, John. Is the relic you're seeking for you or for a third party?'

'I'm acting as a broker,' said Docker.

'Have you the authority to actually pay for the goods?' asked Morton.

'The final yes or no won't be mine.'

'Does your client have any idea what sum might be involved?'

'I'd have to see the goods first.' Stubbing out his cigarette, Docker went back to the bookshelves.

'We should have Clive and Willi in the room if we're to talk business,' said Morton, lifting the handpiece of a phone off its cradle. He murmured into it and hung up.

Gaffney was first through the door. 'The doctor has left,' he said. 'Bridgette's asleep.' Gaffney didn't say how he knew, but Docker had an uneasy vision of the man peering into Bridgette's bedroom.

Rühmann arrived and immediately crossed the room to Docker. 'This is nothing personal, but we are going to frisk you.'

Docker was thankful his jacket, with the .38 in the pocket, was draped over the arm of a nearby chair. If the weather had been cooler, he might have been wearing it. He stood up and slowly lifted both arms away from his sides.

The tap-down was quick and expert.

'Let's go,' said Morton.

Docker followed the others into a central passageway, wondering what was going to happen next and wishing he could get to his jacket. Near the rear of the house, the men finally stopped at a metal door with its rivets and cross struts painted dark brown in a failed attempt to make it fit in with the other décor. Docker wondered if he'd have noticed the paintwork at all if he wasn't so edgy.

Morton used a slab-sided key to unlock the door then flicked a light-switch and led the way down steep wooden stairs which descended to a cellar and another steel door. Morton splayed his fingers against the wall near the door and pressed. A panel slid sideways, revealing a twin tumble lock. He flicked the tumblers. There was a creak and a hiss as the steel door opened. Rühmann caught the edge of the door and pulled it back enough to allow the other men through. He stepped inside and gently closed the door.

Docker had only been in a bank vault once, but the eau de Nil walls and polished steel of that vault bore no resemblance to what spread out before him. The side walls held at least two dozen paintings, so tightly packed it was as if they were edging each other out. It was a buffet approach to showcasing art. At the far end of the vault there were two safes standing head high. On either side of the safes were glass cabinets with lights picking out the individual treasures inside.

Docker noticed just one chair in the room. Lightly built with a comfortable back and padded seat, it looked ideal for Morton to carry around the huge vault to appraise his possessions. A heavy desk with leather inlay was positioned directly under two low lights dangling from the ceiling. Docker strolled to the paintings pretending to be impressed. Small plaques next to each artwork gave the artists' names and brief descriptions of the paintings. The plaques saved Docker the embarrassment of asking who'd painted what. Holbein, Bosch, Poussin, Bellini and others were on display.

Most of the frames were identical – mahogany with gold around the edges and swirled gold initials 'RM' in each corner. Even to a layman like Docker, it seemed odd that these paintings should be in uniform frames.

Morton laughed, clearly guessing Docker's thoughts from his expression. 'For reasons I won't bother you with, we bring them in from Europe without their frames. Gaffney used to be involved in the importing process but things became a little tense in Europe and he had to hand the travelling over to someone else.'

Docker frowned, trying to decide if the 'someone else' was Rühmann or Bridgette. She'd said she liked to travel and . . . how did she phrase it? *'If I can travel and get paid for it, then what could be more ideal?'*

Rather than raise the question, Docker changed tack. 'Nothing illegal?' he asked, raising an eyebrow in what he hoped was a conspiratorial fashion.

'It's a complex world, full of ambiguity,' said Morton.

Docker was about to comment when Morton cut him off. 'Let's discuss art another day, John. I actually brought you down here to show you something else.' Morton went over to one of the safes and positioned himself so that Docker couldn't see the combination lock. Gaffney and Rühmann watched from the side as Morton spun the lock through a series of soft clicks.

An airtight seal gave way and Morton withdrew a bulky object wrapped in dark red cloth. Morton's hands shook slightly. Whether it was the weight or the excitement, Docker couldn't tell. Handling the cloth-wrapped object as gently as an egg carton, Morton carried it over to the desk and positioned it under the lights.

The men crowded around. He pulled away the cloth, revealing a modern brass box. Looking up at Docker,

Morton caught his expression. 'You're disappointed. What were you expecting – a reliquary with a bit of Byzantine pizzazz? The sort of thing you'd see in Venice to lure the tourists? What I'm about to show you is far more aesthetically pleasing.'

'And more expensive,' added Gaffney.

Morton turned his head sharply at the sound of Gaffney's voice – it was the first time he'd spoken. 'Not that money is a prime consideration when dealing with an object of historical worth,' said Morton.

'Of course not,' said Gaffney. 'Let's say it's a secondary one.'

Flourishing a key that he had fished from the fob pocket of his pants, Morton unlocked the brass box. Inside, on a bed of velvet, was a 12-inch-long jewelled case in the shape of a curved sword.

'It has the contours of a scimitar or, as the Persians would have called it, a *shimshir*. It was crafted in the seventh century – 628 AD to be exact,' said Morton, his voice quavering as he lifted the reliquary from the brass box, placed it on the table and undid the clasps on the side.

The interior of the curved case was lined with leather. Inside were a slim muslin package and a tiny golden scimitar the length of a man's index finger. Morton pulled white cotton gloves out of his jacket pocket and gently picked up the package, unwrapped it and placed it on the table. Docker looked down at a grey sliver of wood about seven or eight inches long and ragged on the side where it had been stripped from a larger piece.

'Christ has touched this piece of wood and so have I,' said Morton. He pulled his right-hand glove off, and reached down to touch the wood.

Morton paused, then slipped his glove back on and reached in again to lift out the miniature sword. He handed it to Docker.

Docker drew the sword from its scabbard and held the delicate object towards the light. Tilting it, he saw there was intricate Arabic lettering along the blade.

'The inscription reads: "Cross and honour restored by Siroes,"' said Morton. 'This is one way we can be sure of the provenance of the Cross.'

'It may be the real sword, but is the wood from the real Cross?' Docker asked.

'You're not a trusting man, John. Virtually without exception such wooden relics are bogus. Those with the most credible provenance like this one can be traced to Constantine the Great's mother, Helena. You know her, of course?'

'No,' admitted Docker.

Morton took a hard look at Docker, as if to say what kind of antiques dealer are you?, then continued. 'In the fourth century, Helena had been overseeing excavation and building work in Jerusalem when labourers uncovered three wooden crosses. Helena was adamant that the crosses were those of Christ and the two thieves who were crucified with Him. A dying woman was asked to touch each cross. When she touched the third cross she was cured. Helena proclaimed that *this* was the Cross of Christ.'

'Where's the rest of the Cross?'

'You're too impatient. I was about to say that all of Christendom soon wanted a piece of the miraculous wood, but Helena and her family only parcelled out small amounts. Helena, strong on sentiment but not on security, insisted that the bulk of the Cross should remain in Jerusalem. It turned out not to be a good idea. In the seventh century, the Persian king Chosroes sacked the Holy City and stole a portion of the Cross. Chosroes was eventually beaten in battle by Emperor Heraclius. Although Chosroes was defeated he wouldn't hand back the Cross. A bad decision. As a matter of family honour, his son Siroes killed the king and returned the Cross to the Christians.'

Docker turned the sword over and over in his hands. The thin blade was ragged where the years had corroded the metal. He leant forward and saw the impression the tiny scimitar had left in the leather lining of the reliquary. He slipped it back into place. It was a perfect fit.

'You *say* you're in the antiques game,' said Morton, a note of frustration in his voice, 'and you say you're repre-senting a client. It's time to fish or cut bait. I have another offer on the table for the Cross, from a European collector. It's a genuine offer and I don't think it can be topped, but they don't currently have the cash in hand. So, what's your offer?'

Docker recalled how Laurent had left the office with a warning – no, two warnings – carry a gun and don't offer more than $250,000 for the relic, even though he knew the relic was worth perhaps half a million. He'd told Docker to bid low and keep Morton's attention.

'Two hundred and fifty thousand,' said Docker and waited for Morton's reaction. It was slow in coming. When it did come, there was an added sigh.

'A disappointing figure. Your client must know it's worth far more.'

'That's the amount I've been advised to offer,' countered Docker.

'Pitiful,' said Gaffney. 'The Cross last changed hands at –'

Morton held up his hand to stop Gaffney and there were a few seconds of silence before Morton said, 'John, I'll suggest a sum. Let's see how your client reacts. I need to make a small profit. Let's make it $500,000.'

'He won't like it. But I'm prepared to take it back to him as an ambit claim.'

'That's the figure I'm suggesting. As I mentioned, I already have a very keen buyer in Europe.'

'But you say he's short on the dough,' said Docker.

'Temporarily. But from what we've heard he's very close to securing the funds.'

'When did you hear this?'

'Willi put in the call a short time ago. This may be Connecticut but we're not using carrier pigeons these days. I should also point out that your competitor is the preferred buyer.'

'Preferred?'

'We've done business in the past but I'm not a sentimentalist. I'd rather have cash in hand than promises. Talk to your client and then set up a meeting. You've got 48 hours.'

ELF

It was nearly lunchtime. A new day and the same problem. The puzzle just wasn't fitting together. He felt like he was back at boarding school, sitting up in bed with a wooden tray holding the jigsaw pieces – blue sky, sections of a castle battlement, hooves of charging horses, gaps of wooden tray and a knight's plumed helmet suspended between sky and turf. Good training for being a copper, except as a child he'd had the picture on the box for guidance. All he had now was a sheet of Armed Forces paper and his case notes.

He tried jotting down and underlining the information he had. Rewriting names, actions and locations somehow clarified things in his mind. After 20 minutes he had almost reached the bottom of the page, leaving enough space for him to draw a box in the right-hand corner of his pad in which to scribble the name of the American lieutenant, 'Docker', and the two words 'copycat snatch?'.

Laying down his pen, he picked up a mug of tea, took a sip, grimaced and got up to get a fresh pot from the canteen. Major Cooper-Wright was talking to a staff sergeant on the landing and completely ignored him as he walked past. It suited Beauchamp just fine.

Three female clerical staff in the canteen smiled at Beauchamp. He knew he was considered an oddity. Other officers ordered their tea to be delivered. Beauchamp would appear in the canteen, politely ask for a pot of tea, pick up a cup with the least amount of tannin stains and head back to his office. For Beauchamp it wasn't so much a matter of egalitarianism as the fact that he was restless by nature. He couldn't sit still for longer than 30 minutes at a stretch and walking down to the canteen was an ideal excuse for getting away from his desk. His in-tray was usually a daunting pile of folders detailing petty crimes committed by petty minds. At least with Kessler's death he had something more interesting to think about than pilfering or traffic violations.

Back in his office, Beauchamp continued to mull over the case details.

He smelt Elsa before she entered his office. Sandalwood and lemon zest. She was dressed for an early summer's day and Beauchamp spent a moment appreciating his guest's beauty before offering her a chair. He caught a glimpse of Corporal White at the door and nodded *that'll be all*, realising as he did so that it was a caddish thing to do. There had to be some perks to being a captain, though.

105

Elsa opened her sleek black handbag and took out a scrap of paper. It was a list of the people her father had associated with up to the end of the war, together with her attempts at finding their various addresses.

'I thought this might be helpful, captain,' she said. 'Should I give it to your corporal?'

White would have hated the 'your', thought Beauchamp as he quickly assured her that he'd look after it. Studying the list, he saw it was next to worthless. Most of the scientists would have fled and many of the addresses would now be bombsites. Nodding thoughtfully nevertheless, he put the paper aside.

Elsa began discussing the details of her grandmother's heart problems. She railed against the inadequacies of the German health system, or what was left of it. All this information washed over Beauchamp as he speculated about just how unprofessional it might be if he invited her out for dinner. Very unprofessional, he decided. Lunch might be safer.

'There is some further information we need,' he said, using 'we' because it had an official air. 'It's nearly one o'clock, perhaps we could discuss those details over lunch.' He picked up his pen to appear businesslike.

'An excellent idea. But where do you eat around here?' asked Elsa.

Beauchamp panicked. He hadn't thought about that. Somewhere reasonably smart with decent food, where they couldn't be overheard. The officers' mess was out on all grounds. The name 'Poppa 8's' slipped out before he had a chance to consider the consequences. In the centre of the city, it was favoured by officers from the three Western Allied Forces. Poppa 8's had a raffish air that Beauchamp enjoyed. Working girls were often perched at the bar, while in the restaurant section the menu featured dishes that were impossible to find elsewhere in the city. Part of Poppa 8's mystique lay in its history – it didn't have one. One month the site was an abandoned *Weinstube*, the next a thriving restaurant and bar. Who owned it and who came and went were questions the *Polizei* – local and Allied – didn't ask. Poppa 8's exuded a tawdry innocence that never seemed to make it a policing priority.

As Elsa nodded enthusiastically and gathered up her handbag, Beauchamp hoped Major Oswald wasn't in the mood for lunch.

On the positive side, Beauchamp recalled, there'd be few prostitutes at the bar this early in the day. Thank God for the nocturnal sex habits of the Allies. He made an excuse to Elsa that a public discussion would be more discreet if he wasn't in uniform. He didn't mention the possibility of American MPs being at Poppa 8's.

After a few minutes in the locker room, Beauchamp returned to his office in the mufti outfit he kept for plain-clothed work – white shirt, dark grey trousers, black shoes and a brown woollen sports coat.

It appeared all Elsa could do was gawk at his highly polished shoes. Disheartened, he accepted the fact that he was kitted out like an off-duty copper. Since there was little he could do about it, he guided her to the parking area and ushered her into his Jeep.

Moments after he reached the main road, Beauchamp realised a van that had been parked in Rominter Allee near his headquarters was on his tail. He slowed down to allow it to catch up. As the van slowed Beauchamp thumped the Jeep into third gear and pressed hard on the accelerator. The van slipped behind, its two male occupants clearly realising they'd been seen. He saw the van reappear a few minutes before he and Elsa reached Kurfürstendamm. Again the vehicle doggedly followed them. Beauchamp was determined not to let the two men follow the Jeep to Poppa 8's.

Deliberately slowing yet again, Beauchamp allowed a tram to rumble in front of the Jeep. He checked the rear-vision mirror. The van was just a few yards behind his vehicle. Who the hell were these bastards? He could see their bland, seemingly uninterested faces staring directly ahead as if trying not to acknowledge his eyes reflected in the mirror. The haircuts gave them away. Americans. British Army barbers adopted a heavy-handed approach to back and sides, but the Americans had more style. They had to be Oswald's men, but were they tailing Elsa or him? Just at that moment, he didn't intend to find out.

The tram had halted briefly to pick up a passenger, then moved off. This time Beauchamp put his foot down so hard that he heard the tyres spin on the roadway before the Jeep hurtled forward. Elsa held on to her hat and the seat as Beauchamp swung the Jeep in front of the tram, then aimed the vehicle at a narrow alleyway. As if shot out of a cannon, the Jeep raced between the high walls and emerged in a street one block north. Another turn of the wheel and a further stab at the accelerator put the Jeep half a mile ahead of the shadowing van.

As Beauchamp eased off the accelerator, Elsa turned to him with a look of puzzlement rather than fear.

'A little short cut I know,' he explained.

Elsa appeared entirely unconvinced but she didn't say anything and simply leant in front of the rear-vision mirror to adjust her hat. Beauchamp was delighted by the unexpected intimacy of her shoulder touching his own while she hovered in front of the mirror. Out of the corner of his eye he could see the careful brushstrokes of her make-up, as unreal as a mask.

When Elsa moved away from the mirror, Beauchamp took the opportunity to check the road behind, relieved that there was no sign of the van. It was a matter of minutes before they arrived at Poppa 8's, the street number 8 picked out in neon tubing. This early in the day, however, the sign wasn't lit up.

As Beauchamp and Elsa entered the bar and restaurant the jukebox was playing. In a far booth, four US airforce officers were harmonising along to the gospel rhythms of The Song Spinners' 'Comin' in on a Wing and a Prayer'.

Beauchamp knew how that felt.

He ignored the maître d's offer of a table in the open area of the restaurant and chose a corner away from the singing crewmen.

The waiter who served them was an older man in a black apron that touched his toe caps. Addressing Elsa, he asked in

German if they were ready to order. Elsa chose quickly while Beauchamp puzzled over how the waiter would know she was German without her speaking. It wasn't as if she was dressed in national costume. I'm overly paranoid, he decided. After all, how many foreign women were there in Berlin? Precious few who weren't in WAC or nurses uniforms.

Watching the waiter push his way through batwing doors into the kitchen, Beauchamp thought there was something disturbingly familiar about the gaunt, erect figure. Surely it couldn't be the organ grinder from outside the US MP headquarters. He had only seen the man at a distance, but the stiff walk triggered a faint memory. No, he decided again, it must be pure paranoia. Dredging through his limited German vocabulary, Beauchamp attempted to discuss life in Berlin, while Elsa politely corrected his errors.

The food came and Beauchamp was pleased that the waiter didn't linger. He probed at the yellow cubes on the plate, praying they were tinned pineapple. Between bites, Beauchamp continued speaking in halting German before he admitted defeat and switched to English – to his relief and hers.

'Who do you think killed my father for his secrets?' Elsa asked, bringing the conversation back to the investigation.

'It's too early to say.'

'You are being evasive. Tell me, who do you think did it?'

'The Americans already have the knowledge, the French can't afford it, the Germans have no way of using it and that leaves the Russians. But they wouldn't leave his body in western Berlin. If they'd snatched him, he'd be in Moscow within a day.'

'So who did it?'

'We have a number of leads which perversely aren't leading us anywhere.' He impaled the last of the pineapple and chewed on it while trying to think of a delicate way to discuss how her father died. 'There's another question,' he said. 'Did your father's killers get the information they wanted?'

'They were fools to have tortured him. They should have just offered him money and fame.'

'Unfortunately torture is cheaper.'

It was her turn to spear something on her plate, the final cube of the knuckle meat. 'Why do you bother with this case? Why do you not leave it to the Americans?'

'He was found on my patch – my territory. This is my case . . . and you asked for my help.'

'That is very noble of you,' she said with a small smile that carried a 'thank you' with it.

Beauchamp wondered if he was floating an inch above his seat. To celebrate he took a sip of water. One of the US aircrew in the far booth laughed loudly and the sound snapped Beauchamp back. He adopted a more official tone as he asked Elsa about her life in Germany and the States. Schools, friends, jobs. It could be relevant.

Carefully Elsa took him through her life, and Beauchamp nodded thoughtfully. Either she was tactful or she didn't go on dates – whatever the reason, and he doubted the latter, Beauchamp was grateful that Elsa didn't raise the subject of men.

A few minutes later, gazing over the rim of his coffee cup and watching Elsa take a sip from her own, Beauchamp wondered how other nervous men coped with making small talk with beautiful women. It was a pity, he concluded, that the British weren't as socially confident as Americans. The Yanks always seemed able to cope with public speaking, being interviewed on the wireless or asking a girl on a date. In fact, Beauchamp decided, he'd never met an American who wasn't completely in control.

ZWÖLF

Docker woke with a start, wondering where he was. Through the window he heard birdsong and the breeze rustling the leaves. Connecticut was turning on another perfect morning. This is the life, thought Docker, but sadly it's someone else's. He showered, had breakfast alone and went to Bridgette's room. She was gone.

Trying to stay calm and not run, he moved quickly through the house and swung open the front door. He was surprised to see a rumpled Bridgette sitting in the front passenger seat of Gaffney's car, looking nervous.

'I'm leaving with you,' she said, noting his open mouth. 'The doctor said my ankle is badly sprained. So, if I'm going to be laid up, I want to be in my own apartment.'

Docker nodded in agreement and went to find Gaffney to take them home. Gaffney looked shocked when he saw Bridgette in the car but Morton, who suddenly appeared in the doorway, looked unfazed.

Docker slipped into the rear seat, running the palm of his hand over the cream upholstery. Even with the hood down he could smell the erotic aroma of warm leather. From the back seat of the convertible, he had a fine view of the sweep of Morton's gravel driveway, the clipped lawns and, more importantly, the nape of Bridgette's neck.

Bridgette stared straight ahead while Gaffney sat stiffly behind the wheel, trying not to look like the resident chauffeur. Walking to the passenger door, Morton leant down to kiss Bridgette's cheek but she twisted her head and the intended kiss ended about a foot short of its cold target. Morton sighed, stepped back and clicked the passenger door closed.

The car accelerated gently and the wheels crunched towards the gates. There was no cheerful farewell from a man in workman's dungarees who came out of a guard-house to swing the gates open. Docker waved a 'thank you' and then pointed to where the butt of a revolver was jutting out of the bib of the man's dungarees. Pushing the gun out of sight, the man shut the gates with what sounded to Docker like an *and-stay-out* clang. He'd be happy to comply.

The Sportsman's V8 engine powered it along a steep road which looped back towards the coast.

After tying a large silk scarf around her head to keep her hair in place, Bridgette squirmed around in her seat and grimaced at Docker. 'Do you have any headache powder?'

'I'll look,' he said, and began patting all his pockets. He found a Goody's powder at the bottom of his jacket pocket, next to the barrel of his .38. 'No water though,' he said, handing her the paper sachet of powder. He tapped Gaffney on the shoulder. 'Can you stop somewhere for water?'

Gaffney sighed and turned off the main road at a sign for Prevost's Hill. He parked near a roadside diner. 'Wait here,' he snapped, disappearing into the diner.

Bridgette turned awkwardly in her seat. 'I said I'd thank you. I'm sorry I didn't get the chance. But I needed you. You were my excuse to get away.'

'Why didn't you just leave?'

'Randolph would never have let me. Not with what's happened.'

'What *has* happened?' he asked.

She looked nervously at the diner door. 'Not now. I'll tell you another time. But I needed a guardian angel to rescue me.'

'I'm no angel.'

'I hope not,' she said cheekily.

'Who pushed you off the path?'

'No one. I jumped.'

Docker looked startled. 'I don't believe it. You can't be that crazy.'

'But I am *that* scared. I'm frightened enough of Randolph to jump off a cliff. Okay, I screwed up. I didn't mean to fall that far – I misjudged it. I walk that path every evening and I thought I knew the area. It was a dumb thing to do but I was just desperate for an excuse to have you take me back to New York.' She stopped speaking when she saw Gaffney came out of the diner with a dixie cup of water.

Within minutes they were back on the main road. 'When we get to the city, I'll set you down first,' Gaffney said over his shoulder to Docker.

Bridgette didn't look like she liked that idea.

By the time Gaffney pulled up outside Docker's apartment, the sun was banking towards what passed for a horizon in this part of Manhattan. 'Thanks for the ride,' Docker said as he got out of the car. Gaffney didn't look at him.

'My pleasure.'

'Aren't you going to hail me a cab?' Bridgette quickly got out but her bandaged foot barely touched the concrete before she let out a yelp. Docker steadied her until she was upright.

Gaffney looked surprised and began to protest. 'One minute you're bitching about how you need to rest, the next you're refusing a lift home. Randolph won't like it.'

'Tough,' declared Bridgette, taking a few tentative steps backwards.

Gaffney looked at her, then glanced over to Docker, appearing to weigh up whether to continue the argument. Mind made up, he put his foot on the accelator.

Bridgette and Docker watched him leave. It was good to be back in the city. Before Docker could invite her in, a cab drew up without either of them making a move. Docker took out a business card, the one with just his name and number, and handed it to Bridgette. 'Give me a call if you need a specialist.'

'In antiques?'

'That too.'

Docker waited until the cab was out of sight, then headed to his own apartment. Inside, he put on a record and fixed a drink before calling Laurent.

'What's that music in the background?' was Laurent's only greeting.

'"How High the Moon."'

'Well, turn the thing down.' Laurent waited until Anita O'Day fell silent. 'Did you find the Cross?'

Docker smiled. 'What? No "Good to hear from you"?'

Laurent ignored him. 'Well, did you?'

'Gaffney took me to meet a man who's a good host but a tough bargainer.'

'Forget the character insights. I want to know if you found the Cross.'

'I might need some information from *you* first,' said Docker. 'What's your real interest in the Cross?'

'I specialise in antiquities and the Cross is the greatest one of all. It's just as I told you.'

'All that was before I met Gaffney and the pack he runs with. They're crooks and that makes me suspect you.'

'I've paid you for your services,' Laurent said, his voice cold. 'What's that make you?'

'Not particularly grateful.'

'Well, you should be,' said Laurent, before adopting a softer tone. 'Look, let's meet. What about the Algonquin at six?'

DREIZEHN

The fact that he'd once shared a cigarette with her made inspecting the body even more of a chore than usual. Beauchamp had respected her resilience. It was a tough life for any woman in Berlin, but for prostitutes it was even worse. The war had desensitised many men to the suffering of others. Easy prey for emotionally traumatised clients, the city's tarts were often used for the release of more than sexual frustrations. Murdered prostitutes were all too often found.

For Beauchamp, this victim was different. She'd faced adversity with hands on hips, condoms in her pocket and a vague attempt at femininity. When he'd last seen her she'd been wearing a woollen coat over a dressing gown. Today it was just a thick tarpaulin, wrapped mummy-like around her and secured by short ropes that, in turn, were tethered to stones. Whoever killed her hadn't used heavy enough weights: she'd floated to the surface and drifted into the canal bank where she'd been spotted by a passing barge.

Beauchamp and White crouched side by side on the muddy bank, studying her body. She hadn't been tortured but she had the same jagged hole in the middle of her forehead as Kessler. Same calibre, same no-nonsense approach to murder. The body had been found that morning but she'd been dead for days. Although Beauchamp was confronted week after week with the bodies of victims, it hadn't yet hardened him. Many in the RMP prided themselves on their professional detachment but Beauchamp was still willing to admit that brutality made him sad and angry. Whatever this woman had done since he last met her wasn't enough to warrant this outrage. Before he stood up he carefully covered the body with a grey blanket. He began to pace the area. As he studied the mud, reeds and waterline, he thought back to the first time he'd met the prostitute.

Stuff Oswald and Cooper-Wright, he decided, he would use the prostitute's death to spread the Kessler investigation across all of western Berlin.

Leaving another RMP to finish photographing the area and wait for the morgue cart, Beauchamp and White stacked the cardboard-tagged tarpaulin, ropes and rocks in the rear of the Jeep before driving back to headquarters.

Beauchamp had barely washed the grime of the canal from his hands when he was ordered to report to Cooper-Wright. He arrived at his superior's office to find him doing a blimpish turn.

'Haven't you got any sense of priority?' spluttered

Cooper-Wright. 'You and your men shouldn't be sidetracked by parochial police work. Death is an occupational hazard for whores. For God's sake, captain, the local plod could look after that dead woman's case. I want you to concentrate on Operation Bird Dog.'

'I believe the prostitute's murder is not just a random killing. It could be linked to –'

'I don't give a stuff what you think it's linked to. Bird Dog is scheduled to launch on the 20th, the first day of the distribution of the new Deutsche Marks. You're going to be heavily involved.'

Blast it, thought Beauchamp. Maintaining crowd control at banks would drain most of the RMP's resources. But he was pragmatic enough to know that the distribution was inevitable. The introduction of the Deutsche Mark was far more than a means of replacing the inflation-prone Reichsmark and stabilising the German economy, it was a direct counter measure to Russia's supposedly secret plans to print a new currency. Beauchamp sensed there would be a Kremlin backlash to the Deutsche Mark because the Russians were, in fact, the first to plan to introduce new German notes. In response, the Western Allies had rapidly prepared a fresh money supply that would be in their control, not the Soviets'.

A vast cellar under the Reichsbank building in Frankfurt now held the bulk of the new blue-backed notes which had been produced at an extraordinary rate by the Bureau of Engraving and Printing in Washington. The currency was being systematically trucked across Germany in wooden boxes marked 'Clay' and 'Bird Dog'. The British in Berlin were in charge of the local distribution and were guarding over 250 million Deutsche Marks.

The city was hissing with rumours that the currency reform was imminent. With many citizens believing they'd only get one new Deutsche Mark for 10 Reichsmarks, there could be panic. Certainly the public was currently on a spending spree.

Cooper-Wright wagged a finger at Beauchamp. 'As we're all too aware, there's little doubt that everyone, including the criminal elements, know the currency switch is coming. But they don't know the *exact* changeover date or the *actual* exchange rate.'

'And that rate is?' asked Beauchamp.

'One new Mark for one old Mark,' said Cooper-Wright, looking as if he was pleased he finally had information Beauchamp didn't. 'It's a fair exchange that will keep the populace from panicking, unless they have trouble accounting for how they earned their Reichsmarks.'

'The Germans may be happy, but the Russians will be well and truly pissed off.'

As Beauchamp headed back to his desk, he decided that before he found himself immersed in the Bird Dog assignment, he should see Speer again. Now *there* was a German who would never be happy unless he got his own way.

Trees shaded the garden path, flowerbeds ran alongside the main wall and there was a potting shed in the corner with one side made entirely of glass – presumably to warm the seedlings with sunshine and provide a line of sight of those inside.

A sentry in a tower rested his rifle on top of a balustrade and watched Speer and Beauchamp as they admired the Spandau garden.

'Only Hess and I care about the flowers,' said Speer, looking Beauchamp in the eye. 'This area, by the way, covers 6,000 square metres. I have measured it.'

'It's always good to know the size of the challenge you're faced with.' Beauchamp bent down and ran the dirt through his fingers. He looked around, casually trying to see if Rudolf Hess was in the walled garden. There was no sign of the lantern-jawed former Deputy Führer.

'Do you get along with Hess?'

'*Nein*. He sits over there and watches me walk around the garden. He calls me the village postman. I would not describe him as a friend, but then this is no place to make enemies.' Speer corrected himself: 'More enemies, that is.'

Speer moved off down a pathway. Just like a good host showing his guest around the estate, thought Beauchamp as he stood up and followed him. He was intrigued by his feelings towards Speer. He felt neither pity nor anger towards the proud man leading the way down the path. But, Beauchamp admitted to himself, he did find it easier than he imagined talking to someone who was, literally, a leading architect of the Third Reich's global ambitions. Beauchamp suddenly realised what Speer's appeal was –

show business. Speer had the glamour and public profile of a star. He knew it and was using it. He wanted Beauchamp to feel privileged that someone so internationally famous should confide in him, a mere copper. Sod that, concluded Beauchamp.

When they reached a small, immaculate vegetable garden, Beauchamp stopped, forcing Speer to halt too. 'Amistead wasn't giving anything away.'

Speer admired the carrots for a minute before he set off again. 'I imagine the visit to Amistead's house was not a complete waste of your time.'

'He's smooth, with some civilised trappings,' said Beauchamp. 'But I have a hunch – *ein Gefühl* – that he's somehow involved.' He stopped to acknowledge the presence of a guard in a nearby watchtower and nodded a greeting. The guard stared blankly back at him.

'Unsociable prick,' muttered Beauchamp.

'You wait until you meet the Russians,' said Speer. They continued walking until Speer stopped suddenly, turned to face Beauchamp and asked bluntly, 'Do you like Berlin, *Kapitän?*'

Beauchamp was temporarily thrown by the question and stared at Speer, saying nothing.

'Do you know what it is *really* like to live in this city?' Speer continued. 'You are tucked away in your safe little barracks with your batman pressing your uniform while the population struggles to survive.'

Beauchamp wasn't going to let the remark about the batman pass. 'I'll introduce you to Corporal White one day.

Let's see if you can convince him to play batman. He and I are out on the street every day, we know the people are struggling, and . . .' he paused and looked at Speer, 'we know *why* they're suffering.'

'Surely you cannot hold me responsible three years after it is all over?'

'Can't I?'

Speer straightened a fraction. 'Do you ever listen to the radio program "Die Insulaner"?'

'No.'

'"Die Insulaner" means "The Islanders". It is satirical. The name alone says how everyone feels about Berlin. While other cities are building skyscrapers after the war, Berliners are building what we call a *Teufelsberg* – a devil's mountain – out of rubble.'

'It's not that I don't appreciate the social insights, Herr Speer, but I think we should get back to the subject of the Cross. Who was that mysterious Russian visitor you say blackmailed you with plans naming you as the architect of the Blechhammer concentration camp?'

'I have explained already. I have no idea. He appeared one day and blackmailed me. It was quick and efficient. I never saw him again.'

'That makes it very hard for me to trace the relic. I've had one of my men check the records of your visitors. There are no details of the person you mentioned.'

'You do not surprise me. But if you hunt down Dr Kessler's killers then they will lead you to my Cross.'

'*Your* Cross?'

'I risked my life to hide that Cross. I have a duty to see that *das Kreuz von Berlin* is returned to this city.'

'You're going to have to wait.'

'Then let me give you another piece of information. I have been told that Amistead makes a habit of making a night crossing into the Russian sector at the Brandenburger Tor once a week. Tonight is one of those nights.'

'That could be for any reason – checking on his stable of prostitutes or trading cigarettes to the Soviets. It's risky for me to get involved for a few cartons of cigarettes. Who told you?'

'There are still some in the city who have not forgotten me. I have my informants, just like you. *Now* may I suggest that you continue your investigation?'

With that, he turned abruptly and walked towards the potting shed, leaving the Englishman standing on the pathway.

Beauchamp wondered if he should tap his heels together before he left the garden.

VIERZEHN

The Algonquin was humming when Docker arrived. He crossed the lobby area and went to the bar. On his right, a bartender was busy serving a number of hunch-shouldered men evenly spaced on the bar stools. Laurent had already cornered a small table as far away as possible from a group having pre-theatre drinks. Laurent signalled a waiter, ordered a martini and a single malt, and delivered a crushing handshake to Docker. 'So, is it good news?'

'That depends on how much money you want to spend. The person you're dealing with is a man called Randolph Morton. He's asking 500,000.' He watched Laurent's eyes when he mentioned Morton's name. There was no flicker of recognition at the name, but Docker saw a reaction to the money.

Laurent leant forward slightly to take a sip of his drink and said, 'Half a million. That's high but not out of the question.'

'Morton told me you have a competitor – someone in Europe.'

'Did he say who?'

'No, he's too cagey to show his hand. There may not even be another buyer.'

'Someone else certainly wants the Cross – and he's in Berlin.'

That city again, thought Docker. He put his whisky glass on a coaster. A little slopped over the rim. He fiddled with the coaster and began to rotate it as he went over each moment in that Berlin street. As always he couldn't decide whether he'd still pull the trigger if he'd known what the consequences would be. Ah, for the clarity of the movies. But life wasn't *My Darling Clementine*. There was no Wyatt Earp getting the glory while the bad guy got the bullet. Real life was Docker being advised to hightail it out of town as if he were the bad guy in the black hat.

Laurent also looked distracted. With a toothpick, he chased his olive around the bottom of his glass, lancing it on the second try.

'Why didn't you tell me you knew there was someone in Berlin chasing the Cross?' Docker asked.

'I was interested to hear if that person was mentioned or even named. The man in question is almost certainly linked with a Frenchman named Alaine Amistead, who deals in black-market contraband and women. We're very interested in Monsieur Amistead.'

'We?' Docker's reaction was immediate.

Laurent came back just as quickly, 'I meant "I".'

Docker knew he was lying. Trying to appear calm, he took a gulp of whisky and set the glass aside. The 'we' confirmed what he suspected. If the 'we' had been a slip-up by Laurent, the casual mention of Amistead was almost certainly deliberate. Docker had dealt with Amistead, back in the days when Docker could walk the Berlin streets without glancing over his shoulder. Back when Docker had a reputation for being a smart military policeman rather than an assassin's target. Amistead was a name dropped in the conversation to judge Docker's reaction. He studied Laurent. So, he's no frustrated relic hunter and he's not a cop – not with that tailoring. He must be a damn spook, possibly OSS. But why would an undercover agent be interested in antiquities?

Laurent kept dealing the clues. 'There's also someone else in the game. A Russian, Nikolai Popov. He trades anything that hasn't been nailed down, mainly artworks, antiques and secrets. He's the one who sold the Cross to Morton. His masters in the Kremlin know nothing about his art and antiques sideline. Nor do they know that secrets flow both ways. Bridgette Hunter was seen meeting with Popov in a restaurant in the west of Berlin and then they went back to his safe house. Bridgette's a smart operator. I'm not certain what happened next but she caught the night flight to Frankfurt and then flew to the States with the Cross and with Morton's 250 Gs still in her luggage. Morton obviously doesn't know that Bridgette cheated him and Popov, otherwise he would've killed her by now.'

Docker was angry. 'First you tell me not to bother with this girl and to concentrate on Gaffney. Then she turns up as a house guest at Morton's. It's too much of a coincidence. You've known all about Morton's pals.'

'As you said, "coincidence". It's a small world.'

'Particularly with people like you in it.' It was fitting together and Docker didn't like the picture. He could imagine Bridgette standing innocently at Customs with a hand on her hip, the Cross in her bag and Morton's money stashed out of sight. Docker bit his bottom lip to regain his composure. Bridgette's stage training was clearly being put to good, if dangerous, use. 'It's hard not to be impressed by Bridgette,' he said.

'If you like thieving actresses with a death wish,' said Laurent without rancour.

'Why the hell didn't you tell me about all this before I met Gaffney?'

'Simple. I wanted your reactions to everything that happened to be 100 percent natural – no acting. I know your background, John, but I don't know how good you are under pressure.'

'It would have made it a damn sight easier on my nerves.'

'You're a tense man at the best of times; I believe it would have made you more twitchy.'

Docker changed tack. 'Popov sounds like the sort of guy who takes his money and his goods seriously. That makes him a good business partner for Morton. So, do you still want to meet Morton?'

'Sure. You're the middleman, so set up the meeting.'

Docker could feel his jaw tighten. Middleman. Patsy. Pawn. He knew he was being screwed. The whole game had been fixed from the start. He'd been asked to find the Berlin Cross by a client who already knew who owned the relic. It had all been too easy: Laurent points Docker at Gaffney and Gaffney then leads Docker to Morton and the Cross. Laurent, whatever his line of business, wasn't a collector, at least not of relics. Docker took a deep breath and ordered more drinks. He counted to 10, then what was left of his poker face vanished. 'I'm sick of being fucked around,' he said in a hard voice. 'Tell me the truth, you piece of shit. What the hell is all this about?'

'All what?'

That did it. Docker's hand shot out and he grabbed Laurent's tie just below the knot. Jerking his fist upwards, he pulled Laurent out of his seat, glasses rattling on the table. 'Listen, asshole, you drop names like Amistead to see my reaction.' Docker tightened his grip. 'You didn't need me to track down that relic and find Morton. Talk.'

The tip of Laurent's jaw was pointing at the ceiling. 'Talk? You're strangling me.' Docker squeezed harder on the tie. 'Okay. Okay. Let's not make a scene.'

Docker looked around. Every face in the bar was turned towards him. A tableau of disbelief. This was the Algonquin. Customers didn't attack each other, at least not physically. Chastened, Docker lowered Laurent back into his seat and straightened his tie for him.

A frightened waiter appeared with their drinks and

Laurent regained his composure. Downing the fresh martini in one gulp, he said, 'You're right. We knew about the Cross and Morton, and we know all about you. You were the military police's blue-eyed boy in Berlin. You worked closely with the British and the Russians on fighting cross-sector crime and you even had a reputation for being politically astute. It's ironic, then, that you had to get the hell out of the city because you shot the wrong guy.'

'I shot the right guy, I just didn't know who the son of a bitch was.' Battling to keep his anger under control, he added, 'And I know jack about you.'

In a slow, deliberate movement Laurent pulled out a blue ID holder and flipped it open. Docker studied the ID card. Andrew Laurent, National Defense Research Committee. No title. In the bar's gloom it was impossible to judge if the ID was a forgery. During the war, he'd heard the committee's name mentioned in corridor conversations. It had been closely linked to America's wartime secret service agency, the Office of Strategic Services – the OSS. The committee's Division 19 had developed special weapons for the OSS operatives. No more cloaks and daggers for modern spies. These days they needed a new arsenal from a modern armoury.

Docker leant against the back of the booth. 'So, *Agent* Laurent, you couldn't get a job as a real cop?'

'I could say the same about you, *Lieutenant* Docker,' Laurent said, putting his ID away and flicking the rim of his empty martini glass with his fingernail. It made a ping that caught the attention of the waiter as well as a man and a woman at a nearby table. The pair glanced nervously at Laurent and Docker before getting up and moving.

The waiter, simultaneously trying to judge which of the men was the less aggressive and most likely to leave a tip, began to hover – first close to Docker then finally near Laurent.

'Why don't I buy you another drink with our government's money?' Laurent asked.

'Get a couple,' said Docker, holding up two splayed fingers in what could have been a victory sign.

When the fresh drinks arrived, Laurent leant towards Docker and smiled. 'We've been interested in your career since you came home. We got the word from the military police that you were on your way back here from Germany after that unpleasantness in Berlin. You're the type of guy we like to keep tabs on.'

But Docker had stopped listening. The words 'unpleasantness in Berlin' had sapped him behind the ear. He sat stunned. One squeezed trigger and his life had changed irrevocably. On the positive side, he consoled himself yet again, if it'd been him who'd been killed it *really* would have changed his life.

Docker heard Laurent's glass come down heavily on the table.

'So,' Laurent said, with a slight slur, 'someone with great connections in the Berlin underworld, someone who speaks German and someone who needs the money. Who better to be involved in this matter than you?'

'What *matter*?' Docker snapped.

'I'm coming to that and, take my word for it, I need you.'

'Why? An OSS agent could lean on Morton, Amistead and Popov, make them sweat a little and get whatever it is he wanted.'

'Firstly, the OSS is history. The CIA was set up last year. Secondly, the CIA takes care of business outside the States and the FBI has jurisdiction here. We couldn't have the CIA approach Morton.'

'And where does the National Defense Research Committee fit into this gallery of spooks?'

'Oh, we're just a small group on the sidelines. Our brief is to defend the United States and its interests. Sometimes those interests fall outside the US.'

'Like Berlin?'

'Of course, it's the detonator for Europe. If Berlin goes up, our hopes for a stable Europe also go sky high.' Laurent lit a cigar and Docker tapped the bottom of his cigarette packet to pop up a Camel. Laurent had emptied his glass – again. Docker wondered if it was a ploy or whether his 'client' was a lush.

Laurent leant forward and Docker could smell gin and a drop of vermouth. 'I'm in the secrets business, John, and I'll tell you some secrets. Not everything goes to plan, nothing is simple and no one tells the truth all the time.'

'No kidding.'

'Take this little caper. It started simply enough. Over in Berlin is someone who doesn't play by the rules. Popov. He's a Russian agent. That we can deal with. He also sells stolen treasures. Who cares? Well, I suppose the Kremlin does. But, unlike the Russians, we're not opposed to free-lance capitalism. What we don't like about Popov is that he supplies information to the highest bidder. That's a concern. That's destabilising. If we're buying, okay, but if he's selling, *whoa*, we're in trouble.

'We got word that he was out to make a final killing before quitting the city. Berlin was too hot for him. He wanted cash and, to save his hide, he also needed a big prize before running home to Moscow. He put the Berlin Cross on the market to get the cash, and attracted two bidders. One here, Morton, and one in Berlin, Amistead.

'The sale of the Cross was to boost Popov's piggy bank. As I said, that's not a problem. But he's also hungry for information because he wants to go home a hero.'

'I can never understand why people want to be heroes,' said Docker.

'For Popov, it's a case of covering his ass so that if the Kremlin finds out about his moneymaking ventures he won't be thrown into Lubyanka Prison. Between you and me, I doubt it'd work. The Kremlin would simply take whatever secrets Popov had and still put him in Lubyanka – or shoot him. Nevertheless, Popov is convinced he needs to bring back a top secret to Moscow that would make the MGB give him a standing ovation at the airport.'

'MGB?'

'Didn't they teach you guys anything?' Laurent gave a discreet hiccup. 'The NKGB was renamed the MGB after the war. The KGB is now a Ministry – the Ministry of State

Security. Just think of it as alphabet soup with sharks swimming in it.' He gave another hiccup. 'Anyway, we needed to ensnare Popov before he went home. We needed someone as a plant who'd set Popov up so we could blow his credibility with the home team. Those Russians have no sense of humour about freelancing on the job.'

This time he gave a quiet burp. 'John, we all make mistakes and we sure made one in this case. We found Bridgette Hunter, an actress who specialised in little-rich-girl roles. She spoke German and Russian, had been to NYU's Institute of Fine Arts and she was someone we knew we could train. We set up a meeting with Gaffney. That boy was desperate. He was persona non grata everywhere east of Wiesbaden and he needed someone to go to Europe to do deals and then smuggle the goods home. He took the bait. Gaffney introduced Bridgette to Morton and she got to play a role she was born for.'

'Why all this screwing around? You could've just bumped Popov off.'

'He was an MGB operative. We couldn't take a chance on his bosses getting upset at us removing one of their players. You mightn't guess it from the recent tension in Germany, but the Russians are *meant* to be our allies. We planned to leave Popov's punishment to his colleagues. As I said, the Kremlin doesn't take kindly to capitalism, especially amongst its own kind.'

Laurent pushed his new olive up the side of his glass and watched it slide back to the bottom. 'The plan didn't quite work out. We chose the wrong woman,' he continued.

'Like I said before, Bridgette somehow got her hands on the Cross and then stiffed Morton for the quarter of a million. What a woman. She's a smart cookie and I'd love to know how she got Popov to hand over the Cross and leave her with the cash. As for Morton, it seems pretty obvious he still doesn't know she cheated Popov and kept the dough. All Morton would see was the end result – he has the Cross. The fact she cheated that shit in a silk-lined suit and kept the money doesn't faze us. The big problem is that she's now spoiled goods on both sides of the Atlantic. No one trusts her and Popov would love to bump her off – or have someone here do it for him. Popov might even want Morton killed too.'

Docker decided to take a gamble and force Laurent to acknowledge the final Berlin connection – a link between Kessler's disappearance and the Cross. He knew there had to be a tie-in, otherwise there had been more coincidences in the last few days than in a Hitchcock movie. 'And how is Friedrich Kessler involved?' Docker asked as innocently as possible.

It was the first time Docker had mentioned the name but Laurent didn't even flinch. 'The *late* Dr Friedrich Kessler.'

'Dead?'

'The British found his body. He'd been tortured. Our guess is he talked. Kessler's knowledge was the big prize I mentioned. That's what Popov was after.'

'So Popov killed him?'

'Not directly. If Popov already had the secrets he wouldn't hang around.'

136

'Perhaps Kessler didn't talk.'

'Unlikely, but whatever the case, we know the Cross is at the heart of this mess. It seems all of Berlin wants the Cross and fast. We need to have a pow-wow with Morton.'

'I still say it'd be easier for the committee to take out Popov and Amistead and let me go on running a nice, quiet little detective business.'

'Fortunately, or maybe unfortunately, we aren't as trigger-happy as you. We like to make certain of the facts before bumping off foreign nationals. And if we hit Popov and Amistead we wouldn't know what happened to Kessler's secrets. Your problem, John, is you're too straightforward.'

'I never realised that was a fault.'

'In business it is,' said Laurent. He waited a moment before adding, 'I want you to arrange a meeting with Morton for Tuesday in a suite at the Plaza Hotel. Tell Morton to bring the Berlin Cross and I'll have the money ready for him.'

Docker looked concerned.

'Cheer up, John,' said Laurent. 'We decided some time ago to find a fresh face to help us set Popov up. It took us a while to find the right person.' He smirked before leaning forward. 'Congratulations. You're our fresh face.'

FÜNFZEHN

Looming against the twilight sky, the arches of the Brandenburg Gate dwarfed the outline of the man Beauchamp was tailing. It had been over an hour since the pair had left the comparative safety of Wilmersdorf and zig-zagged their way across the city, edging closer and closer to the dangerous area around what the Germans called the Brandenburger Tor – dangerous for Beauchamp because he had no authority to be there.

Having taken as many precautions as he could, including driving an anonymous delivery van and wearing drab workman's clothing, Beauchamp was certain Amistead would not spot the tail. In a small canvas bag by his side he had his Browning side-arm, warrant card, a wad of Reichsmark's and faked German identity papers. Beauchamp hadn't told Corporal White about the forged papers, which had lain hidden in a desk drawer for just such a job, or about his planned foray into the Russian sector. The corporal was a by-the-book copper who wouldn't have approved of either.

When Amistead had parked his car a few hundred yards from the gate and begun walking, Beauchamp had also abandoned his vehicle, grabbed the canvas bag and quickly followed the Frenchman.

Amistead's conversation with the two Russians at the Brandenburger Tor checkpoint was brief. The Frenchman passed through and disappeared from sight.

Following a discreet distance behind, Beauchamp reached the checkpoint. As the guards stepped forward, he greeted them in his schoolboy German, breathing an inward sigh of relief when the Russians responded in even poorer German. They were asking for his identification papers while at the same time sweeping their eyes up and down his body looking, Beauchamp presumed, for any sign he was more than a local worker eking out a living in the western sector. Under the hard yellow glare of an overhead light, they checked his papers and waved him through.

With a coat slung over his shoulder, Amistead was acting the boulevardier as he ambled down the once grand avenue Unter den Linden. He stopped when he reached the remains of the Hotel Adlon. Beauchamp had read about the glory days of the hotel, which once had been described as 'the smartest place in town' – until it was badly battered by Allied bombing. The Adlon had been demolished after the war and was now a near-vacant lot dotted with scattered bricks, several high mounds of masonry rubble and the occasional shard of glass.

Beauchamp wondered if some of the glass came from the 400,000 bottles of wine that Herr Adlon had stashed in his cellar before the bombing began.

Amistead began picking his way towards the centre of the lot. Beauchamp skirted up a side street and approached from the rear. In the soft evening light, he could see another figure waiting with one foot resting on a pile of bricks. The man was smoking a cigarette and concentrating on Amistead as the Frenchman came closer.

Beauchamp crept behind a mound of rubble about three yards from the smoking man. He could see the men greet each other with a firm handshake.

The stranger was the first to speak. 'I am delighted to see you. Thank you for coming.'

'*Je vous en prie*,' replied Amistead. 'I am interested to know what this is all about, Monsieur Popov.'

'Comrade Popov,' came the quick correction, followed by a quicker smile.

Amistead nodded, lighting a cigarette and offering another to Popov. The Russian stubbed out his own and eagerly took one of Amistead's.

'I heard about Kessler. A great scientist. A terrible loss to the international community.'

'*C'est ça*,' agreed Amistead. 'A tragedy.'

'Did the doctor talk?' Popov asked.

Amistead said nothing, instead rolling his cigarette around in his fingers, dropping it on the ground and then crushing it under his heel. 'Pain is a very persuasive means of extracting information from soft men.'

'You sound as if you enjoy torturing such men.'

'It's the control I enjoy,' said Amistead, then added quickly, 'Can you get the Berlin Cross back?'

'Of course,' said Popov. 'More importantly, will you be in a position to exchange what I want for that relic?'

Amistead was quiet for a moment. When he spoke it was in a low voice. Beauchamp could only catch the word 'Kessler' – nothing more.

Fortunately for Beauchamp the Russian's reply was louder. 'Good. Now I have some questions for you.'

Looking over his shoulder towards the street, Amistead appeared nervous. 'Come, comrade, let us move further away.' He cupped Popov's elbow and led him towards Beauchamp.

Beauchamp pulled the gun from the bag, lowered himself onto the ground and lay stretched out alongside the rubble mound. Gravel crunched nearby. He drew in his breath, waiting. More footfalls – they were inches away. Beauchamp tensed. Would the first bullet go cleanly through his head or would they aim for the broad of the back?

'This will do,' came Amistead's voice.

Beauchamp could smell them – tobacco and shoe leather. If either glanced down that would be it. He could see the cuffs on Amistead's trousers. Oh shit, thought Beauchamp, if that Frenchman moves just a fraction to the right he'll tread on my hand. There was nothing Beauchamp could do. The slightest movement of the gun in his hand would almost certainly create a gleam of metal in the half-light. He closed his eyes.

This time Popov spoke. 'You have not said why you want the relic so badly.'

'You need the Kessler information to smooth your way back to Moscow but, for me, the Cross is the key.'

'To what?' asked Popov.

'I *may* tell you later. First get me the Cross.'

'Sadly, I have to trust you.' He added a farewell, '*Nadejus', my eschjo uvidimsja.*'

'I have to trust you too, *hélas.*'

Beauchamp heard the Frenchman begin to walk away. A moment later Amistead stopped and called softly back to Popov, 'Don't you communists believe in the power of the Cross?'

'Fairytales to entertain the gullible.'

'Not this time,' said Amistead. 'Not this time.'

SECHZEHN

As an exercise in managing debt it wasn't particularly sophisticated, but for Docker it was somehow satisfying. He sat behind his desk sorting bills into two piles – unpaid and unlikely-ever-to-be-paid.

He tossed a New York Telephone Company bill onto the unpaid pile just as the handle of his office door turned. There was a brief pause before the door was pushed open and Bridgette hobbled in. He leapt up, guided her to a chair and sat himself down on the edge of the desk.

Bridgette's hands fidgeted on her lap before she gripped her handbag, snapped open the clip and pulled out a small piece of notepaper with a Manhattan phone number scribbled on it. 'He's after me,' she said.

'Morton?'

'Worse – Willi. I got back to my apartment this afternoon and the building super said a foreigner who refused

143

to give his name had been banging on my door. The man left this number to call him.'

'Have you?'

'I came to see you first. If it's Willi then I don't want to be alone when I make the call. I'm frightened.'

'I'm here,' said Docker in what he hoped was a reassuring tone. He wasn't quite sure if he was reassuring her or himself. If Laurent was to be believed, Bridgette was a one-time government agent, a con artist and a rich man's mistress. It didn't make for a happy mix.

She stared into his eyes. 'When you gave me your business card you said to contact you if I ever needed a specialist. You're not an antiquities dealer, are you?'

'I guess you can tell that from the office furniture,' he said warily. 'Let's just say I'm available to help people.'

She gave the hint of a smile. 'Admit it. You're some sort of investigator.'

Docker pushed the phone closer to Bridgette, lifted the receiver and handed it to her. 'Make the call.'

'I can't do it.' She pushed the receiver away.

Docker slid off the edge of the desk, pulled a chair beside hers and sat down. Under other circumstances, being so near to her would have felt intimate, he thought, but sadly not today. She kept looking down at her hands. He shook his head, stood up and began pacing the small office. 'So where's the missing 250 grand?' he asked.

Bridgette looked surprised. 'I don't know what you mean.'

'Funny, everyone else across two continents does.'

Bridgette bent forward with a pained expression, as if she'd been winded. Docker hoped she wouldn't throw up on his desk. He moved his pile of unpaid bills further away from her.

'Morton, Gaffney, Rühmann and you. You're all in this together,' she said straightening up.

'You can skip the indignant act. It plays better on Broadway.' Docker sat down again next to her. Pussyfooting around wasn't going to get him anywhere. 'I've been speaking to someone you know, Andrew Laurent. He tells me you've taken up robbery as a new career. Let's see,' he said, starting to tick off points on his fingertips. 'You realised the guy who had the Cross in Berlin couldn't bitch to the authorities when you disappeared with the goods and his money. You screwed Laurent around after he chose you to help him. But, what the heck, you're only double-crossing the US government. Finally you did one smart thing . . . you gave the Cross to Morton, otherwise you'd have had *everyone* wanting a piece of you.'

'I'm used to that,' she said, attempting nonchalance.

'I can imagine.' He took a breath. 'We both know that Morton would be very pissed off if he heard you'd pocketed the cash. But why do you think Rühmann hasn't told Morton about your Berlin disappearing act?'

'Willi's client is the man who gave me the Cross. The client thinks I've got his money but I've no idea where the hell it is. That doesn't matter to Willi. He believes if he told Randolph anything about me then Randolph would keep the Cross, force me to tell him where the money is and then kill me.'

'So, Rühmann is trying to keep Morton in the dark so he can get that piece of wood, take back the 250 Gs and go home.'

'That's what he may think. But I haven't got the money.' She narrowed her eyes.

Docker altered course. 'How long have you known Rühmann?'

'Not long. He's a broker. A runner. Morton needs him around because Gaffney's name stinks in Europe. But being a broker means that Rühmann handles both sides of a deal – and now he's putting his Berlin client's priorities ahead of Randolph's.'

'What about this guy you met in Berlin, the one who originally had the Cross?'

Instead of answering, she again opened her handbag and searched through the detritus. 'Damn,' she mouthed.

Guessing that she was looking for a cigarette, Docker offered her one.

After two long drags, she began speaking in a tense, defensive fashion. 'It's straightforward. I went to Berlin and met with a man, Nikolai Popov. Russian, in case you hadn't guessed. I picked up the Cross and the reliquary as Randolph told me to and brought them back to the States.'

'That's all? You came here because you wanted my help, now you're holding out on me.'

'I came here because I didn't want to be alone in my

apartment. I didn't come here to get the third degree from you.'

'Can you trust the guy in Berlin?'

'Trust?' Bridgette repeated, her voice taking on a melodramatic edge. 'Given the chance, he'd sell Stalin's soul for a rouble.'

'Probably too late for that,' said Docker, then paused. She wasn't the only one who knew how to be theatrical.

Suddenly horn blasts sounded from the street. Docker went to the window and saw a sloppily parked cab next to the kerb and two trucks from the warehouse down the block trying to squeeze past. One of the drivers was shouting at the cab. The passenger was ignoring the chaos behind him and climbing the short flight of steps to the front door of Docker's building. Docker turned back to Bridgette. 'Rühmann's tracked you down. You better hide or leave quickly!'

'I've nowhere to go to.'

'And I've nowhere to hide you. Come on, take the back stairs.'

She got up and reluctantly hobbled to the door. It opened before she could reach it.

Rühmann wore a dark three-button, single-breasted suit and a snap-brim fedora. He grabbed Bridgette's upper arm and, his tone impatient, said, 'We trusted you.'

'You're too sensitive, Willi,' she replied and tried to pull away.

Rühmann kept his grip and swung to face Docker just as he was getting up from his desk. 'Stay where you are,

Herr Docker. This has nothing to do with you.' He squeezed Bridgette's arm. 'My client in Berlin believes you have his money.'

'He's lying,' said Bridgette. 'I handed over Randolph's money and was given the Cross.'

Rühmann's voice became harder. 'My client denies it. He tells me that you cheated him, took the relic and kept the money. Now the deal is off. He wants the Cross back as well as the 250 thousand dollars you stole from him.'

'I haven't got the money.' There was a quaver in Bridgette's voice. 'And you can't get the Cross back. It's locked in Randolph's vault.'

'You are a thief, Miss Hunter.'

'Your client stole that relic from the Germans.'

'That is not relevant. What is important is that you have money that rightfully belongs to my client, and Randolph is in possession of a valuable artefact that has not been paid for. One way or the other, I will make you pay.'

'Let her go,' said Docker. He stood behind his desk, weighing up his chances of reaching the gun in his drawer without alerting the German.

Bridgette turned her head so she faced Rühmann. 'I don't have your client's dough and, as far as Randolph is concerned, he knows he has paid 250,000 for that Cross. He won't give it up. He'll kill you if you try to take it.'

'Leave the relic to me,' said Willi. 'In the meantime I intend to collect my client's money. So, Fräulein, I have come here to give you a deadline.'

'What good is a deadline if I haven't got the money?' asked Bridgette.

'Why don't you both take a seat,' said Docker, attempting calm. 'I've got enough chairs.'

Rühmann let go of Bridgette's arm, picked up the nearest chair and threw it through the closed window. Glass and timber showered onto the pavement, followed by a sharp obscenity from the street below.

'What a rough neighbourhood,' said Rühmann. 'People swearing, furniture being thrown. It is just what you would expect around here. You should move uptown.'

'Thanks for the real estate advice,' said Docker through gritted teeth. Launching himself off his desk, he threw himself onto Rühmann, the visitor's hat rolling away as the two men struggled. Neither man would release the other as they wrestled across the floor. Holding Rühmann's suit lapels, Docker rolled over, bringing the German with him. Docker let go of the lapels, swung both knees up and catapulted Rühmann further back into the room. Hauling himself up on the side of the desk, he snatched the .38 from a holster in the desk's top drawer and waved it at Rühmann.

'Get out,' gasped Docker, still out of breath.

Rühmann picked up his hat, tugged at the right-hand corner of his jacket and looked at Bridgette. 'As I said, I am giving you a deadline – you have 24 hours to return the money.' He turned and left.

Bridgette slammed the door shut and locked it as Docker slipped back into his chair and put the revolver on his desk.

'It's not often I see an antiquities dealer with a gun,' Bridgette said.

'Just as well,' said Docker.

'That jerk deserved everything he got,' she said.

'A jerk, yes, but he's a damn determined guy. He's behaving like someone who is 100 percent certain you scammed that dough.'

'You'd believe a gangster who threatens women rather me?'

'I didn't –' Docker began, but it was too late.

With as much dignity as someone with a limp could muster, Bridgette unlocked the door and stomped out of his office. The door banged shut, leaving Docker to sniff what remained of her cologne. *L'air du Temps*.

SIEBZEHN

The trio stood around the bed, staring at it as if willing Elsa's grandmother to appear. Like a starched and ironed chaperone, the matron was standing between Beauchamp and Elsa, watching the young German woman for any sign of imminent hysteria. Seeing none, the matron continued to explain how Frau Kessler had died within days of her son's body being found. The American authorities who had arrived to break the news of Friedrich Kessler's death to Frau Kessler had been less than happy when they found the elderly woman dead in her ward bed. They had demanded and got an autopsy. There were no signs of a struggle or of poisoning.

The matron excused herself for a moment and returned with a satchel. In it were some drugs she believed Dr Kessler had bought for his mother on the black market. They were of no use now.

Elsa made a gesture for the matron to keep them, but

Beauchamp put his hand out, saying the drugs were evidence.

He took the satchel and clipped the clasp shut, then thanked the matron and indicated to Elsa it was time to leave.

Beauchamp's time was fast running out. The announcement to Berliners had been made that on 20 June the Deutsche Mark was to be issued. The Reichsmark would be officially dead in less than 48 hours. Beauchamp felt angry with himself for not having followed up the Frau Kessler lead earlier. The fact that the hospital was in the US sector shouldn't have delayed him.

It was only at Elsa's prompting that he had finally agreed to visit the hospital. Now there was another body to add to Kessler's and the prostitute's – another body to mock his expertise.

Deep in thought, he drove Elsa back to her hotel without saying a word. Just as he couldn't tell anyone at the RMP about his unsanctioned and possibly court-martial-worthy visit to the Russian sector, he couldn't discuss it with Elsa. Now that he'd overheard Popov and Amistead discussing Kessler's death, the link between the Frenchman and the dead German had finally been made. Speer had been right – Amistead was at the heart of the drama, but without firm, legally gained evidence Beauchamp knew he was, as White would have said, 'stuffed'. Sneaking into the Russian sector wasn't an exploit that Beauchamp could confidently raise with his superiors. He'd gone over every second of his twilight visit to the ruins of the Hotel Adlon, and the pieces of the puzzle were coming together – well, almost together.

Beauchamp parked against the kerb directly outside Elsa's hotel and escorted her to the front desk to retrieve her key. She looked quickly around the lobby, ignored the clerk and kissed Beauchamp on the cheek. The nearby lift doors groaned open and she left him. He listened to the steel cage creak its way between the floors, waited until it stopped, and then walked to a wall mirror. He reached for his handkerchief and wiped off the lipstick. Then he tucked the linen, with its slight red smear, into his breast pocket and rebuttoned it before patting the pocket. Probably best to keep it tucked out of Corporal White's sight. He might get the right idea.

White was disappointed. He had been incessantly practising 'Please stay in the queue' in German to get the right intonation of authority. But the long line outside the bank was orderly, with people queuing patiently to change Reichsmarks for Deutsche Marks. These Berliners appeared completely resigned to the currency changeover. His hands clasped behind his back, White was walking alongside the line, doing a reasonable impression of someone in charge, when Beauchamp arrived with a staff sergeant.

'Everything's under control, sir,' said White confidently.

'Because of you?' asked Beauchamp, with a twinkle in his eye.

'Put it down to my superior policing.'

'Any large wads of Reichsmarks?'

'None, unless it's stashed in their knickers.'

'Before I check I'll wait until soap is more readily available,' said Beauchamp.

'Wise decision, sir,' said White.

Beauchamp got back in the Jeep, the staff sergeant following. 'What we need to do is some real policing,' Beauchamp said. 'That's if the major and the Russians allow us to.'

I seem to spend my life standing in front of this man's desk, thought Beauchamp. He looked down at Major Cooper-Wright and forced a smile. 'Everything's going to plan, sir.'

'If your idea of "going to plan" is having your balls firmly squeezed by Marshal Sokolovsky then I'm worried about you,' said Cooper-Wright.

'What's he done now?'

'Doing . . . doing. He's got his men on the move. The barricades are going up, captain, and I plan to be ready for anything. Get your gear, we're invited to a secret briefing.'

Cooper-Wright looked pleased with himself, Beauchamp less so.

The main conference room at York House was crowded with edgy British Army officers, all except Beauchamp concentrating on the low stage in front of them. He was restless and his dislike of formal briefings was intensified by having to sit next to Cooper-Wright. He had no choice though; every other chair in the room was taken. Near the podium was an easel with a map of Berlin pinned to it. Each of the sectors was marked and a red line had been drawn around the French, British and American zones. The Western Allies' zones were encircled by the Russians.

Today's speaker was the newly promoted Major General Sanderson, who clearly enjoyed the attention. In a plummy baritone, Sanderson told the assembled officers that, on the previous night, Berlin's city assembly had been ordered by Russia's Marshal Sokolovsky to introduce a new currency – the Ostmark – and to enforce its use. Sokolovsky planned to ban the Allies' Deutsche Mark. However, the assembly had defied the Russians and voted to keep the Western-backed currency. There was uproar after the meeting and communist agitators, who'd been lying in wait outside the assembly building, attacked the members as they departed. Overnight the Russians had moved to cut off the city. All traffic into the western zones of Berlin had now been halted.

'Frankly, as regards to land routes, we're buggered,' said Sanderson. 'The Russians are refusing to allow deliveries of coal and food across the Elbe. They claim the main bridge is closed for repairs, and they've also halted barges on the river. After conferring with us, the Americans have backed away from a plan to send a unit of combat engineers to the bridge. We believe an armed convoy forcing its way into Russian-controlled territory is too risky. On the bright side, if there is one, we do have six weeks of food supplies stockpiled in the western sectors.'

Cooper-Wright raised his hand. Beauchamp glanced sideways at his superior officer, knowing that the major would never ask a question if he didn't already know the answer. 'I'm assuming, sir,' said Cooper-Wright, 'that it was the introduction of the Deutsche Mark that triggered the Soviet response.'

'Bang on,' said Sanderson approvingly. 'The Russians believe that by stealing a march on the Kremlin's plans to introduce its own new currency, we've taken control of Germany's financial systems. They've responded in a typically brutal fashion. They plan to starve us into submission.'

Beauchamp sat with a notebook on his knee. He'd written '24 June, blockade started'. He had toyed with writing 'siege' but it was too medieval a word. He didn't want to overdramatise the situation; there were enough people panicking as it was. On reflection, 'siege' *was* the right word. The Russians were planning something out of the Middle Ages. As soon as this meeting was over, he'd have no choice but to postpone the Kessler investigation.

'What I'm about to tell you is strictly hush-hush, of course,' said Sanderson. He looked around the room at the nodding heads before smiling. 'A lifeline is being thrown to us by London and Washington. The Russians have left the air corridors open and the Allies are going to feed this city from the air. That's the plan, gentlemen, and every person in this room will play a critical role in the airlift.'

Beauchamp arrived back at his office cursing. Looking at his wastepaper bin he was tempted to kick it across the room – instead he clenched his fists. How could this be happening *now*? Just as he was about to crack the Kessler case, he was being diverted by those bloody Russians from collaring Amistead and that new player, Popov. For a moment, he considered another reason for his frustration. Elsa. How long would it be until he saw her again? Snatching up the phone, he almost tore the cord from its base. His knuckles were white against the black bakelite as he made the call to her hotel.

'I'd hoped to meet you again,' he began, then added, 'to discuss the investigation, of course.'

'But you cannot?'

'Something's come up.'

'I know. I have been listening to the radio. The city is cut off.'

'There's nothing to worry about.'

'The last time the Russians threatened Berlin there was *a lot* to worry about.'

'You're right. We can't underestimate them. But I had hoped to continue working on your father's case.'

There was a brief silence on the line. Beauchamp realised Elsa hadn't considered that issue. He waited for her to say, 'But you cannot?' again.

Instead, she said, 'I understand. The living come before the dead.'

'Just for the moment. I'll be back in touch very soon.'

After they said goodbye, Beauchamp banged down the receiver. 'Damn,' he said and kicked the paper bin against the far wall.

ACHTZEHN

Docker sat in a Plaza Hotel suite swirling whisky around in his glass. Heavy curtains muffled the traffic noise. He took a sip and reached for a complimentary cigarette from the box on the coffee table. If nothing else, he decided, this case was introducing him to the sweet life.

The doorbell rang. As he opened the door the blow caught him in the solar plexus and doubled him up. Morton stood over him pointing a gun at his face. 'Where's the fucking Cross, you piece of shit?'

Docker rolled onto his knees, took a breath and staggered upright. The gun was still pointed at his face. 'I've no idea what you're talking about,' Docker gasped.

Morton's thumb cocked the revolver. 'Last chance.'

Standing just behind Morton, Gaffney urged him on. 'I heard those two bunco artists talking in German.'

'You mean me talking to Rühmann?' said Docker, bewildered.

Gaffney nodded, looking like a man keen not to delay an execution.

Docker walked over to his chair and grabbed his whisky, the gun barrel following him across the room. 'I'd never met the guy before in my life. I spoke to him in German because with a name like Willi Rühmann what other nationality would he be? I thought he was your pal. Why the hell would he have taken the Cross?' The words came out in a rush, Docker's mind whirling.

Morton's eyes were hard. 'Why? Money. That's one valuable piece of wood.'

'Maybe, but this has nothing to do with me,' said Docker.

'First you set up this damn meeting, then I find the Cross has gone missing and Rühmann with it. That doesn't sound like a coincidence to me.'

'I had nothing to do with Rühmann taking the Cross. If I did, would I be sitting here waiting to be used as a punching bag?'

Morton hesitated but there was something in Docker's manner that prompted him to uncock the gun. Gaffney looked disappointed as Morton slipped it into his coat pocket. The three men stood staring at each other.

The doorbell rang again. Morton looked at Docker. 'Your client?'

'Guess so.'

'Open it.' Morton had his hand bunched in his coat pocket.

Dishevelled and still grimacing from the pain of the punch, Docker motioned a wary Laurent into the room and made the introductions, allowing enough time for the men to nod to each other before saying to Laurent, 'There's been a hiccup. A Berliner, Willi Rühmann, has stolen the Cross and Mr Morton believes I'm somehow tied up in all this.' He massaged his sore stomach.

'Where's this Rühmann guy now?' asked Laurent, teeth bared.

Docker sounded defensive. 'How the hell would I know?'

'Fuck,' spat Laurent. He balled up his fists, then unclenched them. He looked across at Morton. 'When did you find the Cross was missing?'

Morton's face contorted for a moment. It was the face of a man who didn't like being quizzed by strangers. His reply was abrupt. 'A few hours ago. When I found it missing, I drove straight here from Connecticut.'

'And you've no idea where Rühmann's gone?'

'I wouldn't have taken a swing at your boy if I knew.'

'Boy?' repeated Laurent, looking amused and taking out his cigar case. Docker watched as Laurent dropped back to what he was most comfortable with – role playing.

'I'm surprised we haven't met before, Mr Morton. You're obviously a keen collector.'

Morton was still guarded. 'And I'm surprised I've never heard of you. If I'd had time, I would've had you checked out.'

'I'd be happy to give you some references,' said Laurent with confidence. 'The Duchess of Windsor is always very generous with her praise as is her friend, Chiang Kai-shek. Then there's Joe Kennedy –'

'Okay, Okay,' said Morton. He swung around to Docker. 'You're punching above your weight working for this guy.'

Docker gave a tight smile.

Laurent brought the attention back to himself. 'Who is Rühmann?' he asked.

Morton answered just as Docker was about to speak. 'He's a broker and he knows his stuff. He'll know where to off-load the Cross to get the maximum return.'

'I suggest we track Rühmann by a process of elimination,' said Laurent. 'Staying in the US is out. The Berlin Cross is too hot and too specialised a commodity for Rühmann to off-load here. It wouldn't be Asia either. There are only a few serious collectors in that region who'd pay for a Christian treasure. Same goes for Arabia. I can't see the Cross attracting much interest east of Istanbul. That leaves Europe and, more specifically, Berlin. My guess is that Rühmann is heading home.'

'LaGuardia,' Gaffney's voice cut in. 'We've got to get to the airport to stop him.'

'Think it through,' cautioned Morton. 'We don't even know how long that Kraut has been gone. Rushing to the airport won't do any good if he's halfway across the Atlantic.'

'Got a better idea?' asked Gaffney, showing annoyance with Morton for the first time.

Morton was too keyed up to sit down, too tense to move. 'The deal still stands,' he finally said to Laurent. 'You want the Cross, I want your money. In fact I want 500,000 of your money.'

'Amounts are academic without the relic,' shot back Laurent. 'We need someone to track the Cross down and bring it back, and I know just the man.'

Docker started backing away. 'Not a chance,' he said. He could see where this was all leading – to him getting killed. There was no dignity in being bumped off in a back alley, not for a few hundred bucks. 'Berlin's a tough town. I'm not risking my life just to make you –' he nodded at Morton, 'wealthier and you –' a glance this time at Laurent, 'the owner of some ancient trinket.'

'Perhaps Mr Morton and I can appeal to your better nature. What if I triple your retainer and Mr Morton picks up the tab for your expenses?'

'Plus a success fee,' added Morton.

'How much?' asked Docker.

'Five percent of the value,' said Morton without blinking.

'Still no deal,' said Docker.

'What would it take?' Morton's voice was now softer, probing.

Would greed outweigh fear? wondered Docker. His greed, that is. He thought for a moment, then said, 'I want four times the original retainer plus 15 percent of the value of the Cross.'

Morton's cheeks reddened in fury, but Laurent said 'What else can we do?'

'Not pay him,' fumed Morton.

'Then we all lose,' countered Laurent.

'Okay, okay,' said Morton.

'That's settled then.' Laurent looked at Docker. 'I'll arrange the tickets and send Mr Morton the bill. All you have to do is find the Cross.'

Docker waited until the hotel room was empty, then sat down heavily on a chair near the phone. He suddenly realised he wanted to see Bridgette again before he left. No, he *needed* to see her.

He reached for the phone.

The Great White Way was looking neither great nor white as Docker trudged up Broadway that Saturday night. The rain was thin and misty, the sidewalks slick and scruffy, the air humid. The neon seemed as sincere as the hooker's smile that greeted him as he swung into West 44th Street and headed for Sardi's, the Theatre District restaurant that for over 20 years had been favoured by show-business folk.

Docker arrived 15 minutes earlier than planned. He found the entrance crowded with men in suits shaking the rain out of their hair and baying at each other as they competed for attention. There was little chance of being overheard here, he thought, as he squeezed past them into the restaurant.

Disappointed that the red leather banquettes were taken, he found himself seated at a table off to one side of the room. But with the showbiz caricatures crowding the walls and the smell of expensive colognes and seared steak rising from nearby tables, Docker still felt himself part of the Broadway buzz.

There was no fanfare when Bridgette arrived 30 minutes later. Docker noticed she still had a slight limp, unless she was faking that too. She slipped into a chair and asked the waiter for a Manhattan. Docker made a lame comment about the weather.

Bridgette swivelled to take in the room. In a quick 'hello', she wiggled her fingers at a man seated at a banquette at the rear of the room. The man had full cheeks, thin hair and was sitting next to a well-built, self-consciously good-looking man. 'Actors,' she explained to Docker.

'Out of work ones, if they're here at this hour,' said Docker.

'The smooth one is Noël Coward, the cute one Larry Olivier.'

'Oh,' said Docker, doubting that any woman had ever used the word 'cute' to describe him. Picking up a menu, he changed the subject. 'Let's order.'

Docker tried to keep the conversation going until the meals arrived. He asked a few bland questions about Bridgette's career and then broke off when the waiter reappeared with their orders. Uncertain as to how Bridgette would react, he waited until she'd had a few mouthfuls before saying calmly, 'I had a meeting with Morton and Laurent today. Morton says that Rühmann has stolen the Cross.'

Dropping her fork onto her plate, Bridgette looked genuinely frightened. But is she faking *that*? wondered Docker.

'Randolph will think I was involved,' she said. 'He'll kill me.'

Docker tried to calm her. 'No, no, I saw him earlier today. He never mentioned you. He just wanted to beat the crap out of me.'

She appeared to find the thought reassuring and pushed her plate aside before lighting a cigarette. Shooting a thin stream of smoke away from the table, she asked casually, 'Tell me about your connection with Laurent.'

'Simple. He's my client.'

'But you're no dealer.'

'How can you tell?'

'They're rarely rude to a lady and, what's more, dealers don't have guns in their desk drawers.'

'I've met Gaffney. I'd say he was capable of both.'

'*And* I saw your office. If you're really in the antiquities game I'd suggest you'd better get a night job.'

'Cruel but fair,' said Docker, taking his *real* business card from his wallet and passing it to her.

She felt the paper quality, turned it over twice and laid it on the table. 'They used to call you folks "confidential agents". Are you?'

'Well, I'm discreet.'

'Not *that* discreet if you're happy to meet me at Sardi's.'

'I like noisy restaurants. I can ask tough questions.' He paused for one beat and asked, 'Just for the record, did you know Rühmann was going to double-cross Morton?'

'For the record, the answer is "No". And, since you've stooped to working for Laurent, you're in no position to criticise me.'

'But Laurent tells me you also work for him.'

'Not any more. I did what I was asked to do – schmooze Gaffney then Morton, convince them I was an expert at the sort of work they wanted done, head to some bombed-out city, practise my German, make the highest offer for what could have been just a worthless piece of wood and smuggle it back to New York.'

'You didn't mention the missing 250 Gs.'

'Do you think I'd be crazy enough to steal the money?'

'For a quarter of a million? You bet. A lot of people would be tempted.'

'If I'd taken the money, why would I go back to Randolph?'

'Self-preservation. If you'd tried to run and this Popov guy had screamed foul, then Morton would have known you'd screwed him. You'd have been a marked woman.'

'Instead of just a fallen woman.'

'Literally, given your habit of jumping off cliffs.'

'Once. Once only. And I told you why.'

'I haven't told anyone else – yet.'

'If you think I'm going to be extra friendly with you just to keep you quiet –' she began, then stopped.

Docker had flushed deep red.

'You know I don't think you're like that,' she said.

Docker wasn't certain if she was teasing him or questioning his masculinity. He looked desperately around for the waiter. There was no staff in sight. He was trapped. He went back to the missing money. 'So you admit you creamed the cash?'

'I admit to nothing.' She touched his hand.

He pulled his hand away but left it on the table, confused. 'One minute you're angry, the next you're playing up to me.' His cheeks were still red.

'You know I like you more when you blush than when you're playing detective.'

'Private detective.' He allowed himself a small smile.

'Okay, Mr Detective. Let's go somewhere private.' She stood up to leave as a hand gently touched her shoulder.

'Can I tempt you with a drink, darling?' Noël Coward was standing close behind her.

Spinning to greet him, she kissed both his cheeks and said, 'I'd be very tempted but we must leave.' She introduced Docker and watched as the men shook hands. 'John was worried you might be looking for work,' she said.

'Anything but,' said Coward, amused. 'Larry and I are off to Jamaica. I've bought a little spot on the north coast and Larry needs a holiday.' He looked Docker up and down, arched an eyebrow at Bridgette and left.

'What was that business with the eyebrow?' asked Docker, knowing the answer.

'He's just a naughty boy,' said Bridgette, steering Docker out of the restaurant and into a nearby cab.

The cab nosed its way through the wet traffic, bringing them to his apartment just after midnight. He pushed open the apartment door, his toe cap kicking a buff envelope that must have been slid under the door. Inside was a new passport in the name of John Davis, tickets for a flight the following morning and two unsigned notes, the first explaining that Kessler's mother was listed as a patient in a hospital in suburban Berlin, the second outlining his new background as Davis.

Bridgette stood behind him taking no interest in the note or the documents. 'Aren't you going to offer a girl a drink?'

'Sure.'

'I suggest you draw the curtains first,' she said.

NEUNZEHN

Are we alarmists? Beauchamp kept asking himself as he and White cruised Berlin, monitoring the mood on the streets. The Russians had been throwing tantrums from the day the war finished. What else was new? Would the locals be as concerned about the blockade as the Allied forces?

Three days later, on 27 June, he had his answer. While on patrol, Beauchamp noted subtle changes in the way the Berliners were going about their day-to-day life. People were carrying extra shopping: two or three loaves of bread instead of one, a few more potatoes, a stack of anonymous tins – whatever was available.

On the wireless at Royal Military Police headquarters, Beauchamp heard news that US General Lucius Clay had arranged for the airlift of coal, food and medicine to begin in earnest the following day.

Over the next week the airlift gained momentum. Berliners were craning their necks to watch US C-47s shuttling in and out of Tempelhof. Beauchamp could see the dread in their eyes. This was no adventure, this was the beginning of a new nightmare.

At headquarters, Major Cooper-Wright took pleasure in giving Beauchamp the news he'd dreaded – he had been assigned to the British Airforce base at Gatow about 10 miles to the west. Even worse, he'd been put in charge of guarding the goods being flown into the base. It was the sort of tactical role Beauchamp loathed. Support roles were designed for organised men who enjoyed drawing up guard rosters, something Cooper-Wright knew Beauchamp was execrable at. The most frustrating part about the new role was that it could only get busier.

And it did. His new life revolved around the unending landings and take-offs on the rebuilt Gatow runways. The Royal Engineers had slaved over the construction of steel-plate strips to replace the grass runways originally created for a Luftwaffe training field. The result was an airport that never slept.

Aside from a few hours' rest in a camp stretcher every day, Beauchamp's only break was to walk to the woods near the hangars and smoke. Each afternoon for half an hour, he'd watch a *Bachstelze* – a wagtail – tend its nest in a hole in a tree trunk. Standing in the shade, cigarette smoke drifting up into the leaves, Beauchamp would plan the next steps once this emergency was over. He'd have to take White into his confidence, otherwise he'd have no support and little chance of nailing Amistead and Popov. Beauchamp knew that it was one thing to go sniffing around the Russian sector alone at night for an hour or two, but it was quite another to carry out a serious, ongoing investigation without the reliable White at his side.

White he could trust, but Major Cooper-Wright was a liability. Beauchamp acknowledged to himself that although Cooper-Wright was a pompous pain in the arse, nevertheless he was also a first-rate political player. Years of bullying down and toadying up had positioned the major for great things in His Majesty's Army, therefore upsetting the Russians or the Americans was not an option the major would even consider. Boats remained unrocked if Cooper-Wright's career was at stake.

Beauchamp's only consolation was that his inside source – Speer – wasn't going anywhere. Whatever happened with the blockade, Spandau's gates were staying shut. Beauchamp suspected that Popov was the anonymous Russian who'd blackmailed Speer into revealing where the alleged Cross of Christ was hidden. The most logical motive was money, but was that all? The conversation between Amistead and Popov on the flattened Hotel Adlon site had been so cryptic that Beauchamp couldn't be sure there wasn't more to all this.

After watching the *Bachstelze* for a while, Beauchamp would find his conscience eventually pulled him back to work.

At night the Gatow airfield was lit by electricity furnished by the Russians. When Beauchamp asked a radar operator why the Soviets didn't flick the switch off, he was told the British, in turn, controlled the power running to a

Russian airforce base. Both sides had decided it was prudent to keep the current flowing.

Bright lights lit Gatow like a theatre. Around the perimeter, darkness hid the scurrying of men and machines, but nearer to the hangars, harsh lighting turned taxiing DC-3s into a chorus line.

Beauchamp studied the planes in their RAF Transport Command livery, knowing he was possibly the only person at Gatow who didn't want to climb aboard and be part of the airlift. Beauchamp didn't like to fly. He distrusted aeroplanes. To him they were no more than dangerous, uncomfortable airborne buses whose drivers appeared to take a perverse pleasure in seeking out pockets of turbulence.

Despite his attitude to flying, he was impressed with the airlift. Before being unceremoniously dispatched to work at Gatow, Beauchamp had heard the engine noise of American C-54s, spaced at 90-second intervals on their run into Tempelhof airbase. Loud and rhythmic, the Americans called it a 'jungle drum beat', but to Beauchamp it was more of a reassuring drone. Like the Berliners he'd spoken to, he found he slept better at night if there was a constant noise from *die Luftbrücke*, the air bridge. Gatow may have been busy, but Tempelhof was manic with 480 landings and corresponding take-offs a day, the incoming planes filthy with coal dust and crammed with canned food, dried fruit and building materials.

Air bridge or not, by the following Friday Beauchamp had had enough. Even the sight of uniformed girls in a German Red Cross Jeep handing out chocolate bars along the main Gatow runway didn't cheer him up. He asked for and got a meeting with Cooper-Wright.

The meeting was very tense. Beauchamp outlined a plan for the *Schutzpolizei* to take a more active role in guard duty at the base. The major was sceptical, saying the *Schutzpolizei* had been relegated to mundane duties in the city now the airlift had begun.

Beauchamp tried not to lose his temper and said through gritted teeth that mundane duties were precisely what was involved at Gatow. The major remained unconvinced.

Beauchamp tried a different tactic, saying that using Germans in such a high-profile policing role would be good public relations and Cooper-Wright would be seen as taking a visionary step forward.

The major immediately got the point and authorised Beauchamp to start researching the opportunities. 'Sort it out with the Germans. Tell the blighters you're doing it at my behest.'

Thank Christ, thought Beauchamp as he gently closed the major's door on his way out. He should have appealed to the bastard's ego long ago.

Over the following 48 hours, Beauchamp held five separate meetings with the *Schutzpolizei* and a British liaison team at York House. Details finalised and with all the credit going to Major Ashley Cooper-Wright, Beauchamp was shot of 'that sodding airfield' – as he thought of it – and back on the case. Almost. There was someone he wanted to see first.

As Beauchamp sped up to Elsa's hotel and screeched to a halt, she was leaving the front door of the building. She looked up briefly from pulling on a pair of light gloves. 'This is a surprise, *Kapitän*. I thought you were involved with the airlift. Why are you here?'

'Research,' he replied, stunned by her studied nonchalance. She was a puzzle.

The gloves in place, she continued down the front steps to the footpath, with Beauchamp at her side. 'I'd be delighted to help you with research.'

'Actually,' he admitted, 'I really came to see you. Research is an excuse.'

Stopping, she turned quickly to face him. 'To see me?'

Beauchamp watched her face to see if there was a hint of warmth in the question. Elsa's eyes remained wide, as if she was surprised by the attention. 'We can also discuss the case.'

'*Einverstanden*,' she agreed. 'Let's sit at a café.'

Side by side with a small table in front of them, they sat in the open air outside a café watching the passers-by. There was a sense of urgency in the Berliners' movements – even the waiter rushed their coffees to their table, spilling some into Beauchamp's saucer.

Dabbing his napkin into the dark liquid, Beauchamp tried to sound calm. 'Once this show is over we'll find your father's killers.'

'I do not think of it as a "show". The Russians are not the entertaining kind.'

'It's just an expression,' he said, trying to think of how

to change the subject. He opted for, 'Do you get out much in New York?'

'Are you asking if I have a boyfriend?'

'Was it that obvious?'

'I am afraid so, *Kapitän*.'

'James.'

'James. I like that.'

'I'm glad there's something about me you like.'

'James, there is a lot about you I like. You are very serious about your job, but not too serious about other things.'

Damn it, he thought, I'm going to say it. 'Ah, well, true in a way. But I am serious about you.'

Her hand rested in the crook of his arm as they walked back to the hotel. Beauchamp stood tall, the visor of his red cap shading his eyes – a man on a mission.

The clerk barely glanced up as Elsa retrieved her keys.

Beauchamp kicked the door shut with his heel. As Elsa backed across the room drawing him towards the bed by his tie, he began dropping a trail of hardware and scraps of uniform – holstered Browning HP-35, ammunition, handcuffs, baton, keys, notebook, belt, gaiters, tie, shirt, vest. God, why didn't I leave this crap at HQ? Beauchamp asked himself.

The sound of a rather low-flying aircraft reminded him that he was still on duty. He'd better get back to the matter at hand – fast. He moved in what he hoped was a manly fashion despite his underwear tugging at his ankles, and fell forward.

***

Elsa phoned for room service, leaving Beauchamp to stand at the window studying the underbellies of transport planes passing over the city. The sun was out and he could see US Airforce C-47 Skytrains bearing the fading black and white stripes of the original D-Day 1944 invasion force.

'They must be dragooning every rust bucket that can fly,' he said.

Elsa put her hand on his shoulder and Beauchamp turned and kissed her. 'I have to go,' he said. 'But I think some more research is required.'

'I look forward to it.'

The door closed softly behind him as he walked down the hotel hallway. Now I'm in a real pickle, Beauchamp thought to himself, I'm in love *and* under siege by the Russian army.

ZWANZIG

'Now this is what I call an airport,' Bridgette said to Docker when their cab pulled up outside the Pan American terminal at Idlewild. The airport had been opened two days and the starkness of the near-treeless landscape made the discus-topped terminal more dramatic. There was a hint of Buck Rogers in the design, forming a striking contrast with the cosy and elegant atmosphere of the Marine Air Terminal at LaGuardia Airport. LaGuardia had its James Brooks murals but Idlewild's architects had made the sky and the runways the main features.

Bridgette and Docker stood at the massive glass window, taking in the view. A triple-tailed Constellation, the sun glinting off its sensuous lines, stood on the tarmac near the terminal. Docker had read somewhere that the Constellation had a cruising altitude of 20,000 feet, which sure beat being bounced around the sky in a low-flying military transport plane.

On the terminal concourse, Docker looked away from Bridgette for a brief moment and saw a man in a badly cut woollen suit, his hat pushed down a little too hard on his head. A tug at Docker's sleeve made him glance down – Bridgette was pulling him towards an information counter. Docker looked back to where the man had been. He was gone. Damn.

Picking airline pamphlets out of a display rack, Bridgette was in a teasing mood. She began reading aloud. 'Did you know Pan Am has introduced tourist class on flights to Puerto Rico? Sounds exotic.'

Docker didn't reply. He felt uneasy. Standing next to her while she flicked through the pamphlets made it all seem too normal. This was business and he was flying to Berlin to probably get his ass shot off in a back street. At least Laurent had booked a return trip for him.

'Nervous?' she asked, putting the pamphlets back and leading the way to the bar.

Their attention was quickly diverted by the scene on the runway. Small trucks were flitting around the aircraft. In the Constellation's cabin, they could see the pilot and co-pilot running through their checklists.

Docker ordered drinks at the gleaming bar and carried them back to the only free table in a far corner. They clinked glasses.

'Got your passport?' she asked after one sip.

Docker tapped his coat and said 'yes'. Not only did he have a passport with his new identity – John Davis – he also had a wallet crammed with US dollars and crisp, freshly minted Deutsche Marks. He took out a Mark note to show her. The situation was becoming increasingly bizarre, he thought. Why had he suggested Bridgette come to the airport? He knew the answer. This might be the last time he'd see her. If he wasn't killed, she'd be long gone with the 250 grand by the time he returned. He didn't want to lose her. The thought was just gnawing at his stomach when she slipped her hand into his.

'I'm going to miss you, do you know that?' Her voice was almost shaking, for the first time since he met her, stripped of the over-confident tones of an actress.

Docker felt light-headed. They'd slept together for one night. Did that matter to her? Her genuineness was a surprise. He folded his hand over hers. Conscious of the crowd in the bar, he said, 'We look like two lovers saying goodbye.'

'After what happened last night, we *are* two lovers. But this isn't goodbye.'

'No, not goodbye.' Slipping his free hand under the table, he tapped softly on the underside of the tabletop. Knock on wood, he prayed. Where was that Cross when he needed it?

Five minutes later they left the bar and stood near the departure gate. They kissed and Docker handed his ticket over to the flight attendant.

Aboard the Constellation, Docker tried to relax. The aircraft smelt new. He tapped on his window, wondering if the material was perspex or glass. But his attempts to distract himself with small details rather than think about

Bridgette were useless. He kept seeing her upturned face after that final kiss.

The Constellation left the runway, climbing and banking towards the Manhattan skyline. He could see the gleam of the Chrysler building. A stewardess leant down to admire the view through his window. 'It's quite a sight,' she said.

As they watched the city glide by the wingtip, Docker caught the green of Central Park, the grey stripes of the avenues and the black of the East River. He said goodbye to New York as the plane banked again.

It was a perfect three-point landing. The plane from Paris slowed, picked up speed, then slowed again before taxiing in to Frankfurt's civilian terminal. Docker collected his bags and made straight for the office of American Overseas Airways, handing over his authorisation to join a Skymaster charter flight into Tempelhof.

According to Docker's papers he was a member of the Operation Vittles coordinating committee reporting directly to US Major General William H. Tunner. Laurent had been positive nobody would question the papers. Docker was more concerned that with such a grand job title he might get too much attention. He needn't have worried. Frankfurt airport was organised mayhem. He was shunted through the press of the crowds and within two hours he was back in the air.

Clouds partly smothered Berlin in a series of pancake

layers and the overall effect was quiet and claustrophobic. The Grunewald forest – flat, green and dotted with lakes – butted into the side of the city, which looked shattered. Docker had seen cities brutalised by war, but he was surprised again at the ferocity with which the conquerors had crushed Berlin.

His mind ticking over, he reviewed his plan – or what there was of one. His first stop was to follow up on Frau Kessler. The old dame may be a passive player, but she was the reason Kessler returned to the city. After that, if he was still alive, he'd visit the site where Kessler's body was found.

Docker asked himself again what the assignment was. If he took his instructions from Laurent and Morton at face value then he was being paid to search out and retrieve a piece of the Cross. Laurent hadn't suggested that Docker try to contact Popov. Nor was there any direction about Amistead. All Laurent had said was 'find the Berlin Cross'. Hell, what could be easier or simpler?

Turbulence suddenly made the aircraft bounce, forcing Docker to grip his whisky glass as the plane, like a boat on choppy water, thudded through the clouds. Crockery crashed in the kitchen galley. Docker forced himself to ignore the turbulence. In his mind he repeated Laurent's instruction to find the Cross. Emptying the remainder of the drink and steadying the glass on the shuddering armrest, he wondered why on earth Laurent was interested in the Cross. Sure, Docker could see why Laurent wanted to stabilise Berlin and block any plans Popov, Amistead, Rühmann and Morton might have. But the Cross? Docker thought back to the Algonquin bar and Laurent's pride in being an agent in the National Defense Research Committee. The committee's role, as Docker recalled it, was special weapons development. Was that why Laurent was so determined to find that piece of wood? Perhaps the wood could be used as a weapon, as part of either an offensive or defensive strategy.

It was too late now to turn back – the plane was breaking through the clouds and the air was calmer, even if Docker wasn't.

Looking out the aircraft window, he glanced back along the fuselage and saw a long queue of aircraft strung out behind his plane. Pressing his face against the window, he strained to see what was ahead. He let out a low whistle of appreciation at the sight – there was a queue of transport planes stretching ahead towards the Tempelhof runways.

The last time he'd arrived in Berlin he was greeted at the airport with a salute and a waiting car. This time there was nobody, just the tense and drawn faces of aircrew and cargo handlers. There was no glamour in this siege busting, only coal dust, sweat and stress. Someone was playing Stan Kenton over the public address system.

Docker sighed and carried his bags to the main doors, tipping an elderly organ grinder at the terminal's main door for good luck before trying to find a cab. The area directly in front of the terminal was as chaotic as the tarmac. Civilian and military trucks edged their way past Docker, while arm-waving US Army personnel with clipboards gestured at the drivers. Hemmed in near the main door were two dilapidated taxis. Docker commandeered one and sat in the rear seat for 10 minutes while the driver attempted to get around the trucks. When they eventually reached a clear road, the driver put his foot down and they sped towards the hospital in Steglitz where Laurent had advised him Frau Kessler was listed as a patient.

Outside the hospital Docker asked the driver to wait and keep an eye on the luggage, then rushed inside and went straight to the reception desk. When the matron appeared he could tell by her expression that he was too late. She led him to a small room where she immediately told him about Frau Kessler's death.

If the matron hadn't been standing directly in front of him he would have spat out an obscenity, instead he could only sigh. The matron reached across and touched his arm. 'Death is always *eine traurige Angelegenheit,*' she said.

A sad business, thought Docker. You bet it is. He breathed in while he fought to control himself. Had that asshole Laurent screwed him around again? Could it be possible that the man who appeared to know everything had missed the fact Frau Kessler was dead? Perhaps it was another set-up.

A few seconds later he politely farewelled the matron before taking his frustration out on the cab door. The driver said nothing as Docker banged the door hard enough to rattle the windows.

Docker looked down at a note the matron had handed him as he left. Frau Kessler's grand-daughter, Elsa, had visited recently and she'd given the matron the name of the hotel where she was staying. At last, a lead. Docker was disappointed the bum steer about Frau Kessler had cost him time, but he consoled himself with the thought that at least he'd be able to question Elsa Kessler. But how would he explain to her that, after first refusing to help her, he was now on a case in Berlin? He realised it was going to be a very embarrassing encounter. If he let her know he was coming, she might refuse to see him. He'd have to surprise her – and was she going to be surprised.

Head tilted sideways like a bird of prey, the hotel desk clerk took in Docker's five o'clock shadow, travel-crumpled clothes and two scuffed bags. 'Do you have an appointment with Fräulein Kessler, *mein* Herr?' he asked with a sniff.

'I'm an old friend.'

The clerk turned to the rows of wooden cubby holes behind him and, out of habit, reached over and tapped the empty one where Elsa's room key would have rested. Room 306. 'She is in,' the clerk said, his voice still laced with doubt about Docker, 'but *erstens*, I must phone her room to announce you.'

'Thanks, but I need to freshen up first.' Dropping his bags at the side of the desk, Docker made for the men's room. As he reached the door, he glanced back and saw the desk clerk had begun serving a customer. Docker moved quickly to the elevator. It clanked loud enough to alert anyone within a 20-mile radius that he was on his way. He knocked on her door, mentally preparing his greeting.

A rangy man wearing a towelling robe partly opened the door. Music played in the background.

Jamming his foot in the door before the man closed it, Docker said, 'I'd like to see Fräulein Kessler. My name's Docker.'

The man calmly ran his fingers through his wet hair as he looked Docker up and down. 'Stay there, please,' he said in an English accent.

Moments later a young woman appeared in a summer skirt and blouse, swinging the door wide open and staring wide-eyed at Docker. The Englishman hovered protectively in the background, his right hand now jammed in the pocket of his robe.

Shit, he's armed, thought Docker, before turning his attention to the woman in front of him.

'Lieutenant Docker? The one who never called?' she said, with a cool edge to her accented voice.

Docker narrowed his eyes. 'Call? Call who? Where's Elsa Kessler?'

'*I* am Elsa Kessler.'

Like hell, thought Docker. Equally well-groomed maybe, about the same age and with a similar accent, but not Elsa.

'I've made a mistake,' he said backing away, trying to give himself time to think. 'I don't want to disturb you folks.'

The Englishman stepped forward. 'Let's not discuss this in the hall. Come in.'

'No, I have to go,' said Docker taking another step backwards.

'I said "come in",' demanded the Englishman, emphasising his words by pointing a Browning directly at Docker.

As Elsa closed the door, the man stepped quickly behind Docker, spun him to face the wall, and began patting him down. Within a second, Docker's .38 was gone from his coat pocket.

'You can turn around,' said the Englishman, satisfied Docker was unarmed.

Docker turned in time to see the Englishman handing the .38 to the woman.

'If he moves aim for his heart,' the man said. 'It'll be somewhere near his wallet.'

The woman kept the revolver trained on Docker while the man stepped into another room, leaving the door open. Docker heard the shuffle of clothes being pulled on before the Englishman, his laces still untied, emerged in Royal Military Police uniform and took the .38 off the woman. He kept it aimed at Docker.

'I'm Captain Beauchamp,' he said. 'Please sit down.'

EINUNDZWANZIG

Beauchamp was to the point. 'What brings you to Berlin, Mr Docker?'

Docker said nothing. Dropping into the nearest chair with an audible thump, he could only stare at the woman.

'I didn't realise Americans were so reticent,' said Beauchamp. 'But if you won't speak to me, then please talk to Fräulein Kessler. She asked if you were the lieutenant involved in the investigation of her father's first disappearance.'

His mind racing, Docker still said nothing.

Beauchamp maintained his patient tone. 'Why did you ask for Elsa Kessler at the door and then try to leave?'

'She's not Elsa Kessler,' said Docker, nodding towards the woman.

Beauchamp swung around and looked at her. She, in turn, stared at Docker, appearing to be genuinely angry. 'What are you talking about?' she asked him.

Docker weighed up whether it was easier to tell the truth or lie. He decided on a limited version of the truth. 'I met the real Elsa Kessler in New York. She tracked me down because I'd been with the military police here. Now I'm a private investigator. She wanted me to trace her missing father.'

'My father is dead. So why are you here?'

'I'm here on another case.'

'Which is?' asked Beauchamp.

'None of your business, captain,' said Docker.

'Only in New York. Here it definitely *is* my business,' said Beauchamp, putting the .38 on a side table as he laced up his boots. He pulled the knots tight with quick jerks then looked across at Elsa. She was sitting upright, tense. Docker looked exhausted. Everything about Docker's behaviour signalled that he wasn't lying. He seemed genuinely confused. Was the woman in this hotel room lying? When he'd first seen her at the US Military Police headquarters he had automatically assumed that she was Elsa Kessler. He'd never seen any identification. But he had seen Oswald's interaction with her. Oswald may have had some strengths, but acting wasn't one of them. The American major would have had access to personal files on Elsa Kessler, and he obviously believed she was the real thing. That's the rational conclusion, Beauchamp decided. But more importantly, if less rationally, he knew he trusted Elsa. Even coppers were allowed to fall in love. Perhaps neither Docker nor Elsa was lying and there had been a counterfeit Elsa in New York. The question was – why?

Beauchamp turned his attention to Docker. 'Let's get back to Fräulein Kessler. I can assure you she is, as you Americans say, the real McCoy.'

Docker ran the fingertips of his left hand over his right knuckle, unsure of who'd conned him but beginning to guess. If Laurent had been standing in that Berlin hotel room Docker would've decked him . . . or at least got in the first punch.

Docker stood up and walked to the far end of the room. Trying to think the puzzle through, he jammed his hands into his pockets to stop himself taking a swing at something – the curtains, a vase of flowers, a framed print.

Let's see, he fumed to himself, in Plan A Laurent plays on my emotional ties to Kessler and sends a woman calling herself Elsa Kessler to hire me to go to Berlin to track down her father. I decline this opportunity to get shot. Laurent then turns to Plan B, a lucrative offer to track down an expensive relic that, not so coincidentally, also forms a strand of the Berlin web. The end result is the same. I wind up in Berlin chasing my tail. Surely Laurent must have realised I would eventually run into the real Elsa. But so what? By then I would be firmly stuck in the web.

Docker stopped pacing and sat down. They must want me because of my track record. I found Dr Kessler the first time, and the US government wanted me to track him down again. Then Kessler is killed but I'm *still* the government's choice to get the relic. Why? Because I specialised in cross-sector crime in Berlin. In 18 months it's unlikely the players will have changed. The same hoods and hatchetmen will be in place, and I've dealt with – and done deals with – most of them.

Elsa interrupted his train of thought.

'Mr Docker, are you willing to help me find my father's killers?'

'That's the second time someone calling herself Elsa Kessler has asked for help. The answer's the same. I'm sorry about your father but there's nothing I can do. Ask the cops. This city is lousy with them.' Then, nodding towards Beauchamp, he said, 'You've even got one stashed in your hotel room.'

Elsa ignored the frustration in Docker's voice. 'Relax, Mr Docker. I will make you a drink.'

With a glass in his hand, Docker was certainly more relaxed.

Beauchamp, in turn, was looking Docker up and down, trying to judge if he could trust this man. Perhaps he could use him. He looked across at Elsa. She was standing in the centre of the room, signalling for Beauchamp's attention.

'As Mr Docker says, he worked here in the American police,' she said. 'He could help you.'

Beauchamp nodded. 'Possibly.'

'Thanks for the vote of confidence,' said Docker. 'But I'm not interested.'

'Because there is nothing in it for you?' asked Elsa. 'Are you the type of man who only does things for money? What about justice?'

'Justice?' Docker repeated, hoping he didn't sound as if he'd just heard the word.

Beauchamp interrupted. 'There have been two killings we believe are linked. First Dr Kessler and now a prostitute.'

'You've got an entire police force behind you, captain. You find the killer.'

'The killer might be someone you met when you worked here – Alaine Amistead.'

Here we go again, thought Docker. Everything in Berlin is intertwined, but here was a chance to get a little help from the RMP to find the Cross. He put his glass down. 'I knew Amistead. When I was stationed here, Amistead was top of the black-market dung heap. I guess nothing's changed.'

'Except you.' Beauchamp smiled, leaning across to where he'd placed Docker's .38. He handed the gun to the American and said, 'Strictly speaking, you shouldn't be carrying that weapon, but you might need it.'

'And you might need me.'

'Correct. I just haven't decided how you can help.' Beauchamp walked to the hotel door and swung it open. 'I'll be in touch. Where are you staying?'

Docker hesitated, then decided the cops could find out easily enough. He wanted to at least appear to be cooperating. 'A hostel called the Friedenstaube near the Rathaus Schöneberg.'

Docker avoided a departing handshake. It was a gesture of trust, and today he didn't trust anybody.

ZWEIUNDZWANZIG

White scooped phials of liquid and metal pill boxes from a grubby cardboard box and placed them directly in the pool of light under Beauchamp's desk lamp. The medicine was part of the collection that Kessler had left at the hospital for his mother.

Beauchamp picked up a phial. 'What's the story?'

'We've traced them, sir. A truck carrying pharmaceuticals with the same batch numbers was hijacked near Reinickendorf in the French sector earlier this year. The driver was dumped and the load disappeared.'

'Any tie-in to Amistead?'

'Nothing direct. In the past he's avoided operating in French-controlled areas. But that doesn't mean he wasn't involved.'

'Agreed. He's a trifle wary of his fellow countrymen. Word is French Military Intelligence have placed a bounty on the bastard's head.'

'Perhaps we could collect it,' suggested White.

'Not a bad thought but the major might kick up a stink,' said Beauchamp. 'However you've given me an idea.'

Beauchamp made a phone call, his French relaxed and colloquial yet too precisely enunciated to be anything but an Englishman's.

Putting down the phone, he said to White, 'According to my contact, Amistead is seen as a poor influence in Berlin and a lousy ambassador for France.'

'Perhaps he should review his bribing priorities,' offered White.

'You've been here too long, corporal,' said Beauchamp, straightening up in his chair and scratching his chin. 'I'm told that the *Deuxième Bureau* has taken our friend aside and advised him that if he doesn't leave Germany by August they'll cook his fat little goose.'

'That's if we don't feel his collar for the Kessler killing,' said White.

'Either way he must be a man who wants to get out of town, fast.'

'What about the other cove you mentioned – Docker?'

'Earlier today I made another call.'

'To the Frogs?'

'To London. MI6.'

'Oh,' said White.

'It's not a place I enjoy calling.'

'I can imagine why. There's a Polish saying: "Touch shit and it sticks to your fingers".'

Beauchamp laughed. 'Nevertheless, I asked the boys at

54 Broadway what they know about Lieutenant John Docker, now of this parish.'

'And, sir?'

'I still haven't heard back.' Beauchamp looked down at his watch. 'And that was eight hours ago. Perhaps they're stalling.'

Suddenly the office door exploded open, revealing Major Ashley Cooper-Wright two beats short of a coronary.

Beauchamp closed his eyes, thinking the jig was finally up. Fraternising with Berliners wasn't an offence but dereliction of duty was.

White attempted to sidle out, but the major's bulk blocked the doorway.

'This is a crisis,' said Cooper-Wright.

All I did was spend some time with a German woman, thought Beauchamp, by now used to his superior's histrionics.

'It'll be a diplomatic incident that will create headlines,' the major continued. 'I could imagine this taking place in a country with entrenched corruption, but for God's sake, the new Germany has only been operating for three years.'

Beauchamp was totally confused. It's not as if he'd slept with the enemy. Well, not a *current* enemy.

'Close that door, corporal,' Cooper-Wright ordered and waited until White and Beauchamp were both in his line of sight. 'There's been an irregularity with the distribution of the Deutsche Marks.'

'An irregularity, sir?' asked a relieved Beauchamp. 'Have some been pinched?'

'No, in fact an audit shows that every incoming Reichsmark and every outgoing Deutsche Mark has been accounted for. The figures match. But there are millions more Reichsmarks than were anticipated and, obviously, millions more of the new Marks have gone into circulation.'

'Sounds like money from the black market is being washed through the system,' said White.

Cooper-Wright looked surprised, as if he'd never heard a corporal speak before. 'Exactly. And as we were assigned to oversee the distribution we've got to find out what went wrong.'

'It could have been bank staff,' suggested Beauchamp.

'I doubt anyone at the German banks was responsible. The auditors can only identify one source for the money flow – the US sector.'

'That sounds like a job for the US MPs,' said Beauchamp quickly, seeing precisely where Cooper-Wright was leading the conversation.

'Don't try to fob off this problem on to the US military police. If those millions of Reichsmarks have been exchanged in the US zone then it's highly likely a rogue element of the MP is involved. The operation to guard the currency in the American sector was overseen by an MP major named Oswald. Know him?'

Beauchamp nodded. 'Nasty bit of work. Very defensive. Very wary.'

Cooper-Wright appeared to take in the information before demanding, 'So, captain, can you imagine why I'm here talking to you and the corporal?'

'Presumably because White and I had a bit of a run-in with the American MPs.'

'Absolutely. You two are my resident experts on their military police so I thought you could sniff around.'

'When you say "sniff", do you mean you want us to go back into the US sector?'

'That's a detail, captain, which I'll leave up to you. Your orders are to find out who did the currency swap. Any ideas on how you'll start?'

Beauchamp lit a Chesterfield. 'What we need is a tame American.'

DREIUNDZWANZIG

Docker drove his fist in hard. No reaction. These German pillows were as solid as planks. He jabbed again. A little better. He propped the pillow under his head and stretched on the bed. Wiggling his feet, he realised he'd either have to take up sock darning or buy a new pair. He opened the window to let in the afternoon breeze and was delighted that the traffic noise was like a whisper compared to New York.

He stared at the light fitting, which began to go in and out of focus. He tried to fight off the fatigue. How long had he been awake? He added up the hours as he felt himself drifting off. He shook his head to try and clear it, then swung his feet onto the floor. The room rocked as if he were on a boat.

He washed his face, got dressed quickly and left to find a cab. An ambulance and two fire trucks went past at high speed, but there were no taxis. Frustrated and tired, he walked to a major crossroads and waited. Whether it was the blockade or just a bad day, he didn't know or care. After 15 minutes he gave up and hailed a double-decker bus. After changing buses to reach Potsdamer Strasse, he walked the quarter mile to the Platz. When he'd left Berlin, the Russian, US and British sectors had come together in this flattened city centre under the jaded eyes of local police who were assigned the thankless task of manning Potsdamer Platz's central clock tower. Now the area was an armed encampment, with the British and Americans facing off their one-time allies, who were bottling up surrounding avenues with troops and armoured vehicles.

Docker had hoped to wander the market stalls and get a sense of what was happening on the black market. But all he encountered was a shabby collection of collapsible card tables displaying chipped crockery and, from the looks of them, third- or fourth-hand shoes. There was more barbed wire in the area than contraband.

Deciding there was nothing to be learnt here, Docker hiked to a bus stop and headed to the Kurfürstendamm and Poppa 8's.

For Docker, it'd been a long 18 months between drinks at Poppa's. He wondered if the joint still had the pulling power it had when it opened, seemingly overnight, just after the war. Then it had been the hot spot for off-duty American and British officers.

Poppa's 8 hadn't changed. Back-slapping officers were still buying each other drinks, eating passable meals and trying not to be tempted by the hookers at the bar.

Docker's first drink tasted so good that he had a second. He noted that the kitchen's batwing doors were still in place, if slightly rickety. They swung open saloon style whenever a waiter pushed through.

Sitting on a stool, elbows on the bar, Docker gazed idly through the swinging doors. Behind a long steel-topped table in the centre of the kitchen were two men in deep conversation. It took Docker a moment to register who the younger of the men was. Swearing under his breath, he slipped off the bar stool and moved out of the line of sight of the men in the kitchen. He'd crossed the Atlantic, schlepped a grudge and a gun all over Berlin, only to realise he should have come straight to Poppa's to find the man he was looking for – Willi Rühmann. The German was with an elderly man who Docker couldn't quite place.

Docker pondered his next move as he watched Rühmann talking to the frog-mouthed man. Rühmann was dressed with the élan of a store dummy, with a neat tie against a white shirt and a dark, anonymous suit. The elderly man shook his head and turned away. Where had Docker seen that face?

Both men disappeared from Docker's view. Tossing what he hoped were enough Deutsche Marks on the bar, he rushed out of the building in time to see the two men heading down an alley beside Poppa 8's. They walked directly to a tram stop where they waited in line. Docker followed them and stood back on the sidewalk until he saw the two men board a tram. Sprinting for it, Docker cursed as the tram took off without him. Another one arrived in seconds and he leapt aboard and pushed towards a seat at the front.

He tried to appreciate the absurdity of being in hot pursuit of his quarry in a tram with a top speed of 10 miles an hour. Sliding his hand into his coat pocket he felt the comforting steel of his revolver and the less reassuring cardboard of his business cards bearing the name 'John Davis'. What a waste of time that ploy had been.

The tram in front slowed and stopped. Docker's tram nudged in behind it. He saw the two men step down and walk quickly up the avenue. By treading on the insteps of two women passengers as well as the toe caps of an off-duty British officer, he managed to jump from the tram before it pulled away. The pair he was following had stopped and were doubling back towards him, the elderly man studying every passer-by. They went into a corner store.

Docker waited, unsure what to do. A few minutes later they reappeared on the street from a side entrance and once again set off. Docker liked to watch a professional attempt to throw a tail. Sudden stops in the street, backtracking, detours, the works. The elderly man and Rühmann would have caught Docker out twice in the last five minutes if the crowded tram hadn't slowed him and if he hadn't been so indecisive outside the store. He congratulated himself for prevaricating as the two men walked down a side street and stopped in front of a plain door. Docker followed 30 feet behind.

Before they could even knock, the door was opened by a man dressed in a black shirt and trousers. A passing truck muffled their greeting and the trio went inside. Docker crossed to the other side of the road and tried to stay as far back as possible from the building. Walking casually down the street, he crossed the road again. The windows of the neighbouring house on the left were boarded over. He went up to the front door and pushed. It was nailed shut. He walked past the target house and tried the door of the house to its right. It opened. Aromas of kerosene, rising damp and cabbage mingled in the hallway. In a side room, a copy of the newspaper *Neue Zeitung* was opened on a rickety table and Docker could see steam rising from a nearby coffee cup. He heard a radio playing somewhere on an upper floor. Taking a deep breath, he tiptoed towards the rear of the house.

He went through a back door into a small yard with a pile of wood in one corner. Clambering onto the pile, he heaved himself over a crumbling brick wall. He brushed himself down as he crept over to the rear door of the target house. It was locked. The neighbour leaves the front door open, thought Docker, while this guy locks his window. What was there to protect? As he tried to push up the sash window with his palms it creaked against a latch. Running his penknife blade between the gap in the two halves of the window, he hooked the latch but snapped his blade. He tried the window again. It creaked open.

Rolling headfirst into the room, he struggled to his feet, left the window open and made his way up a hallway, gun in hand. He could hear loud voices coming from the left and so headed right, taking the first door he found.

Docker felt as if he'd been winded when he saw the photographs. He loosed off the 'Sh' of 'Shit' before pressing his lips shut. He was looking at a photograph of himself and, what was worse, he remembered walking down that cold Berlin street all those months ago. There were also photographs of Kessler, Elsa, Beauchamp and Amistead. A rogues' gallery. Docker felt a tremble go through his body as he tried to guess why the photographs were tacked across the wall. Then he heard a sound and turned to the doorway. The black-shirted man was aiming a Makarov pistol at Docker's stomach while Docker's revolver dangled from his hand, pointing uselessly at the floor.

The elderly man Docker had seen with Willi Rühmann appeared from the hallway, moved quickly to Docker's side and took the .38 from him. Rühmann stood waiting in the hallway looking tense.

The black-shirted man put his own weapon away and came forward, hand outstretched. 'Welcome back to Berlin, Lieutenant Docker. My name is Popov. I have been expecting you.'

In the street outside, White, who had been shadowing Docker throughout the day, checked his watch, picked up a walkie-talkie and contacted Beauchamp. 'That Docker cove gets around,' he told him. 'One minute he's drinking in a bar, the next he's on a damn tram tagging behind two men, then he's sneaking in the front door of someone's house. It's been an hour and he hasn't come out.'

Beauchamp's voice crackled in the earpiece. 'Good work keeping on his tail. Give me your location. I'll get support and be there soon.'

Beauchamp and two lance corporals found White sitting in an unmarked delivery van in light-blue overalls and a black civilian beret.

'What the hell is that?' asked Beauchamp, reaching over and tugging at the beret.

'A disguise, sir.'

'For God's sake, corporal, this isn't Montmartre. How many Berlin men have you seen in a beret?'

'Not as many as I'd hoped.'

White got out of the van and the four men walked in a tight group up the street, discussing tactics.

'We should rush the front door,' said White.

'We don't know who's in there aside from Docker. I wouldn't risk it,' replied Beauchamp.

When they reached the front door Docker had entered, White hesitated. 'Do you think he's okay?' he whispered.

As if in reply, there was a crack of a single gunshot from the house next door. 'Come on,' ordered Beauchamp as he sprinted to the neighbouring building.

Splintering through the front door, the four RMP men spilled into the vestibule like a music hall act. A lance corporal ran into the closest room. There was the sound of gunfire and he came spinning out, his shoulder spraying blood. Beauchamp and White fired blindly into the room. There was a thump but no answering fire and the two men rushed in.

Rühmann was tied to a wooden chair, dead. An elderly man lay sideways against a wall, bullet holes across his chest.

In the far corner, Docker was standing, holding a glass. His eyes were wide. 'What a town. First these bums take my gun, then they serve warm vodka.'

Docker's sardonic tone didn't fool Beauchamp. He noted the clear liquid slopping in the glass as the American's hand shook. Beauchamp smiled. 'Aren't you going to thank us for saving you?'

'Why? As you could see, I had everything under control,' said Docker. In a bitter toast to the dead organ grinder on the floor, he downed the drink and spat 'Na zdorovia,' then flung the and empty glass into a fireplace.

A few shards of glass ricocheted onto the floor. Beauchamp stepped back from the flying glass and pointed at the two dead men. 'Is this all of them?'

'No. A Russian agent named Popov split when you came crashing in.'

'Stay here,' ordered Beauchamp.

With the second lance corporal on guard by the front door and White bandaging up their wounded colleague, Beauchamp began systematically searching the remainder of the house.

Beauchamp noted the homely touches in the other rooms – cotton bedspreads neatly folded, pans and glasses washed and stacked in the kitchen. The shabby furniture must have been scavenged from other houses. The photographic darkroom, however, was modern and professional. All the chemicals appeared to be German. He tried an adjoining room. Photographs covered a wall. He saw Elsa's photo first, then his own. God Almighty, what were they doing there? He left the photos in place and kept searching. Gun cocked, Beauchamp opened the door to a large hall cupboard.

Pressed against the rear wall was an organ on a wooden carriage, reminding him of the music he and White had endured along with the grilling at the US MPs' building. Closing the cupboard door quietly, he continued the search. Room after room was empty. Holstering his gun, he returned to the cupboard, pulled the organ into the hallway and popped the clips on one side of the carriage. A lid flopped down to reveal a large, hidden camera.

Back in the blood-stained room, Docker and White were waiting and the wounded lance corporal was lying on the carpet with folded jackets propped under his head. Beauchamp bent down to the body resting against the wall and began searching it, eventually feeling a small rectangle of cardboard sewn inside the lining of the dead man's coat. He used a penknife to unpick the coat seam. On one side of the card was a brightly lit head-and-shoulders photograph of the elderly man.

'What is it?' asked Docker, trying to see over Beauchamp's shoulder.

Slipping the card into his jacket pocket, Beauchamp said, 'A *postoyaniye propusk* – a "permanent pass". He was an MGB operative.' Turning, Beauchamp pointed at the dead man tied upright in the chair and asked Docker, 'What about him?'

'Willi Rühmann, another person with his own agenda. I met him in the States. The two Russians were giving him a hell of a working over before the old guy got fed up and finally shot him.'

'And you just happened to be standing there, drinking vodka?'

'It wasn't my idea. Popov caught me coming into the house. He seemed pretty damn pleased with himself after he decided I'd make the perfect bargaining chip if he was ever trapped. For a hood, he's hospitable – right down to offering me booze. He told me to stay in the room while they talked to Rühmann.' He nodded at the body in the chair.

'It must have been a tough talk if they ended up shooting him,' said Beauchamp.

'You wouldn't want to jerk around with Popov and the old guy. The Russians were arguing with Rühmann about money. Rühmann said he'd hidden something Popov wanted and wouldn't say where it was until he got some dough. What he got was a bullet.'

'More money for what?' said Beauchamp, sounding puzzled.

'Rühmann was tangled up in that private matter I mentioned earlier. He was the guy who stole what could be part of the Cross of Christ.'

'Around and around we go,' said Beauchamp. His thoughts flashed back to Spandau Prison. He was positive now that Popov was the Russian who visited Speer.

'You don't believe me.'

'Oh, I believe you, Mr Docker. But you're not the only one looking for the Cross of Christ.'

'Who else is on the case?'

'There's me, for example.' It was Beauchamp's turn to study Docker.

'You?' asked Docker.

Beauchamp hesitated, hoping he was making the right decision to trust the American. 'Albert Speer – you know of Speer, of course? – asked me to visit him in Spandau. Speer claims a Russian blackmailed him into revealing the location of what Speer called *das Kreuz von Berlin* – the Berlin Cross.'

'I know all about it. The Russian sold the relic to an American buyer and Rühmann then stole the Cross back. You could say it was double dipping.'

'But Rühmann didn't reveal where the Cross is now?' Beauchamp sounded frustrated.

'Nope. He just sneered and told Popov he would have to guess the next steps. He said, for a Russian, that would be easy. That's when the old guy pulled the trigger.'

'Guess the next steps? Easy for a Russian? Some sort of riddle?'

'How many steps are there in Berlin? Ones big enough to make a final joke about.'

'Possibly St Hedwig's Cathedral or the Altes Museum or even around Gendarmenmarkt. I don't know. Big steps and Russians. The Reichstag has massive steps. When the Russians arrived in Berlin in '45, they hoisted a red flag over the Reichstag building.'

'If we've worked it out, so has Popov,' said Docker.

Turning to White, who was still tending the wounded lance corporal, Beauchamp asked, 'Ambulance?'

'On its way, sir.'

'Then let's go,' ordered Beauchamp.

Docker stepped forward. 'I'm coming too.'

'We don't need your help,' said Beauchamp.

'I can identify the Russian.'

'True,' said Beauchamp, having second thoughts. 'Are you armed?'

'No. Popov took my gun.'

'Very wise of him. Okay, come with us.'

'Hey, I'm not going into another fire fight without a weapon,' said Docker.

'In that case, you can stay here.'

'Forget I mentioned it.' Fed up, Docker led the way out of the building.

As the Jeep wheeled into the traffic, Beauchamp asked Docker, 'Do you think the Cross is genuine?'

Docker shrugged. 'The only person who'd know for sure was crucified.'

VIERUNDZWANZIG

White squinted into the twilight as the Jeep screeched up to the Reichstag. The three men clambered out and made their way towards the entrance of the once grand building. It was a shambles. The Soviets may have planted their flag on the Reichstag to symbolise the fall of Berlin, but nobody had bothered to begin rebuilding the old parliament. It hadn't been a priority for Hitler in 1933 when the main hall was gutted by fire and it wasn't important for the conquering armies in 1945 either.

At the front of the ornate building, a wide flight of stairs led up to six Doric columns and a massive portico. Chiselled above the entrance was the inscription *Dem Deutschen Volke* – To the German People.

When the three men were 30 yards from the building, Docker pointed at large pieces of the shell-peppered façade that had broken away and were jumbled across the top step. 'What about up there? It's a good, memorable place to hide something.'

'Could be – let's see.' Beauchamp drew his weapon and strode forward while Docker kept three paces back. White, lugging a light machine gun, moved cautiously on the left-hand flank.

They had only gone a few yards when Docker hit Beauchamp hard between the shoulder blades, flattening the Englishman. A bullet had taken a bite-sized piece out of the ground behind the sprawled pair. 'You okay?' Docker whispered.

'Thanks. I think,' groaned Beauchamp.

'I owed you one,' said Docker keeping his head down.

Another bullet sent up a small spray of dirt nearby, forcing both men to press their faces into the stones and grit. Off to the side they heard White open fire. In the half-light it was impossible to see who he was shooting at.

Beauchamp and Docker heard the scatter of falling stones and then the sound of running footsteps, growing fainter as the gunman headed along Ebertstrasse.

'He's headed for the Brandenburg Gate,' shouted Beauchamp.

'Are we going to follow?' asked Docker.

'And get shot by the Russian army?' Beauchamp shook his head. Thinking back to the night he crossed over into the eastern sector in civilian kit, he realised how lucky and how foolish he'd been.

The three men climbed the long flight of steps towards the entrance of the Reichstag. 'The Cross could be anywhere,' said Beauchamp, flashing his torch over shattered bricks.

'Rühmann wouldn't have stashed it any old place,' said Docker. 'It'd be too hard to find again.'

White, who'd reached the fallen pieces of façade Docker had pointed to earlier, called out, 'This could be it.' Beauchamp and Docker ran towards him.

White's torch beam picked up several new shell casings. 'The gunman was firing from here,' he said to Beauchamp.

A flick of Beauchamp's torch showed where the gunman had dragged away a slab of masonry, exposing stacked bricks formed into a makeshift cubby hole. The hiding place was empty. The Berlin Cross was gone.

'Ah, shit,' said Docker. He sat down on the Reichstag's top step, pushed his hat back on his head and lit a cigarette. Off to the left he could see the broad slash of the Strasse des 17 Juni and the thick growth of the Tiergarten. He smoked in silence as the two Englishmen prodded and poked around the entrance way. Eventually Beauchamp sat down beside him and together they watched pairs of head-lights moving through the Tiergarten.

'The bugger escaped with the Cross,' said Beauchamp, stating the obvious in order to break the silence.

'Shit,' Docker repeated.

There was further silence until Beauchamp, dusting down the front of his uniform and trying to look official, asked, 'If I help you find the Cross, can you assist me on another case?'

'Unrelated to the Cross?'

'Possibly. However, Berlin is a place where everything is linked – either by design or coincidence.'

'Which was it – design or coincidence – that had you guys tailing me today?' asked Docker.

'Ah, well,' began Beauchamp, scratching his chin, 'that was definitely by design. Now, if you can spare me a moment, let's discuss this other matter.'

'Shoot,' said Docker.

'We've discovered that millions of old Reichsmarks have been illegally exchanged for new Deutsche Marks in the US zone and, according to my superiors, it's highly likely that someone in the US military police was involved.'

'But you're not sure?'

'Corporal White and I had a run-in with a few MPs and their reaction was totally out of proportion to what we did.'

'Which was?'

'A little investigating in their sector. Normally it'd be seen as run-of-the-mill, but this time a certain Major Oswald blew his stack.'

'Where would this Oswald guy have got millions of the old currency from?'

'Who else but Amistead? I hear he has until August to get out of Berlin.'

'And what's my role?'

'Bait. I want you to tempt Oswald.'

'Bait? More like a sitting duck. What if Oswald isn't guilty?'

'Look at the facts – Oswald's job was to guard the currency and now the auditors have discovered irregularities.' Beauchamp, seeing Docker was wavering, continued quickly. 'However, in the unlikely case that Oswald is actually kosher, then we'll step in and explain the real situation.'

'Can I have a gun?'

'The Russian souvenired yours and that, I'm afraid, is that. Besides, you don't need a weapon. As I said, we'll look after you.'

Docker snorted. 'I'll be like a goat tied beneath a tree while you guys sit safely in the branches waiting for the tiger.'

'First you're a sitting duck, now you're a goat. Under Allied regulations, Mr Docker, investigators are only allowed one hunting metaphor per case.'

FÜNFUNDZWANZIG

Docker stood in the hallway of the boarding house holding the phone's mouthpiece a half-inch from his lips. The line made Bridgette sound as if she were speaking inside a large tin drum. Occasionally he heard the echo of his own voice, edgy, defensive and lacking the energy he'd hoped for. Had he made a mistake calling her? He didn't even know what the time was in New York. At least she was in her apartment. He couldn't ask what she was doing – instead he tried one word: 'Busy?'

'I'm understudying for a role in *Mr Roberts* at The Alvin. There's only one woman in the cast.'

'Anybody in it I'd know?'

'Henry Fonda.'

'Oh,' said Docker, a short, sharp stab of jealousy making him catch his breath. He'd been hoping for a less glamorous actor. He decided to come to the point. 'There's been a new development here and I might be delayed. The

Brits want some help on a case involving currency fraud. They want a patsy to take all the risks and receive none of the credit.'

'Sounds like an irresistible offer,' said Bridgette.

There was a pause and Docker asked the question he couldn't put to her face-to-face. 'Just how did you manage to get the Berlin Cross away from Popov?'

'Do you really want to know?' she asked.

'I don't *want* to know but I *need* to know.'

'Let's just say that you can take anything off a man when his pants are down.'

'Couldn't you have said he accidentally left it at a bus stop?' said Docker, trying to lighten his pain.

'You wanted the truth.' She softened her tone. 'When are you coming home?'

'What have I got to come home to?'

There was the faint hissing of static on the line as Bridgette took her turn to stay silent, then she said, 'Thanks to my last job for Randolph, you've got 250,000 reasons. No, make that 250,000 and *one*.'

After he put the phone down, Docker stared at the handpiece for a full minute. Her final words made him think of the old radio quiz show 'Dr IQ', in which the host jingled silver dollars into the contestants' palms. If it came down to it, he'd take the girl not the money. Money only seemed to bring him bad luck.

An hour later, he was sitting on a tram heading to the US MPs' headquarters. The route looked painfully familiar. Would his former colleagues in the building recognise him, grill him, ask what the hell he was doing back here? It'd been a year and a half, and no doubt a few of the guys would still be in their places, probably rusted to desk jobs. Before he'd left British headquarters he asked Beauchamp to check when Oswald had been posted to Berlin. The answer: 11 months ago. There was no chance of Oswald recognisng him. It would be just plain bad luck if one of Oswald's squad knew him.

When he reached the US MPs' building he'd have to play it straight and skip the John Davis ploy. If he went into the building using fake ID it could create even more problems.

The US MP on duty at the reception desk showed little interest when Docker asked to see Major Oswald. The MP called up to Oswald's office, then cupped the mouthpiece, listened and asked Docker what he wanted.

'To discuss an opportunity,' Docker answered.

The MP checked and told Docker to wait. Half an hour later a corporal interrupted Docker's reading of a three-month-old *New York Times*. Erza Pound had won a $1,000 poetry prize, or as the *Times* delicately put it: 'Pound, in Mental Clinic, Wins Prize for Poetry Penned in Treason Cell.' Docker tossed up whether to ask the corporal if he'd ever read any Pound. Perhaps not, Docker thought, looking at the corporal's dull eyes as he was first asked to raise his arms for a pat-down to ensure he was unarmed and then asked to 'Step this way, sir.'

Docker knew every staircase, every corridor. Two men, in close conversation, went past. One glanced at Docker, nodded a 'Hello' and kept walking. God, that was close, he thought. The last time he'd seen the man was in Munich in early '46. He was a transport specialist for the US Constabulary and, because Docker was forced to secretly leave Berlin, unlikely to have heard of his hasty departure. Fortunately the corporal leading Docker up some stairs had missed the greeting.

Docker began to breathe deeply to calm himself. It didn't work. The corporal knocked on a door and ushered Docker into Major Oswald's office.

Oswald shook Docker's hand with little enthusiasm, then indicated a chair. Docker dutifully sat down.

Oswald, still standing, began tapping on his desk with the edge of a piece of notepaper. Stopping, he held the paper up and squinted at it. 'Docker,' he read out. He tossed the paper down and asked, 'Who are you, Mr Docker?'

'Someone who might be able to help you.'

'I asked who you were.' Oswald's voice was steady.

'A businessman with contacts all over the city.'

'That doesn't impress me. Berlin's full of carpetbaggers and conmen.' Again he picked up the paper with Docker's name on it. 'The only reason you're sitting here is so I can find out who would front up unannounced and demand to see me. Now, what's this "opportunity"?'

'A chance to save your thieving hide,' said Docker.

Oswald reacted by going scarlet in the cheeks then turning white as the blood drained away. Docker wondered if this sting was going to work.

Oswald took a seat. 'Are you threatening me, Mr Docker?'

'I'm going to give you a chance to stay a rich man,' countered Docker evenly.

'Obviously you don't know anything about military pay scales.'

'I'm talking about a little scam I hear that you and some of your squad pulled,' said Docker.

'Scam?' repeated Oswald, with a touch of bewilderment. To Docker, the major sounded unconvincing.

Docker kept going. 'According to my sources, you did a deal and exchanged a fortune in the old currency for new Deutsche Marks.'

'How could I possibly benefit?'

'The Reichsmarks belonged to a crook – Alaine Amistead. I'd say you took a cut off the top during the exchange.'

'Where'd you get this story from?' asked Oswald, now seemingly indignant.

'Good contacts in the wrong end of town.'

'And which end is that?' asked Oswald.

'Out Spandau way. Not a bad location if you like sports.'

'Let me guess, the Royal Military Police at Olympic Stadium.'

'Right on the money,' Docker said.

Oswald didn't excuse himself, he just got up and walked out the door. A minute later the major returned with a surly military police captain. Oswald sat down again and picked a pen from a chipped mug on his desk. 'Well, Mr Docker, shoot.'

Docker tried to ignore the captain standing directly behind him, the back of his head feeling very vulnerable. He took a breath and went through the story he'd rehearsed with Beauchamp. It sounded less plausible in front of Oswald than it had when he and the Englishman had shared a mug of strong tea.

Docker ploughed on, watching Oswald's eyes. They hadn't blinked. He wasn't buying the story.

'Bullshit,' broke in Oswald before Docker could finish. 'First of all I've no idea what you're talking about. Secondly, I can't imagine that the Brits would send an American as their bagman.'

'Let's take the second point,' said Docker, just keeping a tremor from his voice. 'My British contacts aren't going to come strolling up to your front door. They tell me you're not a very good host.'

'So, it's that Limey clown, Boo-chump.'

'I knew that piece of shit was trouble when we caught him playing cop here,' said the captain.

Docker could see Oswald's mind working, trying to connect the dots between what he knew about the money, Beauchamp and this uppity newcomer.

Docker heard the door being locked.

'That's better,' said Oswald. 'Now we won't be disturbed. So, Mr Docker, why don't we start again – right from the beginning?'

***

Beauchamp sat in the van 100 yards from the Americans' building, trying to imagine Docker spinning the tale. White was in the driver's seat, black beret pulled down low, giving a good impression of a none-too-bright French delivery-man. He'd assured Beauchamp that the Americans would think he was a local. Beauchamp still had his doubts. The shutters on the window they knew to be Oswald's were closed and there was no way of knowing Docker's fate.

A taxi went past and slowed, revealing a tall man in the rear seat also studying the building. With a light-coloured suit and dark tie, his hat brim shading his eyes, he didn't look like a Berliner to Beauchamp. The taxi picked up speed and vanished around a corner. Five minutes later the tall man reappeared, on foot. He lit a cigarette and walked slowly past the front of the US MP headquarters.

Eventually Docker came out of the main entrance looking pale and stressed. He walked to the adjacent tram stop.

Beauchamp watched the man in the light suit follow the American and board the same tram. White started the engine and the van slid forward.

Following a tram was frustrating even in thin Berlin traffic. Each time there was a stop, White was forced to pull over to the side of the road. The tram and the van kangaroo-hopped towards the Kurfürstendamm, White stopping when Docker alighted from the tram and, without pausing, walked to a sidewalk café. The tall man also got off the tram, strode past the café and continued up the Ku'damm. Beauchamp saw Docker order some-thing, wait a minute and then leave as soon as the waiter disappeared inside. Docker was now moving in a different direction from the man.

White kept pace about 20 yards behind Docker until he turned into a side street, then pulled the van up alongside the American. Beauchamp swung the door open and Docker climbed into the cramped cabin.

Beauchamp was squeezed into the centre. 'You were being followed,' he said.

'I know, and whoever it was knows that I know. I think he was sending me a little signal.'

'Any idea what it's about?' asked Beauchamp.

'I can guess.'

White did a three-point turn and the van pulled into the Ku'damm again. The man had disappeared.

In the RMP headquarters, Beauchamp played host, offering Docker tea.

'You could extract confessions with that damn brew,' said Docker, shaking his head.

'Then you *must* try some of the British Army coffee,' said Beauchamp, getting up to prepare the worst coffee in Berlin. He put heaped teaspoons of what may or may not have been powdered coffee into mugs, then added the hot water. The resulting aroma was sharply chemical with just a hint of open drains.

Docker gingerly took a mug and immediately set it aside. 'I may not have convinced Oswald that we know all the details of the scam, but I did get his attention. He wants to meet you.'

'You mentioned me?' asked Beauchamp, surprised.

'No, but Oswald guessed. I just offered to line up a meeting with my British contact.' As he said the words, it occurred to Docker that he was spending his life setting up meetings in which he was the most likely person to get shot.

'Did Oswald admit to the currency deal?'

'Not a chance. He's probably leaving himself the option of claiming he wanted to trap you by arranging this meeting.'

'So he doesn't trust you?'

'A stranger arrives in his office and accuses him of a crime, then says the British military police want a slice of the action. What do you think?'

'Admittedly, you don't look trustworthy. I think it's the suit. Have you ever thought of having it pressed?'

Docker tried a sip of his coffee before abandoning it. 'The meeting is set for 11 tonight at the Kaiser-Wilhelm-Gedächtniskirche.'

'Good choice. It's in our sector.'

'I wanted somewhere Oswald would feel off guard.'

Docker sat back to wait, with Beauchamp going about the fruitless task of tidying his office. He soon lost interest in the clean-up and went to a blackboard, chalking up the elements of the puzzle. He stayed in front of the blackboard playing the schoolteacher. He waved a piece of chalk and muttered, 'Let's get it in some sort of order. A few months ago Popov blackmails Speer into saying where the Cross is hidden. Popov retrieves the Cross and sells it for a lot of money to what's-his-name –?'

'Randolph Morton,' said Docker, deliberately leaving Bridgette, Laurent and Gaffney out of this discussion.

'Popov then arranges for that German, Rühmann, to steal the Cross back from Morton and bring it to Berlin because someone else wants it very badly. Rühmann tries to get more money out of Popov and is killed for his trouble. Popov now has the Cross and, from what I learnt during a little outing to the Russian sector, he's going to exchange the Cross for the secrets.'

'You heard him say that?'

'Almost. That was the drift of the conversation he had with Amistead.'

'But why is Amistead desperate to get the Cross?'

Beauchamp scratched Amistead's name on the board. 'He doesn't strike me as the religious type and surely he doesn't believe that piece of wood has any power?'

'He may not, but some might – like Speer and –' Docker stopped himself guessing out loud why Laurent might want the relic. Instead he finished with, '– others.'

'That's a bit far-fetched. My guess is that Amistead, like the black marketeer he is, has got someone else who's going to take the Cross off his hands.'

'Maybe,' Docker said, but the only name he could think of was Laurent's. He doubted Laurent was Amistead's customer. He decided to change the subject. 'If we're going to hang around, why don't we eat?'

'I'll arrange for a tray to be sent in. You can try to guess what it is.'

Docker couldn't guess. Whatever it was had been

thoroughly overcooked and was stone cold. Badly cooked food and lousy coffee – he may as well be back in the forces.

At 10 o'clock, Docker walked with Beauchamp and White to their Jeep. Next stop, the Kaiser-Wilhelm-Gedächtniskirche rendezvous – and still no gun.

When they arrived, Beauchamp turned to the back seat where Docker was sitting. 'Stay here, we'll do a recce.'

Docker was happy to oblige. Ten minutes later, the Englishmen returned.

'It's all clear,' said White to Docker.

Climbing out of the Jeep, Docker stood beside the other two men as they looked up at the front tower of the ruined church. After the Allied attacks the tower was the only part of the church left upright. It was a dismal sight no matter which side of the battle you'd been on.

At 10.45, the three men picked their way over the rubble in the nave of the church and waited near the vestibule. From overhead came the steady hum of aircraft moving across the sky. Heavy cloud cover, lit by the very few bright city lights, hid the planes. Docker felt tense. There could be a gunfight and he was unarmed. These damned Brits were obsessed with controlling the firepower.

As he looked around for cover, he spotted two sets of headlights on Tauentzienstrasse. Engines stopped, lights were switched off and two men left the lead vehicle and walked in the darkness towards the church. There was no movement from the second vehicle.

Docker nudged Beauchamp, who in turn signalled White. The corporal was crouching on what remained of the floor above, perched near a blast hole in the wall. Docker prayed White had a clean line of fire. The sound of footfalls culminated in a single obscenity as a boot slipped on loose stones. Then Oswald and his captain came up the front steps at a trot and entered the vestibule.

Oswald didn't offer his hand. He kept his voice low. 'Well, it's our pal, Boo-chump.'

'*Beech-um* is the pronunciation,' corrected the Englishman.

'You could be pronounced dead on arrival,' said the captain.

Beauchamp took a step forward. 'Ah, that'll be what you Americans call a joke.'

Docker raised a warning hand to avoid a schoolyard brawl. 'Let's get to the point, major. You and your captain made a lot of money and we want a share.'

Oswald didn't appear to want to be rushed. 'You keep mentioning some scam we're meant to be running, but you don't have any proof.'

Beauchamp was firm. 'I have the proof. I was involved in the audit of the missing money and I've traced it back to your office. Now let's talk business.'

Docker was impressed. Beauchamp's tone was part exasperation, part threat.

Oswald looked down at his feet, then slowly shifted his gaze. 'Let's say it was true. What sort of share are we talking about?'

'Fifty percent,' said Beauchamp.

'*Fifty* percent?' Oswald repeated. 'Why be so modest? Why not make it a hundred?'

Before either Docker or Beauchamp could answer, Oswald reached for his cap.

Sensing something was wrong, Beauchamp took one step forward. It was too late. Oswald pulled his cap off with a flourish. From the darkness came the metallic sound of cocking weapons.

Oswald put his cap back on. 'Actually, I've changed my mind. How much you want doesn't matter any more. You,' he said signalling to Beauchamp, 'take out your gun and drop it on the ground.'

Beauchamp did so. The US captain picked up the Browning and pointed it at Beauchamp. Docker felt vaguely offended that he wasn't seen as a risk.

'I want to hear how you found out about the swap,' said Oswald, sounding peevish.

It was the admission of guilt Beauchamp had been waiting to hear. 'Why don't we put the guns away and talk business? You seem like reasonable men.'

'Smart ass,' said the US captain, raising the gun suddenly and pressing it against Beauchamp's head.

The burst of fire from above knocked the captain off his feet. Docker and Beauchamp flung themselves at Oswald. He went under in a tackle that sent a cloud of dust up from the floor. Two guns began firing from the sidelines, one aiming at the upper floor near White, the other in the direction of the three struggling men.

Oswald's voice was panicky. 'Shoot –'

Docker hit him. Then, scrambling for cover, he saw White's bullets chipping the area near the main door.

'Jesus, I'm in the middle of a shooting gallery,' Docker said. He lay flat, and lifted his head in time to see another spray of bullets from White's gun. Docker heard a grunt as an unseen man fell. The second gunman in the darkness stopped firing. There were scrabbling sounds as the second man ran away, crashing over the rubble mounds on his way to the street.

Docker sat on Oswald's back while Beauchamp retrieved his gun from the blood-spattered captain and went over to the dead gunman lying beneath a mosaic on the wall. He had a thin moustache, hair that touched the collar of his turtleneck sweater and an expensive watch.

Docker hauled Oswald to his feet and pushed him towards the dead man. 'Who's he? He doesn't look like a soldier.'

'No idea,' said Oswald. 'Maybe he just liked old churches.'

White appeared with a torch and played the beam over the dead man's body. 'I know him,' he said. 'He was an enforcer in the markets. A nasty piece of work. His name is, or was, Jean-Pierre Gambon. He was one of Amistead's boys.'

Gesturing at Oswald, White asked, 'What shall we do with him?'

'He's a senior member of an allied military force,' said Beauchamp. 'I suggest we do the only responsible thing.'

'Which is?'

'Arrest him.'

SECHSUNDZWANZIG

Friedrich Kessler had liked the good life, said Elsa, holding the portrait of her father that Beauchamp had taken from Popov's house. The other photographs from the Russian's gallery were in a manila folder on a side table, but she ignored them, carrying the photograph of her father to the hotel window to catch the light. The portrait had been taken before the war, with Kessler looking dashing in a double-breasted suit.

'More a successful businessman than your stock-standard scientist,' said Beauchamp.

'Sadly, yes. My father was interested in luxury, not patri-otism. The highest bidder had his loyalty. When he heard that von Braun and 500 rocket scientists had surrendered to the Americans, he knew where his future lay.'

Beauchamp took the photograph from her and slipped it back on top of the others. He reached down, opened a khaki canvas holdall and pulled out a small glassine bag.

Inside was a Longines watch with a distinctive combination square and round face.

Elsa began to cry.

'I'm sorry,' said Beauchamp. As a copper he'd said the words many times before. This time he meant them. He offered her a very starched white linen handkerchief, but she waved it away. Beauchamp put the watch back in the bag. 'We found the watch on Jean-Pierre Gambon. Had you ever met him?'

She shook her head.

'He was a hard man and an enforcer for black marketeers,' Beauchamp continued. 'Wearing your father's watch was either stupidity or arrogance – perhaps both. On top of all that he was also driving a Volkswagen with a new set of tyres.'

'Is that a crime in Berlin?' she asked.

Beauchamp put her testiness down to stress. 'Not yet,' he said.

'And where is Herr Gambon now?'

'He's at the British Army morgue.'

'I want to see him.'

'It's no use going there. You'd have to join a queue of people with hatpins wanting to make certain he's dead.'

'I am going anyway.' Elsa got up and started for the door.

Beauchamp knew it was better not to argue. Taking her by the arm he led her to the lift. As the steel cage ground down between the floors, he asked, 'Would you care to join me for dinner tonight?'

'*Gewiss.*' She smiled.

When the lift door opened on the ground floor they saw White sprinting across the foyer. He halted before them, almost breathless. 'Amistead is on the run, sir. He was spotted trying to drive into the Russian sector near Potsdamer Platz. From what I hear, it looked like the Russians were expecting him – they'd cleared away a road block.' White sucked in more air, then continued. 'One of our lads stepped in front of Amistead's car to stop him, and the Frog ran him down. A couple of other RMP opened fire and Amistead spun round and headed back into the west.'

Beauchamp let go of Elsa's arm and jammed his cap on. 'Any idea where he's headed?'

'No, sir.'

Turning to Elsa, Beauchamp looked apologetic. 'The morgue trip is off, I'm afraid. I'll call you.'

'Be careful.'

'I've got Corporal White to protect me.'

'He looks very capable,' said Elsa, glancing at White in time to see his cheeks burn red.

'Ah,' said Beauchamp, 'wait 'til you see him in a beret.'

News of Oswald's arrest was creating friction between the Americans and British. Oswald had complained long and loud that it was *he* who'd been ambushed by hidden gunmen and that Beauchamp had got it all wrong.

What Beauchamp described as Oswald's 'bleatings' had successfully caught the attention of the Joint Allied Command in the city. But, to Beauchamp's surprise, his superiors were actually backing him, and Oswald was still locked in the RMP holding cells.

The American–British hostility was clearly evident in the street outside Amistead's mansion, where a US senior officer was standing toe-to-toe with Beauchamp explaining in alternating bursts of profanity and scorn how unhappy he was about Beauchamp's participation in a raid in the American sector.

The officer was even less happy that Docker was tagging along. 'Is he armed?' he demanded.

'No,' Beauchamp replied.

'Good,' the American officer snapped before signalling his men.

A fraction of a second later a US Army truck with reinforced fenders raced along the drive, picking up even more speed before bouncing across the portico and through the double front doors. As the steel and wood splintered, the American force went in. Beauchamp and Docker followed in the rear, allowing enough time for the American military to sweep the house. It was empty.

The soldiers left, backing their truck down the driveway and dragging what remained of the door off its hinges. Beauchamp and Docker were left alone. They checked the ground floor and then began searching the two upper levels. On the top floor they found yet another room choked with furniture and paintings. This time Beauchamp was free to inspect the hoard. He stood inches from a gloomy offering entitled *Island of the Dead* in which a white-robed figure was being rowed to a forbidding island.

It was a genuine Böcklin. The last Beauchamp had heard, this particular Böcklin was hanging in the eastern sector. The works he'd seen on his first visit must have also been world-class original art, not fakes. There was little doubt Amistead had excellent taste and good contacts with a high-ranking Soviet supplier.

Docker's only interest in the artworks was what was behind them. He lifted the corner of each painting away from the wall, searching for a safe or a loose brick. There was nothing behind the paintings nor behind the rows of books on a long bookcase taking up most of a far wall. He ran his eyes over the room again, then looked up. A raked ceiling sloped down to casement windows, but one section of the ceiling was flat, as if the builder had created a large cavity between the ceiling and the roof.

He dragged a table under the flattened area and hefted a chair onto the table's polished surface. Then, standing on the chair seat, he pressed his palms up against the ceiling. A recessed trapdoor flipped up and Docker hauled himself through the small opening. Beauchamp stood below and called out, asking if Docker needed any help. In answer, a striped, belted dressing gown stiff with blood was dropped through the trapdoor. It landed on the chair back and swayed in Beauchamp's face. Then came a man's shoe. It bounced off the table and landed at Beauchamp's feet.

Docker appeared at the hole and lowered himself down. 'That's all I could find,' he said, picking up the gown. 'It doesn't look like Amistead's. I see him more in a brocaded smoking coat.'

'You're right. It isn't his. It belonged to a prostitute I knew,' said Beauchamp.

'On police business?'

'Yes. She wasn't my type . . . more your cup of tea actually.'

'What was she doing here?' asked Docker.

'I'd say she picked the wrong man to blackmail,' said Beauchamp.

Beauchamp lifted the shoe off the floor and checked the maker's mark. Johnston & Murphy. 'So there was nothing else up there?' he asked.

'Just a couple of bullet holes in the wall.'

'No doubt made by a Walther P38,' said Beauchamp.

'Why a P38?'

'That's what was used for the coup de grâce.' Beauchamp turned for the door.

Docker hesitated before following. Was he getting closer to the Berlin Cross or further away? Countless clues had led to zip. As he left the room, he consoled himself that at least he was still alive.

Beauchamp and Docker drove towards the American's boarding house. On several street corners there were bright new posters advertising comedian Bob Hope's coming USO visit to Berlin to boost morale. 'As if this city hasn't suffered enough,' Beauchamp said.

When they pulled up outside the boarding house, their goodbyes were mechanical. Beauchamp was in a hurry and Docker wanted a bath.

Docker climbed the staircase, let himself into his room

– and smelt fresh cigarette smoke. He slammed the door and ran back down the stairs.

The door was jerked opened and a bullet took the knob off the top of the stair banister.

In the street outside, a cab was waiting, its engine ticking. Docker jumped in and, crouching, shouted, 'Go, go!'

'Go, go where?' said the startled driver.

'Just move!' ordered Docker in a tone that made the driver immediately put his foot down hard on the accelerator.

Docker looked out the rear window as a tall man in a light grey suit ran out onto the sidewalk outside the boarding house, stopped and stared at the disappearing cab.

Docker was tempted to scuttle off to Tempelhof Airport, like a rat deserting the sinking city. Instead he asked to be taken to RMP headquarters – fast. Through the cab's grimy windows, Docker could see the trees of the Tiergarten lit by the sunset. Another day, more gunfire. 'What a city,' he sighed out loud.

'*Jawohl*,' agreed the driver, taking in the beauty of the golden light.

Beauchamp was pressing coloured pins into the map on his office wall – the hotel where Kessler's body was found, the river bank where the prostitute was washed up, Frau Kessler's hospital, Amistead's house, the Reichstag, the Hotel Adlon site, Elsa's hotel, the US MPs' headquarters and Popov's hideaway. Would he bother with a pin for

Poppa 8's? 'Poppa? Popov?' He said the names again, then jammed a pin into Number 8, Uhlandstrasse. It was too clumsy a play on words, surely? Unless, of course, English wasn't your first language. When had the place opened? Beauchamp made a quick phone call to the *Schutzpolizei* to confirm the details. The bar and restaurant had opened in mid-1946 with private funding and soon drew in a mixed Allied clientele, invariably officers. Since Amistead's attempt to flee the Allied sectors and head for the Soviet-controlled area had failed, perhaps the Frenchman would be forced to rendezvous with the Russian somewhere central, somewhere they both knew. Somewhere like . . .

The phone rang, drawing Beauchamp away from the map. He was told Docker was at the front desk. 'Bring him up,' said Beauchamp, hoping Docker had had that promised bath.

He hadn't. Unshaven, suit crumpled, tie loosened and shirt collar unbuttoned, Docker looked like an unsuccessful tramp. He dropped his hat onto Beauchamp's desk and lowered himself into a chair, asking, 'Got a drink?'

'You're in luck,' said Beauchamp, handing Docker back his hat. 'I'm just heading for a bar.'

Flicking an intercom switch near his phone, Beauchamp called to White, 'I'll see you downstairs in two minutes. Bring another man and a spare walkie-talkie for our American friend.' Beauchamp smiled at Docker. 'Have you ever listened to "Two-Way Family Favourites" on the wireless?'

Docker shook his head.

'It's all about keeping in touch. And I want to make sure we keep in touch with you.'

'Because I'm going to be unarmed . . . again.'

'Spot on,' said Beauchamp, heading for the door.

Docker looked across at the lance corporal sharing the rear seat of the Jeep with him and then ahead at Beauchamp and White. All Docker could see were silhouettes of their heads against the few streetlights. For a moment he allowed himself the luxury of remembering the return trip to New York in Gaffney's car, with the nape of Bridgette's neck – curved, elegant, sensual – in front of him. It sure beat staring at Beauchamp and White. Leaning forward, he tapped Beauchamp's shoulder. 'How're you going to play this?'

'By ear. We don't even know if Amistead or Popov will be there. Want to get out now?'

'If those two are planning to swap Kessler's secrets for the Berlin Cross, then I want to be there.'

The Jeep stopped one block short of Poppa 8's. Beauchamp turned to White and the lance corporal. 'You two go around to the front, but keep out of sight. Corporal, give Mr Docker the spare walkie-talkie; he'll be staying in the Jeep. Your call sign, Mr Docker, will be "*Golf India*". Corporal White's is "*Foxtrot Delta*".'

'What are you going to do, sir?' asked White.

'I'm going in through the kitchen.'

'So that's the grand strategy?' said Docker.

'Part of it,' replied Beauchamp. 'The rest I'll make up as I go along.'

White and the lance corporal set off at a trot, keeping in the street shadows. Beauchamp worked his way down an alley to the rear of the restaurant. Aromas from a ventilation shaft reminded him that he hadn't eaten. The wide, circular duct was screened by a wire grille. Teetering on a garbage bin, Beauchamp used his penknife to prise off the clips holding the grille in place, then he put his head into the opening. He judged he could squeeze along the steel tube that ran above the kitchen.

Heaving himself into the duct and trying to ignore the film of grease coating the tubing, Beauchamp inched his way past two extraction fans near the cooking areas before stopping at a mesh-covered opening above a combined office and storeroom. From back down the duct he could hear the sound of kitchen staff banging saucepans, but the room below was quiet. He pushed the mesh cover downwards and it bounced off a chair. He swore quietly then dropped into the room with an even louder thud. Cat burglary is obviously out as a career option, he decided.

Beauchamp wiped his greasy hands on his trousers and glanced around the room. In the far corner was a filing cabinet. Unclipping the flap of his holster, he drew out his Browning 9mm, walked carefully to the cabinet and attempted to open the top drawer.

A voice behind him said, 'Whatever you are looking for, it is not there. Drop your gun on the floor and turn around slowly, *pozhaluysta*.'

Beauchamp crouched down, lowered his gun onto the floor and stood up as he turned. Amistead was in the doorway, standing behind a man whose rock-steady hand held a pistol.

'Mr Popov?'

'Comrade Popov,' came the correction. Without taking his eyes off Beauchamp, Popov said to Amistead, 'Take my men in the kitchen and check the back and front. He will not have come alone.'

The Frenchman left immediately. Crossing the room to where Beauchamp's gun lay, Popov swept it aside with his foot. 'Sit,' he ordered. Beauchamp found a chair next to a table and sat facing Popov.

Amistead returned within minutes. 'We could find no one.'

Popov looked surprised. 'The British are not brave enough to work alone. But . . .' he looked at Beauchamp, 'this one might be stupid enough to.'

'Where is his gun?' asked Amistead, entering the room and pushing the door shut behind him. 'I will kill him.'

'And lose a hostage? Earlier I lost the American, but this policeman is even more useful. Take his handcuffs and – what is the word?'

'Cuff,' offered Beauchamp.

'*Spasibo*. Cuff him to the table leg.'

Pinning Beauchamp's right hand to the table leg and clipping the handcuffs shut, Amistead looked worried. 'We cannot do business with him here.'

'He will be dead by dawn. That is my promise to you.' Popov gave Amistead a tight smile. 'But before I give you this relic, I want to know what you plan to do with it.'

Amistead looked nervously at Beauchamp.

Popov was becoming irritable. 'Time is running out,' he said. 'Forget him.'

Amistead spoke quickly. 'Berlin is too dangerous and unprofitable. I am leaving for Rome and the Cross is my key to freedom. I plan to give it to the Vatican in exchange for protection.'

'Protection?' Popov appeared bemused. He glanced over at Beauchamp as if to gauge his reaction. Beauchamp was impassive, continuing to watch the pair.

'From police interference *and* the Cosa Nostra,' said Amistead. 'When I set up business in Italy, I doubt the Cosa Nostra will welcome the competition.'

'Why not do a deal with the government?'

'Governments are unstable, ever changing. The Vatican is permanent.'

'Built on a rock, I believe.' Popov lit a cigarette, inhaled and blew smoke out his nose. 'And how do you know the priests will accept your offer?'

'How could they refuse?'

'I do not trust priests. But a man needs a plan so I wish you good luck. Now, let us do it.'

Amistead stood up and began unbuckling his belt.

'That is kind of you,' said Popov, 'but I have more conservative tastes in matters of sex.'

The Frenchman continued unbuttoning his trousers and dropped them to his ankles. He pulled hard at an oilcloth package taped to his right thigh. It came off with a tearing sound. Amistead bit on his lower lip and placed the package and the hair-covered tape on the table. He pulled up his trousers and did them up before opening the package and handing the contents to Popov.

It was a sheaf of papers – the pages fine and waxy, almost translucent. Popov spread them out on the table. There were 10 pages of text, diagrams and calculations written in a shaky but methodical hand. Two of the pages had blood spattered on the upper corners.

Beauchamp leant forward an inch or two. Even with his limited German, he caught references to heavy water before Popov scooped up the papers and bundled them together.

'Who transcribed this?' Popov asked Amistead.

'No one. Kessler did it himself. I watched him write every word, draw every diagram.'

Popov appeared uncertain. 'How can I be sure Kessler gave you everything about the atomic experiments?'

'My men are experts at making people like Kessler give up their secrets,' said Amistead. 'Now it is your turn. What are your plans?'

Popov tapped the sheaf of papers. 'This is my key to freedom. I am leaving Berlin too. I will be back in Moscow by the end of the week. The Kessler secrets will make me a hero.'

Beauchamp broke in. 'Provided your boss, Lavrenty Beria, never discovers your sideline in trading art and antiquities.'

The mention of the name of the chief of the internal security force made Popov freeze. For the briefest of moments, he lost his composure. His fist shot out, cracking

Beauchamp on the side of the mouth. Beauchamp's head snapped sideways and blood ran down his chin.

'It would be wise not to use that person's name again,' said Popov. Wiping blood off his knuckles with a handkerchief, he turned his attention back to Amistead.

'In five years I will retire with a *dacha*, a mistress and more than enough roubles under my mattress.' He swapped his pistol to his left hand and reached inside his overcoat, pulling out the scimitar-shaped reliquary. He placed it on the table, well clear of Beauchamp.

'Are you taking a piece for luck?' Beauchamp asked, his head still pounding from the punch.

'That is a superstitious, bourgeois thought.'

Amistead said nothing. He was absorbed by the scimitar case. He prised open the case's catches and reached inside.

His lips moved as he read the Arabic words on the blade. He picked up the muslin parcel that lay near the sword, unwrapped it and began stroking the wood.

Popov was becoming restless. Sneering at Amistead, he said, 'It is not a magic lantern. Stop rubbing it. We must go.'

'*D'accord,*' said Amistead. Gently he put the sword and the muslin-wrapped piece of wood back in their case.

Popov tucked the bundle of Kessler's papers firmly inside his overcoat while Amistead chose to jam the reliquary into the waist of his trousers. Seeing Beauchamp's 9mm on the floor he pocketed it.

Popov expertly kept his pistol on Beauchamp while searching his pockets for the handcuff keys. Then the

Russian released Beauchamp from the table leg and cuffed both his hands in front of him. He handed Amistead the keys and pulled Beauchamp roughly towards the door. The kitchen staff were standing guard at both the rear door and the batwing doors into the main bar and restaurant area.

Tossing a kitchen cloth over Beauchamp's handcuffs, and wiping the blood off his face, Popov said, 'Walk naturally. Look as though we are all friends.'

With Amistead in the lead, Beauchamp a few feet behind and Popov trailing in the rear, the three men stepped into the alley behind Poppa 8's. The kitchen door was quietly closed behind them, the lock sliding into place with a soft thud.

Amistead stopped, waiting. The only sound was a tram rattling in the distance. He nodded at the others to follow him.

'Come in, Golf India,' said a high tinny voice to their left.

'Indian golf?' said Popov in surprise, a fraction of a second before Docker, flying out of the darkness from the right, crashed into the Russian and sent his gun clattering over the cobblestones. Docker and the Russian rolled into some open-topped rubbish bins.

Beauchamp swung around to meet Amistead, who had pulled the 9mm from his pocket. It was too late. The gun's barrel came up and clipped Beauchamp across the temple, knocking him to the ground.

Trying to scramble to his feet, hands cuffed together, Beauchamp saw Amistead raise the gun, smile grimly and put his finger on the trigger. Beauchamp looked into Amistead's eyes and swiftly brought his clasped hands up hard, hitting him in the crutch. Amistead fell to the ground, dropping the gun by Beauchamp's side. A grunt and then a crash came from the now upturned rubbish bins. Docker and Popov were still struggling, panting, sending garbage across the alley. Beauchamp snatched up the gun, trying to make out which figure was which in the darkness. He fired a single shot.

'Shit,' came Docker's hoarse shout. He let go of Popov and dived for cover. The Russian was on his feet and running. Beauchamp took careful aim at the silhouetted figure which had reached a pool of light beneath a streetlamp. He was tightening the trigger as four workmen, with shovels and brooms flung over their shoulders, strode into the light. Barrel steady, Beauchamp shouted: '*Polizei! Hau ab!*'

The workmen, confused, stared down the darkened alley at him before scattering. Beauchamp blinked. Popov was gone.

Sighing, Beauchamp turned back to Amistead who was in a foetal position on the ground, moaning.

The walkie-talkie in the shadows crackled again. White's voice came through the earpiece. 'I said, come in, Golf India.'

'So *that* was your grand strategy,' Beauchamp said to Docker. 'Hide the walkie-talkie and have White's voice throw them off guard.'

'I wasn't going to sit on my ass and miss the fun. I've been here all the time. When you didn't come back out, I asked White to call me every five minutes while I hid over there.' Docker felt for Beauchamp's handcuff keys and crouched down to unlock the Englishman, then clipped the cuffs over Amistead's wrists. He noticed the reliquary poking from Amistead's waistband.

'I thought I'd never see this again,' Docker said, pulling the curved case free.

Beauchamp rubbed his wrists. 'Amistead planned to move to Italy, and give it to the Vatican in return for protection.'

Amistead groaned again at the sound of his name.

Docker tucked the reliquary in his jacket pocket. 'I've got what I came for.'

Beauchamp stretched out his hand, palm upturned. 'I'll need that as evidence.'

'I've been shot at, threatened, held prisoner and tailed from one end of this town to the other,' said Docker. 'It's all over. I'm going home.'

Beauchamp shook his head. 'I'm surprised. I thought this would be the ideal environment for a private detective.'

'You've been in the military police too long, captain,' said Docker. 'You're getting cynical.'

'A cynic is just a realist with a sense of humour.'

'I'm a realist too. That's why I'm taking the first flight out of here.'

'We'll see,' said Beauchamp as he crossed the alley to collect the walkie-talkie. 'Corporal, get over here on the double. I need the borders sealed from our side.'

'Strictly speaking, I'm Foxtrot Delta, over.'

'For Christ's sake,' said a frustrated Beauchamp. He turned to speak to Docker. Except for the doubled-over, handcuffed Amistead, the alley was empty.

SIEBENUNDZWANZIG

As Docker snuck away from Poppa 8's towards the Kurfürstendamm, a dark cat raced across his path and into a side road. Docker flinched and swallowed hard, wishing he had a weapon.

After waiting for trucks loaded with sacks of flour to pass, he crossed over the Ku'damm. Three Berliners walking towards him stepped clear, taking in quickly his crumpled clothes. Docker was conscious that a scruffy American was a surprising sight to passers-by used to well-scrubbed US military men. He stood in front of a lit shop window, using the reflection to try to make himself look presentable. Even in this light he could see the dark rings under his eyes. When had he done more than snatch a few hours sleep in uncomfortable aircraft seats? After checking his wallet, air ticket and passport were still in place in his inside jacket pocket, he made one last attempt to smooth down his hair. Then he saw the movement of something pale and furtive. He was certain of it. A glimpse of the light grey suit. Docker re-crossed the road and kept walking west, pausing again after five minutes.

The café crowds were beginning to thin out and, except for the occasional drunk, he and the tall man were alone. Docker kept looking straight ahead until he was abreast of a narrow road unevenly lit by a few streetlamps, then turned and walked into the semi-darkness, the heels of his shoes tapping on the cobblestones.

Standing in the deepest shadows, Docker could make out the silhouette of the man as he walked calmly into the road. Then the man stopped just a few yards away, looked around and drew a gun from a shoulder holster.

Now I'm really screwed, Docker thought. Shaking his head, he bent down, finding only a small pebble within reach. If a diversion worked in the alley with Amistead and Popov, maybe it'd work here. He threw the pebble well clear of the man. No reaction. Damn, he's professional. Next Docker slipped off his coat, balled it up and threw it high into the air over the man's head. This time the man spun around, his eyes following the flapping of the now open coat as it landed on the road. Using the scimitar case as a club, Docker hit the man behind the right ear. The blow was enough to knock the man sideways onto the roadway, his gun bouncing a few feet clear.

Docker stepped briskly forward and snatched up the weapon, a lightweight Beretta.

With the scimitar case jammed back in his waistband, Docker stood studying the stranger. 'Thanks, I've been begging for a gun.' He stepped back, levelled the pistol and demanded, 'And, since you obviously know who I am, who the fuck are you?'

'My name's Smith.' The accent was English; the voice deep and controlled.

'Smith?' Docker sounded disbelieving. 'Why are you following me? Who're you with?'

'I'm not following you.' Smith smiled. 'I'm in the export business.'

'And you need a gun?'

'It's a dangerous city,' said Smith, dragging himself to sit upright.

Docker raised the gun. 'At a guess, I'd say you're working for MI6.'

'Never heard of it.'

'Based at 54 Broadway, London, England.'

'My office is in Sevenoaks.'

A car door slammed behind Docker. He made a quarter turn and saw Beauchamp 10 feet away, his Jeep blocking the entrance to the road. 'What in the hell are you doing?' shouted Beauchamp. 'Put that bloody gun down.'

Smith began to get up.

'Stay down,' said Docker.

'Get up,' said Beauchamp.

'Stay down or you're dead,' said Docker.

Smith stayed on the roadway. Looking across at Beauchamp, Smith snapped, 'Are you going to let him kill me? Shoot the bastard.'

Beauchamp ignored Smith, staying focused on Docker.

'I'm the copper here. I've told you once: put the weapon down. I knew there'd be trouble if you got a gun.'

'It's purely for self-defence. This guy's with MI6. He wants to kill me.'

Smith raised his voice. 'I'm on your side, captain.' Very slowly he put his hand inside his coat and pulled out a plain leather wallet. He skimmed it across the cobble-stones towards Beauchamp's feet.

Beauchamp took a few steps forward, bent down and scooped up the wallet. After flicking it open, he said to Docker, 'You could be right about MI6. Unless this documentation is fake.'

Smith was becoming testy. 'You know it's genuine.'

Beauchamp slipped the wallet into his breast pocket. 'Even if it is authentic, why should I shoot this man?'

'Because he's a murderer,' said Smith. 'Ask him why he had to leave Berlin in 1946.'

'It's a fair question, Mr Docker,' said Beauchamp.

Docker waited a moment, wondering how best to answer. When he did he spoke quickly, almost relieved to finally tell someone the story. 'It was back in December that year. I'd been assigned to assist on a missing person's case – to find Kessler. Our MPs were sweeping Berlin looking for him and I was asked to check with some contacts to see what they knew. One of them was Amistead.'

Beauchamp's voice was tense. 'What was your connection to Amistead?'

'Amistead was always willing to cut a deal. Information for cash. In Kessler's case he said he'd help us in exchange for a single shipment of medical equipment and drugs. I told him no. He said he'd help, providing we agreed to be a little less vigilant around the Potsdamer Platz markets. It was vague enough for me to shake hands on it. Thirty-six hours later he called and gave me an address in Kreuzberg. I was told to go alone to an address off Gross-beerenstrasse.'

Smith shifted his position on the cobblestones. Docker twitched the gun barrel an inch and said, 'Sit still. I'm telling all this for your sake too. I want you and the captain to realise I was forced to do what I did. Right from the start, I wasn't happy with the assignment. Too much pressure from Washington and too little time. On top of that, I didn't trust Amistead but I didn't have a choice – we'd been ordered to find Kessler pronto and get him home safely. The Kreuzberg address that Amistead gave me turned out to be in an apartment block with its windows boarded over. The place was a dump. I went up the stairs to find the apartment number I'd been given. There was some guy sitting on a chair in the hallway, reading a newspaper. It was too late to turn around, so I kept going. Then I heard voices from the apartment. The guy in the chair tried to pull a gun so I clubbed him with my nightstick.' He paused and gave Beauchamp a half-smile, 'All those years spent as an MP breaking up bar room brawls finally paid off.'

Beauchamp didn't smile back.

Docker pushed on. 'Then a man opened the apartment door, so I decked him too with the nightstick. Inside was

Kessler, very shaken up. I gave him my coat and we made a run for it. We were halfway up the street when I heard someone shout and then there were shots. I grabbed Kessler and tried to make him run faster, but by then there were bullets flying everywhere. I had no choice, so I turned around and shot the guy who was firing at us. It turned out to be the second man from the apartment. I went through his wallet for ID. There was only a business card in the name of Edward St John. St John was in the export trade. Just like our Mr Smith here.'

Beauchamp guessed the punchline. So this was the reason why Kessler's first disappearance hadn't been on the RMP files – it had been MI6 who'd kidnapped Kessler the first time; and MI6 still wanted the interfering Docker dead. 'You claim you shot St John in defence?'

'Every thug's standard excuse,' said Smith. 'Don't believe a word of it. He's a murderer. He deserves to die.'

'I know him,' said Beauchamp. 'I don't know you.' Holding up Smith's wallet, he added, 'This identification could be fake or *it* might be real and *you* might be an impostor. Either way, I can't risk having you free.'

'Good call,' said Docker. He grinned at the Englishman and thought, in the darkness of the street, he saw Beauchamp wink back.

'Get up and turn around, Mr Smith,' ordered Beauchamp. He clamped on handcuffs.

'Thanks,' said Docker, slipping Smith's Beretta into his pocket.

Beauchamp saw the movement but said nothing.

'Are you insane?' Smith shouted at Beauchamp. 'I'll have you court-martialled. You'll be kicked out of the forces.'

'Tell me when you get to the bad part,' Beauchamp said, picturing Oswald throwing a similar tantrum at the Kaiser-Wilhelm-Gedächtniskirche – part genuine indignation, part fear of having been caught.

White was waiting at the boom gate back at British head-quarters.

Beauchamp left Docker and Smith in the Jeep and led White under the oak tree near the guardhouse. 'You thought arresting Major Oswald was a risk, corporal. Wait until you see who I've got in the vehicle. Claims his name is Smith and he's with MI6. Could be true. But, unfortu-nately, he wants Mr Docker dead.'

'A bit harsh, sir,' said White. 'I know he's an American but –'

'Precisely. So I want you to put the prisoner in a holding cell until we sort out this mess.'

'That'll make one pissed off American major, a Frenchman with sore balls and a possible English spy,' said White, counting the prisoners off on his fingertips. 'All we need is a Russian.'

They returned to the Jeep. White helped Smith out and, gripping his arm, led him towards headquarters.

'Stay near the radio,' Beauchamp called after White. Sliding back into the driver's seat, he said to Docker, 'Now for Popov. We've had the borders sealed from our side, so he can't get back into the Soviet sector. But he could be anywhere in the west.'

'Sherlock Holmes once said the best place to hide something is in plain sight,' said Docker.

'He did?'

'Okay, you got me. Basil Rathbone said it in a Holmes movie. But it's logical. Popov might have gone back to somewhere we've already searched. Somewhere we'd never suspect.'

Nodding, Beauchamp turned the steering wheel, reversed towards the sentry, spun the Jeep around and almost clipped the boom gate on the way out.

Poppa 8's was empty. Customers gone, kitchen and front doors locked and lights off. Beauchamp broke through the front door, found nothing in his search and stomped back to the Jeep. 'Got *another* idea, Sherlock?'

'The Reichstag?'

'I doubt it. Without the Cross, it's just a giant rubble mound.'

'Potsdamer Platz?'

'If he's got that far then he'd have crossed the border by now.'

'What about that place where Popov was holed up?'

There was no argument from Beauchamp this time. Slamming the Jeep into gear, he stamped on the accelerator. The rear wheels squealed on the wet roadway.

Pointing their weapons into the gloom of the hallway, Docker and Beauchamp walked quietly, side by side, through the front door of the house. Someone had torn away the timber boards the *Schutzpolizei* had nailed across the doorway. A police sign reading: *Eintritt verboten!* lay a few feet inside the house.

Reaching the room where Rühmann had been shot, Docker waited for Beauchamp to tap his arm in a 'go' signal before both men rushed in, guns sweeping the area.

In the centre of the room was the antiquated organ. Beauchamp snapped on a torch, the light picking out the shattered side of the organ. The RMP had already taken away the hidden camera, so this damage was new. A blade had been inserted between two sheets of wooden veneer, tearing away the surface and revealing a small hiding place. It was empty.

Beauchamp's voice was low. 'What do you think? Documents? Money?'

'Whatever was there is gone.'

'Along with Popov and –' Beauchamp stopped. A familiar sound came from the road. The sound of a Jeep's engine trying to turn over. 'Bloody hell,' Beauchamp shouted as he ran for the window. He heard the engine turn over again – and again fail to start.

Beauchamp and Docker forced the nailed-down boards from the window. The sound of splintering wood echoed up the street. A darkened shape in the Jeep's front seat suddenly dropped out of sight.

'He's hot-wired it,' hissed Docker.

As they ran up the hallway, shouts came from the street. The two men reached the front steps in time to see the owner of a Stoewer Sedina limousine lying on the road, the door of his car swinging shut as Popov took the wheel. The car took off, leaving Beauchamp and Docker to head for the Jeep.

Finding the ignition wires on the Jeep dangling down, Docker began twisting the leads until the Jeep started.

The Stoewer's owner rolled to the kerb to avoid the Jeep's wheels.

'Popov must've flagged him down,' said Beauchamp, taking a brief glance in his rear-view mirror in time to see the car owner stagger to his feet, waving a fist.

The Jeep sped onto the main avenue, Beauchamp gritting his teeth and clinging to the steering wheel. He could see the Stoewer 200 yards ahead, roaring through the traffic as if on a slalom run. The Jeep hit a pothole, catapulting them both two feet into the air. They thumped back into their seats and Beauchamp kept driving. Popov swerved around a squat British armoured car.

Docker pulled out the Beretta but Beauchamp shoved the two-way radio at him. 'Forget the gun, call for backup.'

Docker slipped the gun back in his pocket and tried desperately to work the radio while still staying in his seat. Beauchamp was in full flight, following Popov's zigzag trail through the suburban streets of Wilmersdorf on the border of the British and American sectors. There was no doubt Popov was heading to the Soviet zone.

Struggling with the radio, Docker heard a squeal of brakes and a crunch of metal. He looked up to see two civilian cars had collided after Popov sped through an intersection. Beauchamp manoeuvred around the crash site and took off up Grunewaldstrasse.

The Stoewer was powering east.

The two vehicles entered the Schöneberg district. The rear wheels of the Jeep skimmed some tram tracks and the vehicle fishtailed. Beauchamp fought to keep the Jeep on the road as Docker braced himself for the crash. It didn't come.

The Stoewer was now less than 50 yards in front, barrelling down empty side roads. It approached the lights of Potsdamer Strasse.

Suddenly, the Russian's car seemed to slow in the bright lights. Beauchamp knew why. The Allies had moved troops and armoured vehicles into the area. Tanks sat awkwardly at crossroads, their barrels pointing east. Bored soldiers watched the chase, nobody raising a weapon as the Stoewer and the Jeep sped past.

'Great lot of help they are,' said Beauchamp.

'Perhaps they think this is normal for Berlin,' said Docker, bracing himself again as the Jeep took a sharp turn.

Searchlights lit up the area from west and east. Beauchamp spied a hastily built roadblock ahead. Popov's car hit the barrier of steel drums at high speed. The car's headlights exploded and two flying drums bounced off the top of the vehicle. It still didn't stop. The drums landed with twin clangs on the Jeep's bonnet as Beauchamp hit the breaks. He and Docker watched as the drums teetered on the bonnet for a spilt second, fell sideways and rolled off into the gutter.

Beauchamp spilled from the Jeep. He whipped out his side-arm and, with a double-clenched grip, tried to steady his aim. Popov's head went in and out of focus as the gunsight followed the Russian's movement. The barrel swung around further and, a second later, Beauchamp saw across the Platz the massed guns of the Russian Army pointed directly at him. Lowering his weapon, he shook his head. He had better things to do than get shot tonight.

Popov slowed down enough to give a cheery wave before carefully driving into the armour-choked streets of the Soviet zone. On both sides of the border, soldiers now watched with open mouths.

'At least we're keeping the guys entertained,' said Docker, offering Beauchamp a cigarette. The unnaturally bright lights gave the border an artificial look, like a night sporting event. Searchlights picked out Corporal White as he stood by the smashed roadblock. Even at a distance, he appeared embarrassed.

'It could be worse,' said Docker.

'How? The Russian has escaped, possibly with America's atomic secrets, and there's a pissed off MI6 agent back at headquarters waiting to hang me and *shoot* you.'

The following morning Beauchamp collected Docker from his boarding house, noting that the American was at least washed, shaved and wearing a fresh shirt. 'What you need now is a decent breakfast,' said Beauchamp.

Weaving through the early morning traffic, the Jeep reached Elsa's hotel in 20 minutes. She was waiting for them at a table in the dining room. She greeted Beauchamp with a kiss on the cheek, then shook Docker's hand before lightly pecking his cheek too. It was a gesture he wasn't prepared for.

They ordered breakfast from a brief menu, then Beauchamp outlined to Elsa the previous day's action.

Elsa waited until Beauchamp had finished before reaching across and squeezing his hand. 'You found my father's killers, but it is a shame the Russian escaped. Is there nothing you can do?'

Beauchamp shook his head. 'Too late. They're probably assembling an honour guard at Moscow Airport for him. He's got the secrets.'

'But we got this,' said Docker, pulling the curved reliquary case from where it was tucked inside his jacket. 'This is what the Frenchman wanted from the Russian. The Berlin Cross.'

Docker opened the case's clasps and unwrapped the fragment of wood.

'It needs to be kept somewhere safe,' Beauchamp said.

Docker nodded.

ACHTUNDZWANZIG

At sunset, Beauchamp stood in front of Albert Speer. The golden light was touching the high barred window behind the architect.

'So, it is all over and you failed to bring me *das Kreuz von Berlin*,' said Speer looking down at Beauchamp's empty hands.

'You're half right. It's over.'

'But the Cross?'

'You asked me to promise to bring the Cross home. I suppose, Herr Speer, it's simply a matter of how you define *home*.'

'Berlin is the Cross's home!'

Anger flared in Speer's eyes then was gone within seconds. Here's a man with excellent self-control, thought Beauchamp. 'I couldn't see why the Cross should stay in Berlin. After all, at one time it had been stolen –'

'It has changed hands countless times down the centuries,' interrupted Speer. 'That is not the point. I wanted it here.'

'You never explained precisely why. It obviously failed you in the war.'

'No, it failed because others interfered. It is only now that I am beginning to understand its power over men.'

Beauchamp stood up to leave. 'So am I,' he said.

Docker was tired of being tired but he had a detour to make on his way home to the States. Using his John Davis travel documents, he boarded the first aircraft whose crew would agree to ferry him out of Berlin. The plane took him along the air corridor to Wiesbaden, where he caught a USAF flight to Munich. The next leg was to Vienna, and finally he boarded a commercial flight to Rome. At the hotel in Piazza Trinità dei Monti there was a message from Beauchamp. The meeting that Docker had asked Beauchamp to arrange had been set for noon.

With his bathroom window letting in the hazy morning sunlight, Docker bathed in a tub and tried to relax. It felt good to be away from the pressures of Berlin, and being in Rome gave him a sensuous pleasure. On the drive in from Ciampino Airport, he'd been pleased to see that neither the retreating Germans nor advancing Allies had damaged Rome's monuments or handsome buildings.

After dressing, he had a coffee at a sidewalk café and watched boxy Lambrettas and curvaceous Vespas scoot past. Unlike Berlin, Rome was vibrant and sexy despite the summer heat and a thin layer of dust covering most surfaces. But I'm not here on vacation, he was forced to remind himself. He paid for his coffee and caught a cab to the Lateran district. The cab dropped him outside the basilica of San Giovanni. There was a clap of thunder and a clutch of Monsignors in black birettas ran for shelter under the cover of the church's massive entrance way. He jogged after them and stood outside the giant bronze doors until the rain passed.

As soon as the sun came out again, Docker crossed the road to the Scala Sancta, stopped and looked back at the basilica.

Statues of Christ and his apostles were ranged along the top of the church. The Christ figure had an arm out-stretched. A good luck wave, perhaps?

The Scala Sancta entrance was crowded with rain-soaked pilgrims. He avoided the knot of visitors waiting their turn to climb the Holy Stairs on their knees and instead took the side stairs which led up to the Sancta Sanctorum, the Holy of Holies. It was dark and cool at the top of the stairs. Looking down he saw the pilgrims in ones and twos creeping up the central staircase on their knees.

A hand touched Docker's shoulder. He turned to find two priests standing behind him – one elderly, the other in his thirties. The elderly priest spoke. '*Benvenuto a Roma, Signor Docker.*'

'Sorry, I don't speak Italian.'

The priest gave a small smile. 'Fortunately our English is reasonable. I am Father Barzini, this is Father Paleario. We are Jesuits. The Curia tells us that it received a call from the authorities in Berlin saying you had a gift for the Vatican. Please come.'

Docker followed the two priests to an arched wooden door and into a room with stone walls. He'd hoped for just a little fanfare, but the priests were businesslike. With a flourish, Docker produced the scimitar-shaped case. Barzini accepted it without a word and undid the clasps.

Taking a magnifying glass from his pocket, Barzini inspected the piece of wood and the miniature sword, before smiling at Docker. 'Fine objects. They look authentic.'

'They are,' said Docker.

Paleario spoke for the first time. 'Unfortunately it is so easy to deceive people who need to believe.'

'If I had any doubts, I wouldn't be here.'

Barzini stepped forward. 'Even St Thomas had doubts. We all need reassurance. If it is what you believe it is, why are you giving it to the Vatican? There are people who would pay a vast fortune for such a thing.'

'I'm going to teach a few people a lesson.'

'It may turn out to be a very expensive lesson,' said Barzini.

'I hope so.'

Barzini placed the relic and sword back into position and closed the case. 'There is someone we would like you to meet.'

Beckoning for Docker to again follow, the priests left the room, taking a flight of marble stairs leading to the floor above.

'Where are we going?' asked Docker, unhappy at being led down a long, poorly lit passageway.

Paleario, still walking, turned and looked back over his shoulder at Docker. 'We're taking you to meet our Superior General.'

The title came back to Docker from a boyhood of having Latin and mathematics beaten into him by the Jesuits at Loyola on Park Avenue. 'Ah,' he said. 'The one they call the Black Pope.'

Barzini and Paleario stopped and turned together. Paleario snapped, 'Conspiracy theories are for the insecure and the paranoid. You strike me as neither, Signor Docker.'

'I wouldn't bet on it,' said Docker. 'And, if I remember rightly, your man is rumoured to be the power behind the Papal throne.'

Barzini came forward and stood a few feet away from Docker. A small smile lifted a corner of his mouth. 'May I give you a very quick lesson in diplomacy?' Before Docker could answer, the priest continued, 'We have heard every rumour, every absurd tale, every lie about the Superior General being the real leader of the Church. Father Paleario and I may even joke about it between ourselves. The Superior General has no such sense of humour. He is in no mood for comments which are – how would you Americans say?'

'Smart ass?'

Barzini lost his smile. 'I was thinking of "flip". So, if you want this meeting to last more than a few seconds I suggest you show some tact.'

'I didn't ask for the meeting,' said Docker. It was too late. The priests were walking ahead. Finally they stopped in front of two guards in elaborate uniforms who stood flanking a massive door. The guards stepped aside and nodded at the elderly priest. Barzini knocked twice and turned the metal handle. The room beyond was draughty. Docker could see at least three tall electric fans blowing the summer air around the room.

Barzini and Paleario led the way in. A thin-faced, bespectacled man with a prominent nose was standing near one of the fans. He held out his hand and both priests kissed it.

Barzini waved a hand at Docker. 'Your Paternity, this is John Docker.'

'*Enchanté*,' said the man. He held out his hand. Docker shook it.

'You're French,' said Docker.

'Belgian. Don't look so surprised, Monsieur Docker, it's a big Church. My name is Jean-Baptiste Janssens. I hear you have brought us a gift.'

'Father Barzini has it. It's a piece of the Cross of Christ.'

Janssens gestured at an armchair. Docker sat down. It was like a meeting with the rector at school. Any minute he expected to be scolded or hit with a leather strap.

The men sat in a circle. Janssens dabbed his forehead with a linen handkerchief. 'My health is delicate. I cannot stand this humidity.' He put the handkerchief away and asked Barzini, 'What were your findings?'

'It is definitely the genuine reliquary.'

Janssens looked directly at Docker. 'Then we owe you, at the very least, our thanks and also an apology.'

'Apology?' queried Docker. He didn't like the turn in the conversation.

'You have given Father Barzini the reliquary for what became known during the war as the Berlin Cross. The piece of wood in the reliquary is just that – a piece of wood.'

Docker was momentarily speechless, then he blurted out, 'No, it can't be. I hear the Nazis used it in their blitzkriegs.'

'They used successful military tactics, not the Cross. The True Cross has been in this room since the 1930s. It was here when the Allies liberated Rome. Perhaps, in some way, it was responsible for the city being saved.'

'Oh Jesus,' said Docker. He didn't apologise. He stood up and quickly and then sat down again. 'What happened? How come everyone thought the Berlin Cross was the real thing?'

'After the Italian Army carried the Cross back from Ethiopia, it was kept in the Vatican for safekeeping. But when Mussolini announced he planned to give the Cross to Hitler as a gift, my predecessor, Wlodimir Ledochowski, a Pole, was horrified. He knew his homeland was under threat and he could not allow Hitler to have the Cross. Father Ledochowski secretly hid the real Cross in this room and substituted a small piece of wood for the holy relic.'

Janssens stood up and went over to a framed photo-graph of Pope Pius XII hanging on the wall. He swung the frame to one side and opened a safe. Drawing out a slim package wrapped in newspaper, he unfolded the paper and showed the object inside to Docker. The sliver of wood was older, drier and more fragile looking than the Berlin Cross. Docker couldn't stop himself. He reached across and touched it, then asked Janssens, 'Who else knows about the switch?'

'Father Ledochowski died in 1942 so, until a few minutes ago, only three people. Now it's four.'

'Why are you telling me?' asked Docker.

'The secret to a secret is only to share it with people you can trust,' said Janssens. 'We believe we can trust you.'

'Did you trust a crook named Alaine Amistead? He was planning to give the Berlin Cross to the Vatican in exchange for protection from the Cosa Nostra.'

Father Paleario shook his head. 'We had some approaches from Signor Amistead's contacts but it all came to nothing. It is just as well. We could not have helped him. As we discussed earlier, many naïve people overestimate our power.'

'Which, of course, in some ways is flattering,' said Barzini.

Docker watched Janssens rewrap the Cross and put it back in the safe, before asking the Superior General, 'So that's it?'

'One more thing,' said Janssens, his back to Docker. 'We do not want people coming to look for the True Cross.

We would like you to keep the reliquary and the piece of wood. Perhaps you can find a use for them.'

Docker needed time to think through the plan that was beginning to whirl through his head. More importantly, he needed a cigarette.

NEUNUNDZWANZIG

The Constellation set down at Idlewild with a bump and a scream of engines. Docker tried not to feel disappointed that Bridgette wasn't there to meet him, and took a cab into Manhattan. The cab dodged and weaved in the congested traffic.

As soon as he'd set his bag down in his apartment Docker put in a call to Bridgette. There was no answer. He tried a press agent who'd worked with her, but the agent couldn't help. Docker was too tired to think about whether she'd taken the dough and left town. He showered, changed, lay on his bed fully clothed and fell asleep.

He woke up four hours later and headed for the Prince Street subway, the Berlin Cross tucked into his inside jacket pocket. He had decided to go to Bridgette's apartment and talk to the building super. Maybe he would know where she was.

After that, Docker planned to track down Laurent.

Docker looked around the unusually crowded platform. The stifling summer air on the street appeared to have sent the population underground to the equally muggy, cramped subway.

As a train approached, he touched his side pocket. Before walking to the subway, he'd gone to his office to get his spare gun. He felt safe at last.

Taking the nearest carriage, he tried to balance himself as the train rocked its way north. This was the real New York, he thought, glancing around the packed carriage, his mood lifting.

He began to hum a tune when he suddenly saw Laurent. The big man was slipping between the strap-hanging passengers. He kept coming, using a hat to cover something in his right hand. Docker jammed his hand into his pocket and fumbled for his .38. Too late. Laurent was barely inches away, his hat swinging upwards. There was a short sharp sound like a hydraulic pump. A silencer. Docker felt a heavy weight pressing down on him from behind. He turned and found a man leaning against him. Docker caught him instinctively and lowered him onto the floor. A brown paper package lay at the dead man's feet. Two inches of black gun barrel poked from one corner of the package.

'He's fainted, give him some air,' called Laurent, pushing back the passengers. 'Help me move him into a corner,' he hissed at Docker.

They pulled the man a few feet, then Laurent propped him into a sitting position. 'He'll be okay soon,' he said to the passengers, most of whom had immediately lost interest in the mini-drama. Docker, however, was staring at the man, particularly his badly cut, heavy woollen suit. Out of the corner of his eye, Docker saw Laurent smoothly scoop up the paper package from the carriage floor and push the gun into the dead man's pocket.

Only a few seconds passed before the train slid into the next station.

Laurent put his arm around Docker and gave him a friendly squeeze. 'This is our stop,' he said. They left the carriage and made their way along the platform.

Docker stopped and held out his hands, palms up. They were both covered in blood. 'Fainted, eh?'

'He was a local MGB operative. One of Nikolai Popov's boys. We intercepted a transmission Popov sent before he finally left East Berlin for Moscow. I don't know what you did to upset Popov, but he wanted you dead. The MGB had known about you all along. You were being monitored by the Russians even before you left here to find the Cross. It seems a lot of people were familiar with your links with Kessler.'

'And how'd you find me here?'

'We've been tailing you ever since you landed at Idlewild.' He paused and then said, 'Let's go somewhere quiet.'

The mid-town Manhattan offices of the National Defense Research Committee were on Lexington, two blocks south of the Chrysler Building. A security guard in the lobby nodded at Laurent and hit the elevator button for the top floor.

'Nice,' said Docker as the wood-panelled elevator swept skywards.

'We're not in the cheap seats,' said Laurent.

Another guard greeted them when the elevator door opened. Docker was ushered into a deep-carpeted office with north-facing windows. The stainless-steel gargoyles of the Chrysler Building stared back at Docker as he waited for Laurent to fix him a drink. Laurent left the room for a minute while Docker sipped and admired the view.

'Where's Morton?' Docker asked Laurent when he returned.

'Appropriately enough for a sugar daddy, he's in Cuba on his plantation. He's not coming back.'

'I notice you haven't asked me about the Berlin Cross,' said Docker.

A soft voice behind him said, '*That's* because he was waiting for us.'

Docker spun around. Droplets of his whisky sailed through the air and onto the carpet.

Bridgette stood there, her arm linked through Gaffney's. Elsa – or Elsa from the diner – stood off to one side.

Docker was transfixed by the sight of Bridgette and Gaffney. 'What the hell are you doing with him?'

Bridgette gave Gaffney's arm a squeeze. 'Clive and I are pals.'

'And colleagues,' said Gaffney, obviously pleased with the shock on Docker's face.

'You're with Gaffney too,' said Docker, staring at the Elsa impersonator. The hoarseness of his own voice surprised him.

'I'm Ingrid Wyler,' the woman said. This time there was no German accent.

Bridgette let go of Gaffney's arm and went to Docker. 'We didn't want you to get hurt.'

'Somehow I don't find that reassuring,' said Docker, backing away from her and sitting down in the nearest chair. Looking from Bridgette to Gaffney to Laurent and Ingrid, he put the empty glass down gently. 'Okay,' he said, 'tell me about it.'

Laurent began to speak but Bridgette cut in. 'Most of what Andrew told you before you left for Berlin was true. We needed your help to discredit Popov and get the Cross. We're certain that Popov's boss, Lavrenty Beria, will doubt the authenticity of the Kessler material once he finds out Popov is a crook who's been selling stolen goods.'

This time it was Ingrid who interrupted. 'When Mr Laurent briefed you at the Algonquin, he just skipped the part about Clive also working for the National Defense Research Committee.'

'Division 19 – the committee's special weapons group,' said Gaffney. 'The emphasis is on "special".'

Docker didn't take his eyes off Bridgette. 'Why the charade?'

'Clive was the original plant working on the Popov-Morton case, trying to screw over Popov and break up the art-smuggling racket at the same time. Morton fell for it, but Popov was very wary of Clive. So I was put under cover. Both Morton and Popov liked me. Really liked me. It helps in my business –'

'So you've said before,' said Docker, stopping her.

Bridgette went towards him. 'We all made a mistake.' She looked around at the others. 'We decided that we weren't going to hand over $250,000 to a Russian spy – even if it was Morton's money. The idea was to make Popov so angry that he'd do something rash. But, except for wanting to kill me, he stayed calm.'

'And the money?' asked Docker.

'It's in the Division 19 account,' she replied. 'I'm not the light-fingered type.'

Laurent broke in. 'We didn't lie so much as edit the truth. Ingrid tried to appeal to your better nature when she met you at the café. That didn't work so I stepped in to guide you.'

Docker looked across to Gaffney. 'And him?'

'Clive was there to make certain you didn't come to any harm. Morton has a reputation for violence – that's one of the reasons Bridgette couldn't just walk out on him without some backup.'

Docker was trying to take it all in. 'Gaffney was my bodyguard?'

Gaffney nodded. 'Morton is an unstable asshole – as you found out at the Plaza Hotel,' he said. 'Sorry about that punch. Morton was too quick – I couldn't stop him.'

Docker sighed. 'But it was snafu from beginning to end. Popov got the secrets and made it home safely.'

'We'll see,' said Laurent. 'Before we let Morton go back to Cuba, we made him sign a document. Clive, show him the copy.'

Gaffney pulled a folded slip of paper from his inside jacket pocket and tossed it to Docker.

Docker unfolded the paper and straightened it on his knee. He skim-read the document. There were accusations that Popov had traded in stolen art and antiquities – objects looted from galleries, museums and private homes in Russian-occupied Germany. At the bottom was Morton's signature.

Laurent looked pleased with himself. 'Now where do you think the original was sent?'

'The Kremlin,' said Docker.

'Right. It went to Beria's office. Popov would be finished even if the document's details weren't true – and they are. Beria can't afford to take a chance with Popov. But, more importantly, the Kessler information which Popov took to the Kremlin will be tainted by association.'

'And the Cross. Why do you want it so badly?'

'The committee – and particularly this division – is in the business of developing special weapons. You saw how effective the Cross was when the Nazis blitzed Europe. We want that capability. Two years ago Churchill talked about an iron curtain descending across the Continent. If need be, we will have atomic weapons *and* the Berlin Cross to push aside that curtain.'

Bridgette crouched down by Docker's chair. Her hand covered his. 'I'm glad you're back.'

Laurent didn't look like a man who was happy *just* to have Docker back. 'I've got a question for you. Why Rome?'

Docker stayed calm. 'I had a feeling you'd know about Rome. Simple answer – I wanted to make sure the Cross was, if you'll pardon the term, kosher. I spoke to an expert.'

'Yes, yes. We know. We had you watched there. From the report, it appears you met with Father Barzini, a smart man when it comes to holy relics. And, of course, he confirmed the Cross and the reliquary were genuine.'

'Sure.'

Bridgette took her hand off Docker's and stood up. 'I'm surprised the Vatican didn't make you an offer for the Cross.'

'It did – $150,000.'

Laurent clapped his hands and laughed. 'Damn cheap. I hope they also offered you the salvation of your soul.' The grin slowly disappeared. 'If those Vatican tightwads have put 150 grand on the table, they must want the Cross badly. So, I'd say, you're hoping we'll beat the offer.'

'I want $200,000.'

Gaffney moved closer. 'We could just take it.'

'You'll never find it. I've stashed it.'

Laurent glanced across at Bridgette. She circled protectively behind Docker. Her hands moved to his shoulders and she began to gently massage the tense muscles.

'It's not very patriotic to demand money from the government,' said Laurent.

'Originally it was Morton's dough,' Docker answered. 'I'll take 200, you keep 50 – and you get the Cross.'

'I've a better idea,' said Bridgette. Her right hand slipped quickly down Docker's chest and tugged at the reliquary in his jacket pocket. He grabbed her wrist but quickly released it. He could feel the cold, hard muzzle of a gun pressed against the side of his head.

'Let her have it,' said Gaffney. He pushed the muzzle sideways, forcing Docker to bow his head.

Bridgette pulled the reliquary free and handed it to Laurent. He inspected it for a full minute.

'It's untouched,' said Laurent. 'You're too trusting, John. When I put my arm around you on the subway, I felt it in your jacket.

The mention of Bridgette's name prompted Docker to look up at her. He'd been beaten up, held hostage, shot at and almost murdered. Finding out the woman he'd fallen for had used him was another blow he'd have to roll with. He looked down at his hands, clenched and unclenched his fists and shook his head.

Laurent, taking a steel cigar tube, a lighter and a cutter from his coat pocket, laid them out in a cross-shape on the desk. 'Remember when you and I first discussed the Cross? I asked if you were a religious man – and all I got was one of your smart-ass comments about it depending on how much trouble you were in.' He scooped up the objects and jammed them back in his pocket. 'Well, you're in a hell of a lot of trouble. But we're going to let you walk away because we know you won't do anything dumb. Guess why?'

Docker leant back in his chair and looked around at the others in the room. 'Because, if I do, you'll tell MI6 where I am.'

'And they'll do our work for us,' said Laurent. 'You're a smart man. It's a shame you're so damn naïve.'

Docker pushed himself upright, taking one last look at Bridgette. There was nothing in her eyes. There were no long goodbyes.

He got in the elevator and, as it sped towards street level, tried hard to find something positive that had come out of the whole damn case. He drew a blank. The elevator doors opened and Docker got out, heading towards the revolving doors at the far end of the lobby. Stepping into the doorway, he mistimed the rotations and received a parting slap on the butt from the spinning door. With a sigh, he set off slowly down Lexington. Merging into the crowds, he finally allowed himself the sweet smile of success. He'd been played for a fool, but *he* wasn't the one left holding the wrong Cross.

The Royal Military Police headquarters had numerous meeting rooms, and the row of officers facing Beauchamp had chosen the largest and most intimidating for his discipline hearing. There were four officers, with Major Cooper-Wright sitting at the far right-hand side like a human full stop. The decision was delivered: Beauchamp was not to be charged following the incident with the MI6 agent. He was, however, to be punished. The RMP officers conferred but Beauchamp could only catch a few whispered words before being ordered to stand.

Cooper-Wright delivered the sentence with a smirk. Beauchamp was to be assigned to a combined Allied military police team overseeing the traffic flow at Tegel, the new airport site in the French sector. Beauchamp knew the place was a featureless ant-heap of swarming people and clogged traffic and that 17,000 Berliners were working in three eight-hour shifts a day to build the airport. The project was going to take months. On the plus side, he'd heard that many of the *Trümmerfrauen* wore bathing suits while working in the summer weather. This was a point he decided not to share with Elsa.

After the hearing he walked stiffly to his Jeep and drove to meet her at the Neuer See, a lacy network of small lakes at the western end of the Tiergarten. In some ways the park reminded him of London. Fortunately the Berliners had taken a stand when the Allies suggested the Tiergarten trees be cut down for firewood.

Beauchamp and Elsa walked by the water. The weather was warm, the sun was out and, if his superiors hadn't just rapped him over the knuckles, Beauchamp would have been a happy man.

'I've got a new job,' he said without self-pity. 'I'm going to be a traffic cop at the new Tegel airport.'

'You have been demoted?' Elsa sounded worried.

Tapping three pips on his epaulet, he said, 'I get to keep these but that's about all.'

'A traffic policeman,' she sighed. 'I feel I am to blame.'

'Nonsense. As long as I remember Germans drive on the right-hand side of the road, it'll be a breeze.'

'I wish I could be here to see you.'

It was Beauchamp's turn to be concerned.

'I cannot stay here,' she said. 'Berlin is a graveyard for my family.'

'I'm disappointed but not surprised,' said Beauchamp. He led her around a large bomb crater and across to a park bench.

'Do you think you'll ever return to Berlin?' he asked.

'Not for some time. But,' she looked into his eyes, 'I will be in London next year.'

'So will I,' he said without hesitation, mentally drafting his resignation letter. He dropped his gaze to the grass at his feet, then after a few moments he lifted his head, wondering if it would be undignified for a captain in His Majesty's Royal Military Police to kiss a woman in public. Elsa solved the dilemma for him.

FACT AND FICTION

The Berlin Cross is a blend fact and fiction. Hopefully, the following will help to sort out what *actually* happened.

The Berlin Airlift

In 1948, not only were movies in black and white, so were politics. The four one-time allies – Russia, the United States, Britain and France – were almost as divided as the country they now ruled: Germany. The Americans, British and French wanted to introduce reforms, including a new currency. The Russians believed the West was attempting to take more control of the conquered nation and, in an attempt to drive them out of Berlin, Soviet military governor Marshal Sokolovsky ordered in June that the Russians cut road and rail traffic to and from the western sectors of the city. The US responded to the Russian blockade by announcing a massive airlift to keep the western zones supplied, which lasted over a year. It's estimated that about two million tons of supplies were carried on more than 250,000 American, British and civilian flights into Berlin. The plan to starve the city failed and after 328 days Russia finally announced an end to the blockade.

To research the Berlin Airlift aspects of the novel, I turned to *Berlin In The Balance* by Thomas Parrish (Perseus Books), *The Unheralded* by Edwin Gere (Trafford) and *To Save A City* by Roger G. Miller (University Press of the Pacific).

Albert Speer

Albert Speer, Hitler's architect and Minister for Armaments and War Production, spent a considerable amount of time after the war attempting to position himself as the most rational and innocent of the Führer's entourage. His argument that he knew nothing of the Holocaust appears disingenuous at best. While in Spandau Prison, he secretly began drafting two books, *Inside the Third Reich* and *The Spandau Diaries*. After his release in 1966, he continued this work as his personal apologist. He died of a cerebral hemorrhage in London in 1981.

To learn more about Albert Speer, I read the memoir *Inside The Third Reich* (Simon & Schuster) and Joachim Fest's *Speer: The Final Verdict* (Weidenfeld & Nicolson).

The Black Pope

The 27th Superior General of the Jesuits, Jean-Baptiste Janssens is described by John Docker in *The Berlin Cross* as 'The Black Pope', a reference to the head Jesuit's perceived influence over the real, white-robed Pope. In a paranoid world, it seemed a splendid plot twist to cast Janssens and his Polish predecessor Wlodimir Ledochowski as the good guys instead of what would have been the Jesuits' predictable fictional roles as music-hall villains. Belgian-born Janssens' one complaint about his leading role in the Society of Jesus was having to endure Rome's humidity. He died in 1964.

Noël Coward and Laurence Olivier

By the time actor Laurence Olivier appears in *The Berlin Cross*, he would have completed *Hamlet*, the Oscar-awarding film which he directed and starred in. Olivier had decided to shoot the movie on location at Elsinore, Denmark, and could well have needed the Caribbean holiday offered by his playwright friend Noël Coward. Coward had recently bought 'Firefly', a home on the north coast of Jamaica. When asked later by a reporter why he chose to live in Jamaica rather than Britain, Coward replied, 'I can answer that in just two words: Income Tax.'

National Defence Research Committee

Although Andrew Laurent is a fictional character, the National Defence Research Committee – the organisation he purportedly worked for – existed. Headed by Carnegie Foundation president Vannevar Bush, the independently funded committee was founded in 1940 to encourage

American research into modern warfare's offensive and defensive armoury, including nuclear weapons, rockets, camouflage and radar. Based at 1530 P Street NW, Washington DC, the committee had 19 divisions, each with its own speciality.

Russia's Atomic Bomb

Russia detonated its first atomic bomb in August 1949, just over a year after the fictional character Comrade Popov took the equally fictional Kessler secrets back to Moscow. In reality, the Soviet nuclear program began in 1943 under physicist Igor Vasilievich Kurchatov, and, after the war, the Kremlin's hard man Lavrenty Beria was chosen to head the atomic project.

Lavrenty Beria

Evil in pince-nez glasses. Beria, the man responsible for the deaths of millions of Russians, was appointed head of the NKVD by Stalin in 1938. Ten years later, at the time when Comrade Popov returns home in the novel, Beria was leading his own internal security force, the MVD.

Berlin in 1948

For a sense of how Europe looked after the trauma of the World War II, I can recommend the stylish photographs in *After The War Was Over* (Thames & Hudson). The prostitute that Captain Beauchamp meets at the beginning of the novel, the elderly organ grinder who traipses around Berlin, and the scenes of scruffy devastation all appear in this remarkable book by the Magnum photographers.

As for learning what life was like across the globe in the late 1940s, I returned to the greatest writer of his (or any other) generation, S.J. Perelman, and his wonderful *Westward Ha!* (Reinhardt & Evans).

The True Cross

In *The Berlin Cross*, the history and the final whereabouts of the True Cross is part fact, part fiction, but I'll leave you to decide which is which.

ACKNOWLEDGMENTS

I learnt two things writing *The Berlin Cross*. The first is that butchers, bakers and bankers are less than enthusiastic about handing over their goods and services today on the promise of a signed copy of a novel in 18 months' time.

The second is that getting a book published requires a team effort. So, my heartfelt thanks go to my literary agent Pam Seaborn, Random House publisher Jude McGee, editors Sophie Ambrose, Vanessa Mickan-Gramazio and Louise Thurtell, and my advisors on matters literary, linguistic, musical and military – Andrew Lownie, Wendy Hamlin, John and Erica Hume, Jan Hill and Doug Fox.

And it would be churlish of me not to acknowledge writers Graham Greene, Raymond Chandler and Dashiell Hammett. The inspiration for the book came from the Greene-scripted film *The Third Man*, and the noir novels of Chandler and Hammett.